Small Fry and Other Stories

Anton Chekhov

Translated by Stephen Pimenoff

ALMA CLASSICS

ALMA CLASSICS
an imprint of

ALMA BOOKS LTD
Thornton House
Thornton Road
Wimbledon Village
London SW19 4NG
United Kingdom
www.almaclassics.com

This collection first published by Alma Classics in 2022
Translation © Stephen Pimenoff, 2022

Cover image: nathanburtondesign.com

Extra Material © Alma Books Ltd

Printed in Great Britain by CPI Group (UK) Ltd, Croydon CR0 4YY

ISBN: 978-1-84749-884-7

Contents

Anton Chekhov (1860–1904)

Anton Chekhov with his
brother Nikolai

Maria Chekhova,
Anton's sister

Yevgenia and Pavel, Chekhov's parents

The birthplace of Anton Chekhov
in Taganrog

The out-building to Chekhov's residence in Melikhovo,
where he wrote *The Seagull*

Olga Knipper as Mme Ranevskaya
in *The Cherry Orchard*

Olga Knipper as Masha
in *Three Sisters*

The House-Museum in Sadovo-Kudrinskaya Street, Moscow,
where Chekhov lived between 1886 and 1890

Small Fry
and Other Stories

Introduction

The stories in this collection date from the early part of Chekhov's literary career, the 1880s, when he was in his twenties. They mostly first appeared in humorous or satirical magazines under the pseudonym Antosha Chekhonte. A few were then published in book form under the titles *Tales of Melpomene* (1884) and *Motley Stories* (1886). They proved immediately and widely popular with the public, and launched Chekhov on his successful writing career.

Later in life, when Chekhov was asked how many works of this sort he had written, he replied, "Around a thousand." Unless he was including trivial sketches, one-act dramas, fillers and jokes, which have not survived (perhaps mercifully), this is almost certainly an overestimate. Four hundred is the figure usually accepted, and not even all of those are of the same high standard. "Oh, with what trash I began!" was his own harsh judgement of his early work. The best stories, however, have been judged by posterity to be among the masterpieces of the short-story form, and it is from among those that this collection has been put together.

To have written so much at such an early age is extraordinary. As Chekhov himself said: "I wrote as naturally as a bird sings. I just sat down, and the writing came... To write an essay, a story, a short sketch, caused me no trouble at all. Like a calf or a foal let loose in a sunlit field, I jumped and sweated, flicking my tail and waggling my head."

The stories show a range of experience remarkable for a man still in his mid-twenties, but from an early age Chekhov had come to know many types of people. His father ran a grocery shop in Taganrog, a small town on the Sea of Azov, and was also active in the religious life of the town, ensuring that his family of five boys and a girl were brought up in the traditions and observances of the Orthodox faith. The French author André Maurois wrote: "In the shop [Chekhov] got to know men of all races and all trades – and, at church, priests, whose special vocabulary he stored away in his mind. A precious apprenticeship, this, though he did not know it, for a writer of fiction."

Of the early stories, Chekhov's friend, the writer Vladimir Korolenko, wrote that they "sparkle with humour and frequent flashes of wit, combined with unusual brevity and powerful images. The notes of pensiveness, lyricism and that melancholy unique to Chekhov, which can already be heard amid the lively humour, only serve to set off their youthful light-heartedness."

Chekhov did feel that he ought to write a novel, and several times tried to do so, but his efforts came to nothing. Like Chopin in music, he was by nature a miniaturist, uncomfortable with longer forms. In a letter to a friend in 1886 he wrote: "I would like to write a novel… but evidently the strength is lacking… I do not have the stamina… until the novel's hour comes I shall continue to write what I love – in other words, short stories." Certainly the short-story form was the one perfectly suited to his talent.

It may well be that the poor health he suffered all his adult life (he died of tuberculosis aged forty-four) made him too weak for sustained literary application. Two years after the letter quoted above he wrote: "I still do not have the ability to write long pieces."

The brevity of the stories is remarkable. The writer Ivan Bunin once said that Chekhov had told him that a short story "should be brief – as brief as possible". Many are just a couple of pages long – sometimes not even that – yet how much Chekhov manages to pack in! In just a few words a character is brought to life with astonishing deftness and given a distinctive personality, as with this description of the lodger in *An Incident with a Classicist*: "Yevtikhi Kuzmich Kuporosov was sitting at his table reading *Teach Yourself Dancing*. [He] was a clever and educated man. He spoke through his nose and washed with soap which had a smell that made everyone in the house sneeze. He ate meat on days of fasting and was looking for an educated bride: this is why he was considered the cleverest lodger. He sang tenor."

The brevity of Chekhov's stories was at least partly due to the demands of the publishers of the humorous magazines he initially wrote for. Space was tight in these publications, and editors persistently called for shorter and shorter pieces. After submitting a few stories to the magazine *Fragments*, he was told: "The form is excellent. Your collaboration has long been desired by us. Write more briefly, and we will pay you more generously."

It was not just brevity that Chekhov strove for, but simplicity. None of the stories have dense passages of description or dialogue, or tortuous grammatical constructions. "No one can write so simply about simple things as you can," Maxim Gorky told him. "Your tales are exquisite phials filled with all the smells of life."

Chekhov thought the reader ought to be able to grasp what a story is about "by the way it is told, without any explanations by the author, from the conversation and the actions of the characters... One must ruthlessly suppress everything that is not directly concerned with the subject." The little details he inserts remind one of the dabs on an impressionist painting, which have significance only when the viewer stands back and views the whole.

Some of the characters have names derived from a word descriptive of their chief characteristic. (This idea originated with Gogol, who did the same in his 1842 novel *Dead Souls*.) For example, a character known for facilitating bribes has the name Sakhar Myodovich, which means "Sugar Son-of-Honey"; *ochumyeli* means "mad", "off one's head", and so a scatterbrained person has the name Ochumyelov; and so on. I considered annotating the derivation of each name, but rejected the idea – perhaps all that is needed is for the reader to be aware that the surnames are often invented.

Many of the stories deal with the baseness, laziness and venality of civil servants and the dishonest practices that permeated every level of Russian public life, not just in the government, but in the police and judiciary. Bribery was endemic, and virtually no official transaction was possible without money changing hands, often quite openly. Patronage and favouritism were rife; bribes were expected and often demanded without embarrassment (the usual euphemism for offering a bribe was "showing gratitude"). Another practice common at the time was for policemen to go from house to house in a neighbourhood on certain holidays, like Easter and New Year's, collecting tips from the residents.

From time to time honest, high-principled officials and administrators tried to eliminate corruption. Tsar Nicholas himself, on acceding to the throne in 1825, was determined to do something about it. But so deep and widespread was the culture that all attempts to eradicate it came to naught.

According to Alexander Herzen, "one regional governor, General Velyaminov, for two years struggled hard at Tobolsk to root out the malpractices – and then, conscious of failure, he gave it all up and ceased to attend to business at all. Others, more prudent than he, never tried the experiment: they made money themselves and let others do the same."

A number of the early tales also highlight the suffocating bureaucracy of official life in the Russia of Chekhov's time. They often feature low-ranking civil servants, "little" men oppressed, downtrodden and forced by their superiors, who could often be arrogant and domineering, into abject servility. They were badly paid, and had to deal with hostile colleagues and perform jobs of often mind-numbing drudgery, like the copying of documents of which they had no understanding. This idea was not original with Chekhov (it was the subject of Gogol's tale 'The Overcoat' as early as 1840), but it was one that Chekhov developed and refined into a fine art. His portrayal of these drudges is characterized by compassion, directness and gentle humour.

Henri Troyat, in his biography of Nikolai Gogol, gives a vivid description of the life of the downtrodden junior civil servant:

Young and old, fat and thin, bald and hirsute, they all shared a deadly dullness caused by their work and the terror of criticism. Years of this discipline had broken their spirits, smoothed away every wart of their personalities and lowered their ambitions. They nourished themselves on ink and paper, and saw no further than the tip of their pen. When their superior asked their opinion on some matter relating to their work, it never occurred to them to say what they thought: they worriedly tried to guess what he wanted to hear. This was the kingdom of servility, of respectable poverty, intrigues for promotion, crude jests and hollow stomachs. On Sunday mornings they went to Mass to please their chiefs. On Sunday afternoons they drank. On Monday they resumed their work with heavy heads. Their only hope was an unexpected gratification, a small bribe.

A culture of saccharine, ingratiating behaviour inevitably became established. "Such indeed is the Russian," wrote Gogol in *Dead Souls*. "He has a powerful passion for rubbing shoulders with anyone who might stand one rank higher than himself, and a nodding acquaintance with a count or a prince he deems preferable to any intimate friendships."

Several of the stories hinge on the practice, customary in tsarist times, of civil servants going to offer congratulations to those of higher rank on the usual holidays. A sheet was kept for visitors to sign at the entrance to a grand house, and a lowly official was unwise to avoid going to sign. The sheet would be read the next day, and a note made of any names that were missing: this would be taken as a sign of disrespect, and an official's position and promotional prospects might thereby be compromised.

The "ranking" of civil servants, military officers and court functionaries into fourteen classes was introduced by Peter the Great in 1722. Alexander Herzen wrote: "One of the saddest consequences of the revolution effected by Peter the Great is the development of the official class in Russia. These *chinovniks* are an artificial, ill-educated and hungry class, incapable of anything except office work, and ignorant of everything except official papers. They form a kind of lay clergy, officiating in the law courts and police offices, and sucking the blood of the nation."

The system soon became rigidly hierarchical. Officials of the highest ranks were looked upon by those of the lower with not just envy, but awe. Minor officials could be humiliated and dismissed by their superiors – as a result, their behaviour was often sycophantic, even grovelling. The stories in this book contain many variations on that theme, and it is because most of them concern those forgotten little men and women caught up in circumstances beyond their ability to control that the collection has been given the title it has. With a few exceptions, the stories have either never or rarely been published in English before.

Because ranks play such an important part in these stories, a list of them has been provided at the beginning of the book.

The decorations awarded to state officials are also frequently referred to. These are (in ascending order of importance) the Orders of St Vladimir, St Anna and St Stanislav. An even higher decoration was the Order of the White Eagle.

There are a few Russian words I did not translate, partly in order to keep the spirit of Russianness and partly because they have no exact English equivalents. Some, like tsar, rouble, copeck, boyar and kvass are well known to English readers and are in any case found in English dictionaries. Others not found in English dictionaries have been italicized in the text and annotated. A few explanations of words and customs that may be puzzling to English readers have also been annotated, though I have tried to keep these to a minimum.

To impart a flavour of Russianness to the text, I have also kept the literal translation of some expressions that are usually rendered freely in English. Russians frequently invoke God, the Devil and sin in expressions translated variously, but I have mostly kept such expressions in their literal form. For example, the expression "I cannot hide sin" is usually given as "I don't deny", or "I must admit", but I have kept it as in the original, as I have the expression "the devil take it", often rendered as "to hell with it". The word *bratyets* (diminutive form of "brother") is usually translated as "old boy", "mate" or "my lad", but I feel these sound rather too "English" and so have kept it as "brother". Examples may be multiplied.

As in my previous two books, I wish to express my thanks to Mrs Masha Lees, a Russian scholar of enviable accomplishment, for checking my translations and pointing out errors I had made.

– Stephen Pimenoff, 2022

Small Fry
and Other Stories

Table of Ranks

Civil Service	Military	Court
1) Chancellor	Field Marshal/ Admiral	
2) Active Privy Councillor	General	Chief Chamberlain
3) Privy Councillor	Lieutenant General	Marshal of the House
4) Active State Councillor	Major General	Chamberlain
5) State Councillor	Brigadier	Master of Ceremonies
6) Collegiate Councillor	Colonel	Chamber Fourrier
7) Court Councillor	Lieutenant Colonel	
8) Collegiate Assessor	Major	House Fourrier
9) Titular Councillor	Staff Captain	
10) Collegiate Secretary	Lieutenant	
11) Ship Secretary*	*Kammerjunker*	
12) Government Secretary	Sub-Lieutenant	
13) Provincial Secretary*		
14) Collegiate Registrar	Senior Ensign	

* *(abolished in 1834)*

An Incident with a Classicist

PREPARING TO GO to a Greek-language exam, Vanya Ottepyelev kissed all the icons. His stomach was churning, and he felt a coldness in his chest. His heart would pound and then stand still from fear of the unknown. What would happen to him today? Would he get a three, or a two? He went to his mother six times for her blessing, and on leaving asked his aunt to pray for him. On his way to school he gave two copecks to a beggar, in the hope that these two copecks would compensate for his ignorance and that, God grant, numerals with *tessarakonta* and *oktokaideka** would not turn up.

He returned from school late, at five o'clock. He arrived and lay down quietly. His gaunt face was pale. There were dark circles under his reddened eyes.

"Well, what happened? How did it go? What did you get?" asked his mother, approaching the bed.

Vanya blinked, twisted his mouth to one side and started to cry. His mother grew pale, opened her mouth and threw up her hands. The short trousers that she had been mending fell from her hands.

"Why on earth are you crying? Didn't you pass, then?" she asked.

"I... I failed. I got a two."

"I knew it! I had a presentiment!" cried his mother. "Oh, Lord! How is it that you didn't pass? Why? On what subject?"

"On Greek... I, Mama... I was asked the future of *fero*, and instead of saying *oisomai* I said *opsomai*. Then... then... a secondary accent is not placed if the last syllable is long, and I... I was hesitant... I forgot that *alpha* in this case was long... so I added an accent. Then Artakserkov told me to enumerate the enclitic particles... I was enumerating them and accidentally introduced a pronoun... I made a mistake... He gave me a two... I was just... unlucky... I studied all night... All this week I was getting up at four o'clock..."

"No, it is not you, but I who am unlucky, wretched boy! I am the unlucky one! I am skin and bones because of you – you persecutor, tormentor, my evil fate! I am paying for you – rubbish, useless boy that you are. I am breaking my back, torturing myself, and, I have to tell you, I am suffering. And what do you care? How do you study?"

"I... I study. All night... You yourself saw..."

"I was praying to God that he send me death, but he doesn't – to the sinner... You are my tormentor! Others have children as children ought to be, but I have one and only one and he gives me no help, has no ambition. Should I beat you? I would beat you, but where on earth would I get the strength? Where, oh where, Mother of God, would I get the strength?"

His mother covered her face with the flap of her blouse and began to sob. Vanya writhed in misery and pressed his forehead to the wall. His aunt entered.

"Well, so... I had a foreboding," she said, having guessed at once what had happened; she went pale and threw up her hands. "All morning I have been feeling sad... Well, well, I thought there would be some misfortune... and so there has been..."

"My wretched boy, tormentor," said his mother.

"Why are you cursing him?" his aunt challenged her, nervously pulling from her head a little coffee-coloured kerchief. "Is he to blame? You are the one to blame! You! Why did you send him to that school? What sort of nobility are you? Or are you trying to enter the nobility? Ah, so you think you will be accepted as a member of the nobility! But it would be better, as I have said, to apprentice him to some trade, to some office, like my Kuzya. You know, Kuzya makes five hundred a year. Five hundred – is that a joke? You tortured yourself, and you tortured the boy with this learning, the devil take it. He is thin, he coughs... look: he is thirteen but looks like a ten-year-old."

"No, Nastyenka, no, my dear! I didn't beat him enough, my tormentor! I should have beaten him, that's all there is to it. Oh... Jesuit, infidel, my tormentor!" She drew herself threateningly towards her son. "I should thrash you, but I don't have the

4

strength. They used to tell me in the past, when he was still small: 'Beat him, beat him'... But I, a sinner, didn't listen. And so I am suffering now. Just you wait! I shall thrash you! Just wait..."

His mother shook a wet fist threateningly at him, and, weeping, went to the room of the lodger. Her lodger, Yevtikhi Kuzmich Kuporosov, was sitting at his table reading *Teach Yourself Dancing*. Yevtikhi Kuzmich was a clever and educated man. He spoke through his nose and washed with soap which had a smell that made everyone in the house sneeze. He ate meat on days of fasting and was looking for an educated bride: this is why he was considered the cleverest lodger. He sang tenor.

"Kind sir!" the boy's mother appealed, flooding with tears. "Be so noble as to thrash my... Do me a favour! He did not pass, to my grief! Believe it or not, he did not pass! I am unable to punish him, because ill health has made me weak... You thrash him instead of me. Be so noble and understanding, Yevtikhi Kuzmich! Help a sick woman!"

Kuporosov frowned and emitted a deep sigh through his nose. He thought for a while, drummed his fingers on the table and, sighing once again, went to Vanya.

"It seems they try to teach you," he began, "to educate you, to give you a start in life, disgraceful young man. Why are you like this?"

He spoke for a long time, delivered quite a speech. He referred to learning, to light and darkness.*

"Well now, young man!"

He finished speaking, removed his belt and pulled Vanya by the arm.

"There's no other way to deal with you," he said.

Vanya obediently bent and put his head between Kuporosov's knees. His pink, protruding ears rubbed against the knitted, brown-striped trousers...

Vanya did not emit a single sound. In the evening, after a family discussion, the decision was made to send him to trade.

The Enquiry

I T WAS NOON. A landowner, Voldyryev – a tall, thickset man with a shorn head and bulging eyes – took off his overcoat, wiped his brow with a silk handkerchief and warily entered the office. A floorboard creaked…

"Where can I make an enquiry?" he asked a doorman who was carrying a tray of glasses from the far end of the office. "I have to get some information, the minutes of the municipal government meeting."

"Probably over there, sir! That's the man you have to see, the one sitting by the window," replied the doorman, pointing with the tray at the far window.

Voldyryev coughed and made for the window. There, behind a green desk, sat a young man in a faded uniform. His face was spotted, as if he had typhus; he had four tufts of hair on his head and a long, pimply nose. He was writing, and had his big nose buried in papers. A fly was walking near his right nostril. From time to time he would push out his lower lip and expel air through his nose, giving his face a deeply preoccupied look.

"May I here… from you," Voldyryev asked him, "get some information about my case? My name is Voldyryev… At the same time I need to get a copy of a decision in the register of 2nd March."

The official dipped his pen and examined it to see if he had taken too much ink. When he was assured that the pen was not dripping, he began to write with a squeaking sound. His lip stretched, but this time he did not have to blow: the fly was sitting on his ear.

"May I apply here for information?" repeated Voldyryev after a minute. "I am Voldyryev, a landowner."

"Ivan Alexeich!" cried the official to the empty air, as if not noticing Voldyryev. "Tell the merchant Yalikov, when he comes, that he has to have the copy of his application certified at the police station. He has been told a thousand times!"

"I am here regarding my dispute with the heirs of Princess Gugulina," muttered Voldyryev. "The matter is well known. I beg you to consider my case urgently."

Still not looking at Voldyryev, the official caught the fly on his lip, looked at it with interest and flicked it away. The landowner coughed and blew his nose loudly in his checked handkerchief. But even this did not help: he was still ignored. The silence lasted about two minutes. Voldyryev drew from his pocket a one-rouble banknote and placed it before the official on the open register. The official wrinkled his brow, pulled the register towards himself with a preoccupied look and closed it.

"A little information… I would just like to know on what grounds the heirs of Princess Gugulina… May I trouble you?"

But the official, busy with his thoughts, rose and, scratching his elbow, went for some reason to the cupboard. Returning a minute later to his desk, he again looked at the register: on it lay another rouble banknote.

"I shall trouble you for only a minute… Give me a little information, only…"

The official seemed not to hear; he began to copy something.

Voldyryev made a face and looked hopelessly at all the scribbling clerks.

"They are writing," he thought with a sigh. "They are all just writing, the devil take the lot of them."

He stepped away from the desk and, standing in the middle of the room, lowered his hands hopelessly. The doorman, again carrying a tray of glasses, probably noticed the helpless expression on his face, because he came up to him and asked quietly:

"Well, then? Did you make your enquiry?"

"I asked for information, but he does not want to speak to me."

"Give him three roubles," muttered the doorman.

"I've already given two."

"You have to give more."

Voldyryev returned to the desk and placed a green banknote on the open register.

The official again drew the register towards himself and started leafing through it. Suddenly, as if unintentionally, he raised his eyes to Voldyryev. His nose shone, reddened and wrinkled up in a smile.

"Ah... What can I do for you?" he asked.

"I would like to make an enquiry about my case... I am Voldyryev."

"It's a pleasure, sir! About the Gugulina case, sir? Very well, sir! What exactly do you need, in fact?"

Voldyryev stated his request.

The official came to life, as if caught up in a whirlwind. He gave the information, arranged for a copy to be made, brought the client a chair – and all this in a single moment. He even talked about the weather and asked about the harvest. And when Voldyryev left, he accompanied him downstairs, smiling with a combination of friendliness and respect, and seeming each minute as if prepared to grovel before the client. Voldyryev for some reason became embarrassed; on an impulse he drew a rouble banknote from his pocket and gave it to the official. Still bowing and smiling, the man took the banknote like a magician, so that nothing was seen of it but a flash in the air...

"Oh, the ways of the world!..." thought the landowner. Going out on the street, he stopped to wipe his brow with his handkerchief.

Surgery

THE DISTRICT HOSPITAL. In the absence of the doctor, who left to get married, the patients are being seen by medical assistant Kuryatin, a fat man of about forty in a threadbare Circassian jacket and worn knitted trousers. On his face is a kindly expression of concern. There is the stench from a cigar that he is holding between the index and middle fingers of his left hand.

Into the waiting room enters the sexton Vonmiglasov, a tall, thick-set old man in a brown surplice with a wide leather belt. His right eye, with a cataract, is half closed, and on his nose is a wart resembling from a distance a big fly. The sexton glances around the room for a moment, looking for an icon. Not seeing one, he crosses himself before a large bottle of carbolic acid; he takes communion bread out of a red handkerchief and lays it before the medic with a bow.

"A-ha... my respects to you," yawns the medic. "What can I do for you?"

"A peaceful Sunday to you, Sergei Kuzmich... I come to Your Honour... Truly and honestly is it said in the psalter, you know: 'My cup is mingled with tears.'* I sat down to drink tea with my old woman the other day and... dear God! I couldn't take a drop – not a single drop. I just wanted to lie down and die. I sipped a little and couldn't bear it! And the pain is not just in the tooth itself, but on all that side. It aches something terrible! It feels, you know, as if a nail or some such thing is being driven into my ear. It shoots such pain! I have sinned and transgressed... I have sinned in my soul and have lived in idleness... For my sins, Sergei Kuzmich, for my sins! After the liturgy, the priest reproached me: 'You were mumbling, Yefim, and couldn't be understood. You chanted, and nobody understood you.' But you try to chant if you can't open your mouth, and everything is swollen, you know, and you can't sleep at night."

"M'yes... Sit down... Open your mouth."

Vonmiglasov sits down and opens his mouth.

Kuryatin frowns, looks into the old man's mouth, and among the teeth, yellowing from age and tobacco, discovers one with a gaping hole.

"The deacon told me to apply vodka with horseradish... it didn't help. Glikeria Anisimovna, God grant her health, gave me a thread from Mount Athos* to wear on my hand, and told me to rinse the tooth with warm milk. I wore the thread, but with regard to the milk I confess I did not follow her advice. I fear God – it is Lent..."

"Superstition..." The medic pauses. "It must be pulled out, Yefim Mikheich!"

"You know best, Sergei Kuzmich. You have been trained to understand when to pull out and when to cure with drops or something else... For that you are a saviour, and have been appointed here, God bless you, to help us day and night like our own father... until the end of our days."

"It's nothing," the medic says modestly, going to the cupboard and rummaging among the instruments. "Surgery – it's nothing... It's just a matter of practice and steadiness of hand... there's nothing to it... The other day, just like you, the landowner Alexander Ivanovich Yegipetsky also comes into the hospital... Also with a tooth... An educated man... asks about everything, is interested in everything, that's the truth. He shakes my hand, addresses me by name and patronymic. He lived in Petersburg for seven years, knew all the professors... We spent a long time together... He prays to Christ God: 'Pull it out for me, Sergei Kuzmich!' So why shouldn't I pull it out? It could be pulled out. You just have to know how: you can't do it without knowledge... All teeth are different. One you pull out with pliers, another with molar forceps, a third with a wrench... as required."

The medic takes up the molar forceps, looks at them momentarily in puzzlement, then puts them down and picks up the pliers.

"Well, sir, open your mouth a little wider," he says, drawing towards the sexton with the pliers. "Now we... this... there's nothing to it... We just need to cut the gum a little... to make a vertical cut... that's all..." He makes a little cut in the gum. "That's all..."

"You are our saviour... It's such a mystery to fools like us, but God has enlightened you."

"Don't talk when your mouth is open... This is easy to pull out, but it sometimes happens that the roots are left... This... there's nothing to it..." He applies the pliers. "Stop, don't move... Sit still... In the twinkling of an eye..." He starts to pull. "The main thing is to get deep down..." He pulls. "So that the crown doesn't break off..."

"Ahhh! Father of ours... Holy mother... Ahiii!"

"Don't... don't... How does it feel? Don't grab with your hand! Let your hand go!" He pulls. "In a moment... Now, now... This really isn't easy..."

"Father above... Saints in heaven... Angels of mercy! Aaargh!... Just pull it, pull it out! Why does it take five years to pull it out?"

"This is really... surgery... It can't be done at once... So... so."

Vonmiglasov raises his knees to his elbows, moves his fingers, opens his eyes wide, gasps for breath... His red face is bathed in sweat, and there are tears in his eyes. Kuryatin snorts, shifts from foot to foot in front of the sexton and pulls... Agonizing moments pass – and the pliers slip from the tooth. The sexton leaps up and feels in his mouth with his fingers. In his mouth he finds the tooth still in the same place.

"It's taking a long time," he says in a tearful and at the same time accusing voice. "I hope you go through this in the next world! Thank you very much! If you don't know how to pull it out, then don't try. I can't stand it any more..."

"But why do you grab me with your hands?" the medic asks angrily. "I'm pulling, and you push my hand away and say stupid things... You fool!"

"You're the one who's the fool!"

"Do you think, you peasant, it's easy to pull out a tooth? Try it yourself! It's not like climbing the bell tower and ringing the bells... You don't know, you don't know," he mimics, mocking the sexton. "Tell me, what kind of authority are you? Look at you... I pulled a tooth for Mr Yegipetsky, Alexander Ivanovich, and he said nothing, not a word... He's a better man than you. He didn't grab me with his hands... I say to you, sit down, sit down!"

"I can't bear it... Let me get my breath back... Oh-h-h!" He sits down. "Don't pull it, just give a jerk... At once!"

"Teach your grandmother to suck eggs! God! Such ignorant people. Live here with such people... you go crazy! Open your mouth..." He applies the pliers. "Surgery is not a piece of cake, brother... It's not like chanting in church..." He squeezes tightly. "Don't jump around... The tooth is coming out – it's an old one... it has deep roots..." He pulls. "Don't move... Now... now... Don't move... It's coming, it's coming..." A crunching sound is heard. "That's done it!"

Vonmiglasov sits motionless for a moment, as if feeling nothing. He stares dully into space, his pale face bathed in sweat.

"I should have used the forceps," mutters the medic. "What a to-do!"

Coming to his senses, the sexton puts a finger in his mouth: in place of the aching tooth he feels two sharp points.

"You wretched devil," he says. "You were sent here, you persecutor, for our destruction!"

"Still cursing me," mutters the medic, putting the pliers in the cupboard. "Boor... They didn't beat you enough in your seminary. Mr Yegipetsky, Alexander Ivanovich, lived in Petersburg for about seven years... he's an educated man... one of his suits cost about a hundred roubles... and even he didn't swear... But what kind of peahen are you? Nothing will happen to you – you're not going to die!"

The sexton takes his communion bread from the table and, pressing his hand to his cheek, goes home...

Sorrow

*To whom shall I tell my sorrow?...**

E VENING TWILIGHT. Heavy, wet snow is swirling lazily around the lamps that have just been lit, and is lying in a thin, light layer on roofs, the backs of the horses, shoulders, hats. The cabby Iona Potapov is all white, like a ghost. He sits on the coach box, hunched over as far as it is possible for a human body to bend, and does not stir. It seems that even if a whole snowdrift were to fall on him he would not bother to shake it off. His nag is also white and motionless. With her immobility, stiffness of form and stick-like straightness of leg she almost resembles a one-copeck gingerbread horse. In all probability she is plunged in thought. For a creature that was taken away from the plough, from its familiar grey surroundings, and thrown here in this maelstrom, full of bright lights and the relentless noise and sound of galloping horses, it would be impossible not to think...

Iona and his nag have not moved for a long time. They drove out of the yard already before dinner, but still have not had a single fare. And now the darkness of evening is descending on the town. The paleness of the lamp lights is yielding place to vibrant colour, and the turmoil of the street is becoming noisier.

"Cabby, to the Vyborg district!" Iona hears. "Cabby!"

Iona starts, and through eyelashes covered with snow sees an officer in a greatcoat with a hood.

"To Vyborg!" repeats the officer. "Are you asleep, or what? To Vyborg!"

As a sign of acknowledgement, Iona gives a tug on the reins, causing a layer of snow to fall from his shoulders and the back of the horse... The officer gets into the sleigh. The cabby makes a clucking sound with his lips, stretches out his neck like a swan, raises himself into an upright position and, more from habit than from necessity, flourishes the whip. His nag also stretches out her neck, bends her stick-like legs and moves off uncertainly.

"Where are you going, you devil?" Iona straight away hears a voice from among the mass of people moving back and forth. "What the devil are you doing? Keep to the right!"

"It's you who don't know how to drive! You keep to the right!" replies the officer angrily.

The coachman of a carriage swears and looks at him, and a passer-by who was crossing the road and brushed his shoulder against the horse's muzzle shakes snow off his sleeve and glares with annoyance. Iona fidgets on the coach box as if sitting on needles, thrusts out his elbows and drives with the eyes of a madman, as if not understanding where he is, or why.

"What scoundrels they all are!" the officer says sharply. "They just try to collide with you, or fall under the horse. They do it on purpose."

Iona turns and looks at his passenger and moves his lips... He evidently wants to say something, but a strangulated sound is all that comes from his throat.

"What?" asks the officer.

Iona twists his mouth into a smile, strains his voice and says hoarsely:

"My son, *barin*...* er, my son died this week."

"Hm! So, what did he die of?"

Iona turns his whole body to the passenger and says:

"Who knows? It must have been the fever... He lay in hospital for three days and died... It was God's will."

"Get out of the way, you devil!" A voice was heard in the darkness. "Move off, why don't you, you old dog! Use your eyes."

"Drive on, drive on..." says the fare. "Otherwise we'll not get there even by tomorrow. Get going!"

The cabby again extends his neck, straightens himself and with awkward gracefulness flourishes the whip. He then looks several times at his passenger, but the passenger has closed his eyes and is evidently not in the mood to listen. After letting off his fare in Vyborg, Iona stops by an inn, huddles up on the coach box and again does not stir… Wet snow again turns him and his nag white. An hour passes, and another…

Along the pavement, loudly stamping in their galoshes and arguing, pass three young men: two of them tall and thin, the third small and hunchbacked. "Cabby, to the Police Bridge!" cries the hunchback in a high voice. "Three… twenty copecks!"

Iona pulls on the reins and again makes the clucking sound. Twenty copecks – it is not a fair price, but he is not concerned about the price. Whether it is a rouble or five copecks, it is now all the same to him, so long as there is a fare… The young men, pushing each other and swearing, approach the sleigh, and straight away all three try to climb on the seat. The question that now has to be decided is: which of the two are to sit and which, the third, to stand? After much squabbling and many reproaches, they decide that the hunchback, as the smallest, has to stand.

"Well, let's be off!" squeaks the hunchback, finding his place and breathing down Iona's neck. "Get going! What a hat you have, brother! You won't find a worse one in all of St Petersburg…"

"Ha-ha… ha-ha!" guffaws Iona. "What a…"

"Well, you, what a, get going! Are you going to drive like this all the way? Are you? Do you want a cuff on the neck?…"

"My head aches," says one of the tall youths. "Yesterday at the Dukmasovs' Vaska and I drank four bottles of brandy."

"I don't understand why you lie!" angrily replies the other tall one. "He lies like a trooper."

"God punish me if it's not the truth…"

"It's about as true as saying that a louse coughs."

"Ha-ha," laughs Iona. "The gentlemen are in a jolly mood!"

"Tfoo, the devil take you!" says the hunchback indignantly. "Are you going to get going, you old pestilence, or not? Is this really the way to drive? Just lash her with the whip. Gee up, devil! Gee up! Give it to her good!"

Iona feels the restless body and quivering voice of the hunchback behind his back. He hears the bad language addressed to him, sees people, and the feeling of loneliness begins little by little to lift from his heart. The hunchback swears until he chokes on an especially vulgar oath and bursts out coughing. The tall youths begin to talk about a certain Nadyezhda Petrovna. Iona turns to look at them. Waiting for a short pause in the flow of talk, he looks around again and mutters:

"This week my... er... my son died."

"We're all going to die," says the hunchback with a sigh, wiping his lips after the cough. "Well, drive on, drive on! Gentlemen, I simply cannot ride like this any longer. When will he get us there?"

"Well, give him some gentle encouragement... on the neck!"

"Do you hear, old pestilence? I shall beat you on the neck!... If one deals politely with people like you, one may as well walk!... Do you hear, Serpent Gorynych?* Or do you spit on our words?"

And Iona hears, rather than feels, the sound of a blow on the back of his head.

"Ha-ha..." he laughs. "The gentlemen are in a jolly mood... God give you health!"

"Cabby, are you married?" asks one of the tall youths.

"I? Ha-ha... Jol-ly gentlemen! My only wife now is... the damp earth... He-ho-ho... That is to say, the grave!... My son has died, but I'm alive... It's a strange business: Death mistakes the door... Instead of coming for me, he comes for my son..."

And Iona turns to tell them how his son died, but at this point the hunchback gently sighs and announces that, praise God, they have finally arrived. After receiving a twenty-copeck coin, Iona for a long time watches the idlers until they disappear into a dark doorway. Again he is alone, and again silence sets in around him... The melancholy which not long ago abated again bursts from his chest with even greater force. Iona's eyes run anxiously and tormentedly over the crowd who are scurrying along on both sides of the street: could he not find among those thousands of people even one who would listen to him? But the crowds hurry on, noticing neither him nor his sorrow... A vast sorrow, knowing no limit. If Iona's heart were to break and the sorrow to pour out, it seems it would flood the whole world and still be invisible. Yet it has found such an insignificant shell to crawl into that you could not see it even by the light of day...

Iona sees a caretaker with a sack and decides to talk to him.

"My friend, what would be the time now?" he asks.

"Past nine... Why have you stopped here? Move on!"

Iona moves several paces away, hunches down and abandons himself to his grief... He realizes now that it is useless to appeal to people. But not even five minutes pass before he straightens up, shakes his head as if feeling a sharp pain, and gives a tug on the reins... It is unbearable.

"Back to the yard," he thinks. "To the yard!"

And his nag, as if understanding his thought, sets off at a trot. An hour and a half later Iona is sitting beside a large, dirty stove. People are snoring on the stove, on the floor, on the benches. The air is stuffy and foul-smelling... Iona looks at the sleeping people, scratches himself and regrets having come home so early...

"I didn't even earn enough for oats," he thinks. "That's why there's such grief. A man who knows his business... who is well fed and whose horse is well fed, is always at peace..."

In one corner a young driver gets up, grunts sleepily and reaches for a pail of water.

"Are you thirsty?" asks Iona.

"Of course I'm thirsty!"

"Well... It'll keep you healthy... But my son has died, brother... Did you hear? This week in hospital... What a tale!"

Iona looks to see what effect his words have, but he sees nothing. The young man has covered his head and is already asleep. The old man sighs and scratches himself... Just as the young man wanted to drink, so he wants to talk. Soon it will be a week since his son died, but still he has not spoken properly about it to anyone... He needs to talk plainly, calmly... He has to tell how his son fell ill, how he suffered, what he said before he died, how he died... He has to describe the funeral and the trip to the hospital for the clothes of the deceased. His daughter Anisya is still in the village... So he has to talk about her... There were all kinds of things to talk about now. The listener has to groan, sigh, lament... It would be even better to talk to women. Though they are fools, two words would make them wail.

"I shall go and see how my horse is," thinks Iona. "I can always sleep... Probably it's what I need to sleep..."

He dresses and goes to the stable, where his horse is standing. Iona is thinking about oats, hay, about the weather... He cannot think about his son when he is alone... It is possible to talk to someone about him, but to think about him, and to see in his mind's eye his son's image, is unbearably painful...

"Are you eating?" Iona asks his horse, seeing her shining eyes. "Well, eat away... If we haven't earned enough for oats, there will be hay... Yes... I'm too old to drive now... My son should be driving, and not me... He would have been a real driver... If only he had lived..."

Iona is silent for a while and continues:

"So that's it, old girl. There is no more Kuzma Ionych... He has departed this life... He went and died for no reason. Now, let's say you had a colt, and you were the colt's own mother... And suddenly, let's say, that same colt departed this life... Wouldn't it be a pity?"

The nag eats, listens and breathes on her master's hands...

Iona gets carried away and tells her everything...

The Lion and the Sun

I N ONE OF THE TOWNS on the western side of the Ural
Mountains the rumour spread that a high-ranking Persian
official, Rakhat-Khelam, had arrived and was staying at the
Hotel Japan. This rumour made no impression on the residents:
a Persian had arrived – well, so what? Only the chairman of the
municipal council, Stepan Ivanovich Kutsyn, having learnt from
the secretary of the board about the arrival of the oriental gentleman, grew pensive and asked:

"Where is he going?"

"To Paris or London, it seems."

"Hm… He must be a big shot."

"The devil knows what he is."

Arriving home from his office, the chairman of the council
dined and again fell to thinking, and this time he thought until
late in the evening. The arrival of a distinguished Persian greatly
intrigued him. It seemed to him that fate itself had sent him this
Rakhat-Khelam, and that at last the time had come for him to
fulfil his dearest, secret dream. The fact was that Kutsyn had two
decorations, the Stanislav third class and a Red Cross badge from
the "Society of Life-Savers". In addition, he had made himself an
amulet (a gold rifle and guitar, crossed), and this amulet, which he
wore through the buttonhole of his full-dress uniform, resembled
from a distance something special that easily could be taken for a
decoration. It is well known that the more decorations and medals
you have, the more you want, and the council chairman already
for a long time now had wanted to receive the Persian Order of
the Lion and the Sun – wanted it longingly, passionately. He knew
very well that to be awarded this decoration it was not necessary
either to go into battle or to make a donation to charity or to serve
on committees: all that was necessary was to take advantage of

a suitable opportunity. And now it seemed to him that such an opportunity had come.

The next day, at noon, he put on all his decorations and his chain of office and went to the Hotel Japan. Fate favoured him. When he entered the room of the distinguished Persian, the latter was alone and doing nothing. Rakhat-Khelam, a huge Asiatic with a long, snipe-like nose and bulging eyes, wearing a fez, was sitting on the floor rummaging in his suitcase.

"I beg you to forgive me for disturbing you," began Kutsyn, smiling. "I have the honour to introduce myself, a citizen of honorary rank and a decorated official, Stepan Ivanovich Kutsyn, chairman of the municipal council. I feel it my duty to pay my respects to Your Honour, so to speak, the representative of a friendly, neighbouring power."

The Persian turned and muttered something in very bad French, which sounded like a piece of wood knocking on a board.

"The Persian border," continued Kutsyn in a greeting he had prepared beforehand, "adjoins the frontier of our vast fatherland, which is why mutual regard prompts me, so to speak, to convey to you a feeling of solidarity."

The distinguished Persian rose and again muttered something in a wooden tongue. Kutsyn, who did not know the language, shook his head in a sign that he did not understand.

"So how will I converse with him?" he thought. "It would be good now to send for a translator, but it's a delicate matter, and impossible to talk about in the presence of witnesses. A translator would go blabbing about it all over town."

So Kutsyn tried to recall some foreign words he had learnt from the newspapers.

"I am the head of the municipal council," he muttered. That is, *lord m'yer... municipal... Vwee? Comprenez?*"

He wanted to convey in words, or by miming, his social status, but did not know how to do it. A picture with a prominent inscription, *The Town of Venice*, which was hanging on the wall, came to his aid. He pointed to the city, then to his head, and in this way

felt he was communicating the sentence "I am head of the town".
The Persian understood nothing, but smiled and said:

"Goot, *moosieur*... goot..."

Half an hour later the municipal head was slapping the Persian,
now on the knee, now on the shoulder, and saying:

"*Comprenez? Vwee?* As *lord m'yer* and municipal... I suggest to
you that we take a little *promenage... Comprenez? Promenage...*"

Kutsyn pointed to Venice, and with two fingers represented
walking legs. Rakhat-Khelam, who had kept his gaze on Kutsyn's
medals and evidently guessed he was the most important person in
town, understood the word *promenage* and grinned courteously.
They both put on their coats and left the room. Downstairs, near
the door leading to the restaurant of the Hotel Japan, Kutsyn
decided it would not be a bad idea to treat the Persian. He stopped,
and, pointing to a table, said:

"According to Russian custom it would not hurt to have...
what's the word... *purée, entrecôte...* champagne and so on...
Comprenez?"

The distinguished guest understood, and a little later they were
sitting together in the very best room of the restaurant, drinking
champagne and eating.

"Let us drink to the prosperity of Persia!" proposed Kutsyn.
"We, Russians, love Persians. Though we are of a different faith,
we have common interests – mutual, so to speak, sympathies...
progress... Asiatic markets... peaceful competition, so to speak..."

The distinguished Persian ate and drank with great enjoyment.
He stuck his fork in the *balik** and, enthusiastically nodding his
head, said:

"Goot! *Bien!*"

"Do you like it?" asked the chairman in delight. "*Bien?* That's
excellent." And, turning to the waiter, he said: "Luka my boy, see
that two of the very best *baliki* are sent to His Excellency's room."

Then the council chairman and the Persian dignitary went to
visit the menagerie. The residents of the town saw how their
Stepan Ivanych, flushed from the champagne, feeling jolly and

very satisfied, led the Persian through the main streets and the bazaar, showing him the sights of the town and even taking him to the watchtower.

Among other things, the residents also saw how he stopped near the gate with stone lions and drew the Persian's attention first to a lion, then upwards to the sun, then to his chest, then again to a lion and the sun. The Persian nodded his head as if to show that he understood, and, smiling, showed his white teeth. In the evening they sat together in the Hotel London and listened to a harpist, but where they spent the night is not known.

On the morning of the next day the council chairman was in his office. The clerks already seemed to know and suspect something, because the secretary approached him and with a mocking smile said:

"Persians have a custom that if a distinguished guest comes to visit, you have to slaughter a ram for him with your own hand."

A little later they handed him a package that had come in the post. The chairman opened it to find a cartoon. Rakhat-Khelam was depicted, with the chairman himself kneeling before him, holding out his hands and saying:

In a sign of the friendship of two monarchies –
Russian and Iranian –
Out of respect for you, honoured envoy,
I would slaughter myself like a ram,
But, excuse me, I am just an ass.

The chairman experienced an unpleasant sensation, like a sinking in the pit of his stomach, but not for long. By noon he was already again in the company of the distinguished Persian, again entertaining him and showing him the notable sights of the town, again leading him to the stone gate and again pointing now to the lion, now to the sun, now to his chest. They lunched in the Hotel Japan, and, after lunch, with cigars between their teeth, both looking flushed and contented, again climbed the watchtower.

The chairman, who evidently wanted to entertain his guest to an unusual sight, cried from above to a watchman who was patrolling below:

"Sound the alarm!"

But the alarm did not sound, as the firemen just then were in the steam bath.

They had supper in the Hotel London, and after supper the Persian left. Seeing him off, Stepan Ivanych kissed him three times in the Russian manner, and even shed a few tears. And when the train set off he shouted:

"Give our regards to Persia. Tell her that we love her!"

A year and four months passed. It was very cold, with thirty-five degrees of frost* and a piercing wind. Stepan Ivanych was walking along the street with his fur coat thrown open, and was annoyed that no one was passing him to see on his chest the Order of the Lion and the Sun. He walked like that until the evening, with his fur coat thrown open, chilled to the bone, and at night tossed and turned and in no way could fall asleep.

His soul was heavy, his insides felt as if they were burning, and his heart was beating restlessly. Now he wanted to receive the Serbian Order of Takov. He wanted it longingly, passionately.

Triumph of the Victor

Tale of a retired collegiate registrar

O N THE FRIDAY BEFORE LENT we all went to eat *blinis**
at Alexei Ivanych Kozulin's. You do not know Kozulin – to
you, perhaps, he is a nobody, a zero, but in our circle of humble
employees he is a great man, all-powerful and very wise. We all,
as his underlings, so to speak, set out to his place. I went with
my papa.

The *blinis* were so delicious that I cannot find words for them,
dear sir – succulent, crumbly, crisp. You only had to take one,
the devil himself knows, dip it in hot butter, eat it, and another
would slip by itself into your mouth. The fillings and toppings
and extras were: sour cream, fresh caviar, smoked salmon, grated
cheese. There was a whole sea of wine and vodka. After *blinis*
we ate sturgeon soup, and after the soup, partridge in a sauce.
We were thus so full that my papa surreptitiously unfastened the
buttons over his stomach and, so that no one would notice him
having taken this liberty, spread his napkin over his front. Alexei
Ivanych, who as our superior was privileged, and to whom all was
permitted, openly unfastened his waistcoat and shirt. After dinner,
without rising from the table, we began to smoke cigars – with
the permission of the chief – and to converse. We listened, and
His Excellency, Alexei Ivanych, spoke. The subjects were still of a
more humorous nature, in keeping with the celebratory occasion…
The chief spoke, and evidently wished to seem witty. I don't know
if he said anything funny. I only remember that Papa kept poking
me in the side and saying:

"Laugh!"

I kept opening my mouth wide and laughing. Once I even
shrieked with laughter, thus drawing general attention to myself.

"Good, good!" Papa whispered. "Well done! He's looking at you and laughing... It's good – maybe he'll indeed give you a promotion to assistant clerk."

"Well now, gentlemen," Kozulin said casually, puffing and panting. "Now we are eating *blinis*, enjoying the freshest caviar and caressing a handsome wife. And our daughters are such beauties that not only you humble men, but even princes and counts gaze at them yearningly. And what do you think of our flat? Hee-hee-hee... There you are! Don't grumble, don't complain, and you'll be all right! Anything can happen, and everything changes... Now you, let's assume, are a nobody, a nothing, a speck of dust... a shrivelled raisin. But who knows? Perhaps in time, ah... you'll be able to seize fortune by the forelock! Anything can happen!"

Alexei Ivanych was silent for a while, shook his head and continued:

"But before, what was it like before? Eh? Good Lord! Your memory plays tricks on you. Without boots, in torn trousers, going about in fear and trepidation... You would work two weeks for one rouble. And they wouldn't give you that rouble – oh no! They would crumple it up and throw it in your face: take it! And anybody could crush you, hurt you, smash you with an axe handle... Anybody could humiliate you... You go with a report and you see, sitting by the door, a little dog. You go up to this dog and take its little paw... its little paw. 'Excuse me,' you say, 'may I go past? Good morning, sir!' But the dog just growls at you – g-r-r-r-r... The porter nudges you with his elbow, but you say to him: 'I have no small change, Ivan Potapych!... I'm sorry, sir!' But most of all I suffered much abuse from this smoked whitefish, from this here... crocodile! From this here very humble-looking man, from Kuritsyn!"

And Alexei Ivanych pointed to a small, bent old man who was sitting next to my papa. The old man was blinking his tired eyes and smoking his cigar in disgust. Usually he never smoked, but if his boss offered him a cigar, he considered it improper to refuse.

Having seen the finger pointing at him, he was terribly embarrassed and began to squirm on his chair.

"I suffered much at the hands of this humble-looking person!" continued Kozulin. "You see, he was the first boss I had. They sent me to him as a humble, inexperienced nobody and put me in his section. And he began to torment me... His every word was like a sharp knife – his every word a bullet in the chest. Now he may look like a little worm, a pathetic little man, but what was he like before! He was a god! I thought the heavens had opened!* He tormented me for a long time! I was writing for him, bringing him pies, sharpening pens and taking his old mother-in-law to the theatre. I did everything for him. I learnt how to take snuff! Y-ess... And it was all for him... I had to have the snuffbox with me constantly, in case he asked for it. Kuritsyn, do you remember? My deceased mother once went to him, and the dear little old lady asked him if he would allow her son – that was me – two days' leave to go and settle his auntie's will. How he fell on her! How he stared at her as he shouted: 'Your son is lazy – he is a parasite. What are you expecting, stupid woman... He ought to be disciplined!' The little old woman went home, fell ill from fright, took to her bed and nearly died then..."

Alexei Ivanych wiped his eyes with his handkerchief and in one gulp drained his glass of wine.

"He wanted me to marry into his family, but luckily at that time I fell ill with fever and spent half a year in hospital. That's how it was then! That was our life! But now? Bah! But now I... am his superior... It is he who takes my mother-in-law to the theatre, it is he who offers me a snuffbox and... look, he is smoking a cigar. Hee-hee-hee... I am the pepper in his life... the pepper! Kuritsyn!"

"Yes, sir?" asked Kuritsyn, rising and standing to attention.

"Present the tragedy!"

"Yes, sir!"

Kuritsyn stretched, frowned, raised his hand above his head, made a face and sang in a thin, tinkling voice:

"Die, perfidious one! I thirst for blood!"*

26

We roared with laughter.

"Kuritsyn! Eat this piece of bread with pepper!"

The already well-fed Kuritsyn took a big piece of rye bread, sprinkled it with pepper and ate it to the accompaniment of loud laughter.

"Everything changes," continued Kozulin. "Sit down, Kuritsyn! When we get up, sing something… Then it was you, now I am the one… Yes… And so the dear old woman died… Yes…"

Kozulin rose and tottered.

"And I… I was silent, because I was insignificant, humble-looking… Torturers… Barbarians… But now it is I… Hee-hee-hee… And now it's you! You! I'm talking to you, clean-shaven man!"

And Kozulin poked his finger in my papa's side.

"Run around the table and crow like a cockerel!"

My papa smiled, blushed winsomely and began to mince around the table. I followed.

"Cock-a-doodle-doo!" We both began to crow at the top of our voices as we ran faster and faster.

As I ran I was thinking:

"I'm going to be the assistant clerk!"

The Lost Cause

I WANT TO CRY MY EYES OUT! If I could howl, it might make it easier.

It was a delightful evening. I dressed carefully, combed my hair, sprayed myself with scent and rolled up to her place like Don Juan. She lives in a dacha in Sokolniki. She is young, beautiful, will have a dowry of thirty thousand, has a little education and loves me, a writer, like a cat.

Arriving at Sokolniki, I found her sitting on our favourite bench under tall, stately fir trees. Seeing me, she rose quickly and, beaming, came to meet me.

"How cruel you are!" she began. "How can you be so late? Surely you know how bored I am. You are a fine one!"

I kissed her pretty little hand, and, trembling, went to sit with her on the bench. I was quivering, aching, and felt that my heart was inflamed and close to breaking. My pulse was racing.

And no wonder! I had come to have my fate decided at last. It's now or never, I thought... All hung on this evening.

The weather was delightful, but I had more important things to think about than the weather. I was not even listening to the song of the nightingale over our heads, even though it is traditional to listen to the nightingale during any even mildly decent rendezvous.

"Why are you so quiet?" she asked, looking me in the face.

"Well... it's such a lovely evening... Is your mama well?"

"She is well."

"Hm... So then... I, you see, Varvara Petrovna, want to have a chat with you... That's the only reason I came... I've been silent, silent, but now... I am a humble servant! I cannot be silent."

Varya bent her head, and with trembling fingers began to pull at a flower. She knew what I wanted to talk about. I was silent awhile, and then continued:

"Why be silent? However silent, however shy, I would sooner or later have to give vent to my feelings and thoughts. You might be offended... perhaps you will not understand, but... so what?"

I fell silent. I had to find the right words.

"Go ahead and speak!" protested her eyes. "You mumbler! Why are you tormenting me?"

"You, of course, already long ago guessed," I continued after a short break, "why I have been coming here every day and plaguing you with my presence. How could you not guess? You, probably, already long ago, with your characteristic insight, guessed the feeling I have, which..." I paused. "Varvara Petrovna!"

Varya bent her head still lower. She began to drum her fingers.

"Varvara Petrovna!"

"Well?"

"I... But what can I say? Of course, even without saying... I love you, that's all... What more is there to say?" I paused. "I'm terribly in love with you! I love you so much that... In short, gather all the novels in the world, and read them through, finding all the declarations of love, vows, sacrifices and... you will understand what... is now in my heart... Varvara Petrovna!" I paused. "But why are you silent?!"

"What can I say?"

"Is it possible... yes?"

Varvara raised her head and smiled.

"Oh, to hell with it!" I thought. She smiled, moved her lips and, almost inaudibly, said, "Why not?"

I desperately seized her hand, desperately kissed her, furiously grabbed her other hand... What a girl! While I squeezed her hands, she pressed her adorable head to my chest, and for only the first time I experienced the luxury of her wonderful hair.

I kissed her head, and the feeling in my heart was as warm as if a samovar had been placed in it. Varya raised her face, and the only thing that remained for me to do was to kiss her lips.

And so, when Varya was already in my arms, when the decision to sign over to me the thirty-thousand-rouble dowry was as good as made – when, in a word, a pretty wife, good money and a promising career were almost guaranteed – the devil must have taken possession of my tongue...

I wanted to show off before my intended bride, to show my principles and to boast. But I myself don't know why I wanted to... It ended very badly.

"Varvara Petrovna!" I began after the first kiss. "Before you agree to be my wife, I consider it to be my most sacred duty, in order to avoid any misunderstanding in the future, to say a few words to you. I shall be brief... Do you know, Varvara Petrovna, who and what I am? Yes, I am honest! I am hard-working! I... I am proud! Moreover, I have a future... But I am poor... I have nothing."

"I know that," said Varya. "Happiness does not lie in money."

"Yes... But who speaks about money? I... I am proud of my poverty. The copecks that I receive for my literary work I would not exchange for those thousands which... with which..."

"Of course. Well, then..."

"I am accustomed to poverty. It's nothing to me. I can go a week without eating... But you! You! Can you, who are not used to walking two steps without hiring a cab, putting on a new dress each day, throwing around money, never knowing need – you, for whom an unfashionable flower is a great misfortune – can you really consent to give up earthly blessings for me? Hm..."

"I have money. I have a dowry!"

"That's nothing! Ten or twenty thousand could easily be spent in just a few years... And then? Poverty? Tears? Believe me, my dear, I have experience. I do know. I know what I'm saying! In order to fight poverty one must have a strong will – superhuman character!"

"What rubbish I'm spouting," I thought, and continued:

"Think awhile, Varvara Petrovna! Think awhile about the step you are proposing to take. Irrevocable step! If you have the strength, come with me... but if you haven't the strength to struggle... refuse me! Oh! It's better for me to lose you than for you to lose your peace of mind. Those hundred roubles that I earn each month for my literary work... are nothing. They are not enough! Please think, before it's too late!"

I leapt up.

"Think! Where there is weakness... there, there are tears, reproaches, early grey hair... I warn you because I am an honourable man. Do you feel yourself strong enough to share my life, which on the surface does not resemble yours, is alien to yours?" I paused.

"I do have a dowry!"

"How much? Twenty, thirty thousand! Ha-ha! A million? And then, besides that, can I take the liberty of accepting that, which... No! Never! I am proud!"

I paced several times around the bench. Varya fell to thinking. I was delighted. If she was thinking, it meant she respected me.

"So then, life with me and hardship or life without me and wealth... Choose... Do you have the strength? Does my Varya have the strength?"

I spoke like this for a very long time. Imperceptibly, I got carried away. I spoke and at the same time felt divided. One half of me got carried away with what I was saying, while the other dreamt: "Just wait, my dear! We'll have no trouble living on your thirty thousand. It will do for a very long time!"

Varya was listening and listening... At last she rose and extended her hand to me.

"I thank you," she said, and she said it in such a voice that made me wince and look into her eyes. Her eyes and cheeks were glistening with tears...

"I thank you. It's good of you to be so candid with me... I'm cosseted... I cannot... We would never make a couple..."

I began to sob. I had blundered... I always become flustered when I see a weeping woman, and now all the more so. While I thought about what to do, she stifled her sobs and wiped her tears.

"You are right," she said. "I would deceive you by marrying you. It's not for me to be your wife. I am a rich woman, cosseted, I travel in cabs, eat snipe and expensive *pirozhki*.* I never have soup or *shchi** for dinner. Mama constantly scolds me, but I cannot go without these things! I cannot go on foot... I get tired... And then clothes... You would have to pay for all these to be made... No! Goodbye!"

And, making a tragic gesture with her hand, she added unnecessarily:

"I am unworthy of you! Farewell!"

She spoke, turned around and walked away. And I? I stood like a fool, thinking nothing, watching her go and feeling that the earth was shaking under me. When I came to my senses and realized where I was and what a huge dirty trick my tongue had played on me, I howled. There was already no sign of her when I wanted to shout, "Come back!"

Disgraced, with nothing to show for my pains, I set off home. The horses were no longer by the gate. Nor did I have any money for a cab. I had to return home on foot.

Three days later I went to Sokolniki. At the dacha they told me Varya was unwell and preparing to go to St Petersburg with her father and grandmother. They told me no more...

Now I lie on the bed, I bite the pillow and beat myself on the head. I feel a gnawing at my heart. Reader, how can I set the matter right? How can I call back my words? What can I say or write to her? It passes my understanding. My cause is lost – and how stupidly lost!

The Chemist's Wife

THE MISERABLE LITTLE TOWN OF B—, consisting of two or three crooked streets, lies deep in sleep. Silence pervades the motionless air. The only sound to be heard is the weak, hoarse yapping of a dog somewhere far away, beyond the town. Soon it will be dawn.

Everything has already long ago gone to sleep. Only the young wife of the pharmacist, Chernomordik, the owner of the chemist's shop in B—, is not asleep. She has gone to bed already three times, but sleep stubbornly does not come to her – and she does not know why. She sits by the open window in just a nightdress, looking out at the street. She finds it hard to breathe, is bored and irritated – so irritated that she even wants to cry, but why... again, she does not know. A lump lies in her chest, and now and again rises to her throat. Several paces behind her, curled up against the wall, Chernomordik himself lies sweetly snoring. A greedy flea is stinging him on the bridge of his nose, but he does not feel it, and even smiles, as if he is dreaming that everyone in town keeps coughing and buying his aniseed drops. He will not be woken now either with pricks, cannons or caresses.

The pharmacy is situated almost on the edge of town, so that a faraway field is visible to the chemist's wife... She sees how little by little the eastern edge of the sky grows light – how it then turns crimson, as if lit by a big fire. Suddenly, from behind a distant shrub, a big, broad-faced moon creeps out. It is red (in general, the moon, rising from behind a shrub, for some reason always seems terribly embarrassed).

Suddenly, amid the night silence, come the sound of footsteps and the jingling of spurs. A voice is heard.

"It's officers from the police inspectorate going to the camp," thinks the chemist's wife.

A little later two figures in white officers' tunics appear: one big and stout, the other smaller and thinner... They idly amble by and trudge along the fence, loudly discussing something. Drawing up to the pharmacy, both figures start to move more quietly and look at the windows.

"There is the smell of a pharmacy," says the thin one. "It's a pharmacy all right! Ah, I remember... I was here last week, and bought castor oil. The chemist here is a man with a sour face and the jaw of an ass. There, my friend, is a jaw! With a jawbone like that, Samson slew the Philistines."*

"Y-y-yes..." says the stout one in a bass voice. "The pharmacy is closed. And the chemist's wife is asleep. The chemist's wife here is pretty, Obtyesov."

"I've seen her. I liked her a lot... Tell me, doctor, can she really love that ass's jawbone? Can she really?"

"No, she probably doesn't love him," sighs the doctor, looking as if he pities the chemist. "The little woman is sleeping now inside. Can you picture her, Obtyesov? Sprawled out from the heat... her pretty mouth half open... her lovely leg hanging over the side of the bed... No doubt the blockhead of a chemist doesn't appreciate what a treasure he has... He sees a woman, probably, as no different from a bottle of carbolic acid!"

"Do you know what, doctor?" says the officer, stopping. "Let's call in at the chemist's and buy something. Maybe we'll see his wife."

"What an idea!... It's night!"

"So what? Surely they have to trade even at night. My dear man, let's go in!"

"If you like..."

The chemist's wife, who is hiding behind the curtain, hears the low, jangling sound of the bell. With a glance at her husband, who is still snoring sweetly and smiling, she throws on a dress, puts shoes on her bare feet and runs to the shop.

Two shadows are visible behind the pane of glass... The chemist's wife turns up the flame in the lamp and hurries to unlock the door; she is no longer bored and irritated, and does not want to

34

cry, but just feels her heart thumping heavily. The stout doctor and the thin Obtyesov enter. Now it is really possible to make them out. The fat-bellied doctor is dark-complexioned, bearded and ungainly. His slightest movement causes his tunic to creak and sweat to break out on his face. As for the officer, he is ruddy-faced, clean-shaven, delicate-featured and as supple as an English whip.

"What can I do for you?" the chemist's wife asks them, pressing her dress to her chest.

"Give us… ahh… fifteen copecks' worth of mint lozenges!"

The chemist's wife, without hurrying, gets a jar from the shelf and begins weighing. The customers look intently at her back; the doctor frowns like a well-fed cat, and the lieutenant looks very serious.

"This is the first time I see a lady serving in a chemist's shop," says the doctor.

"It's nothing unusual here," replies the chemist's wife, giving a sideways glance at Obtyesov's ruddy face. "My husband does not have an assistant, so I always help him."

"So I see… You have a nice little shop! There are so many different… jars! And you're not afraid to move around among poisons! Brrr!"

The chemist's wife seals the package and gives it to the doctor. Obtyesov gives her a fifteen-copeck coin. There is a half-a-minute silence. The men exchange glances, make a move towards the door, then again exchange glances.

"Give me ten copecks' worth of soda!" says the doctor.

The chemist's wife again, moving lazily and sluggishly, stretches her hand towards the shelf.

"Do you have anything here in the shop, anything such as…" mutters Obtyesov, waving his fingers, "anything, you know, like a refreshing drink… seltzer water, perhaps? Do you have seltzer water?"

"We do," replies the chemist's wife.

"Bravo! You're not a woman, but a fairy princess. Kindly get us three or four bottles of it!"

The chemist's wife hastily seals the package of soda and disappears into the darkness behind the door.

"Fruit!" says the doctor with a wink. "You'll not find a peach like that even on the island of Madeira, Obtyesov. Well? What do you think? However... do you hear snoring? It's Mr Chemist himself, who is pleased to sleep."

A minute later the chemist's wife returns and places five little bottles on the counter. She has just been in the cellar, and so is red in the face and a little excited.

"Shhh... quietly," says Obtyesov when she, having opened the bottles, drops the corkscrew. "Don't make so much noise, or you'll wake your husband."

"Well, so what if I wake him?"

"He sleeps so sweetly... he is dreaming about you... Your good health!"

"In any case," says the doctor in his bass voice, belching after the seltzer water, "husbands are so boring that it would be good if they slept all the time. Eh, a little wine would go well with this water!"

"What are you suggesting?" laughs the chemist's wife.

"It would be wonderful! It's a pity they don't sell spirits in a chemist's. However... you should really sell wine as medicine. Do you have any *vinum gallicum rubrum*?"*

"We do."

"Well then! Sell it to us! The devil take it, bring it here!"

"How much do you want?"

"*Quantum satis!*...* Give us first an ounce each, and then we'll see... What do you think, Obtyesov? First with water, and then *per se*..."*

The doctor and Obtyesov sit down at the counter, take off their service caps and start to drink red wine.

"The wine, it has to be admitted, is the most filthy stuff. Vinum Plonkissimum! However, in the presence of... ahh... it seems like nectar... You are entrancing, madam! I mentally kiss your hand."

"I would pay dearly to do it, and not mentally!" says Obtyesov. "Word of honour! I would give my life!"

"You should really stop that," says Mrs Chernomordik, blushing and putting on a serious face.

"What a coquette you are, though!" quietly laughs the doctor, giving her a mischievous sideways look from under his brows. "Your eyes are sending signals. Piff! Paff! I congratulate you: you have overcome us. We are slain!"

The chemist's wife looks at their ruddy faces, listens to their chatter, and she soon comes to life herself. Oh, she already feels so merry! She joins in the conversation, laughs, flirts – and even, at the many urgings of the visitors, drinks two ounces of red wine.

"You officers should come more often to town from camp," she says. "Otherwise it's so boring here. I'm simply dying."

"No wonder!" says the doctor, horrified. "Such a peach... a miracle of nature and... living in the middle of nowhere. It was beautifully expressed by Griboyedov: 'In the middle of nowhere! In Saratov!'* However, we must go. Very pleased to meet you... indeed! How much do we owe you?"

The chemist's wife raises her eyes to the ceiling, and for a long time moves her lips.

"Twelve roubles, forty-eight copecks!" she says.

Obtyesov pulls a fat wallet from his pocket, rummages for a long time in a bundle of money and pays her off.

"Your husband is sleeping sweetly... dreaming..." he mutters, shaking hands in farewell with the chemist's wife.

"I don't like to listen to nonsense..."

"What kind of nonsense is that? On the contrary... it's not at all nonsense... Even Shakespeare said: 'It was blissful in one's youth to be young!'"*

"Let go of my hand!"

Finally the customers, after long exchanges of conversation, kiss the chemist's wife's hand and indecisively, as if changing their mind and wondering whether they have forgotten something, leave the shop.

She quickly runs to the bedroom and sits at the same window as before. She sees how the doctor and lieutenant, on leaving the shop, lazily walk twenty paces away, then stop and begin to whisper about something. About what? Her heart pounds, and there is a pounding also in her temples, but why... she herself does not know... Her heart beats heavily, as if those two, whispering there, are deciding its fate.

Five minutes later the doctor moves away from Obtyesov and walks on, but Obtyesov returns. He walks past the shop once, and again. Now he stops by the door, now he ambles away... Finally he delicately tinkles the bell.

"What? Who's there?" The chemist's wife suddenly hears the voice of her husband. "Someone's ringing, and you don't hear!" says the chemist severely. "What's the matter?"

He gets up, puts on his dressing gown and, swaying half asleep, shuffling in his slippers, goes to the shop.

"What... can I get for you?" he asks Obtyesov.

"Give me... give me fifteen copecks' worth of mint lozenges."

With endless puffing, yawning, dozing off as he moves and knocking his knees against the counter, the chemist reaches up to the shelf and gets the jar...

Two minutes later the chemist's wife sees how Obtyesov leaves the shop and, walking several steps away, throws the mint lozenges on the dusty road. From around the corner the doctor comes to meet him... They meet and, gesticulating with their hands, disappear into the morning mist.

"How unhappy I am!" says the chemist's wife, looking with malice at her husband, who quickly undresses in order to lie down and sleep again. "Oh, how unhappy I am!" she repeats, suddenly bursting into bitter tears. "And no one, no one knows..."

"I forgot the fifteen copecks on the counter," mutters the chemist, pulling the blanket over himself. "Put it, please, in the cash box..."

And he straight away falls asleep.

The Album

TITULAR COUNCILLOR KRATYEROV, tall and as slender as the Admiralty spire, came forward, and, addressing himself to Zhmykhov, said:

"Your Excellency! Moved and touched to the depths of our souls by your many years of leadership and paternal care…"

"For more than ten whole years," prompted Zakusin.

"For more than ten whole years, we, your subordinates, in today's significant for us… ah… day, are presenting to Your Excellency, as a sign of our respect and deep gratitude, this album of our portraits, and we desire in the continuation of your precious life, that is yet… ah… for a very long time, until death itself, that you do not abandon us…"

"By your paternal guidance on the path of truth and progress…" added Zakusin, wiping from his brow some beads of sweat that had suddenly appeared. Evidently he wanted very much to speak, and in all probability had prepared a speech. "And long," he concluded, "may your flag flutter for a very long time yet in the field of enterprise, labour and public service!"

A tear crawled down Zhmykhov's wrinkled left cheek.

"Gentlemen!" he said in a trembling voice. "I was not expecting, and in no way thought, that you would be celebrating my modest anniversary… I am touched… even… very. I shall not forget this minute until I am in the grave, and believe me… believe me, my friends, that no one wishes you so well as I… And if we had our disagreements, I always kept your interests in mind…"

State Councillor Zhmykhov kissed Titular Councillor Kratyerov, who was not expecting such an honour, and grew pale with delight. The chief made a gesture with his hand to show that, from emotion, he could not speak, and began to cry, as though they were not presenting him with a precious album, but, on the contrary, taking it away... Then, having calmed down a little and delivered a few more deeply felt words, he offered his hand to everyone to shake and, accompanied by loud, joyful cries, descended to the street, got into his carriage and, seen off with blessings, departed. Sitting in his carriage, he felt in his chest the onset of a renewed feeling of joy, and again began to cry.

At home, more joy awaited him. There, his family, friends and acquaintances had arranged a great welcome: he was made to feel that he had indeed brought great benefit to his fatherland and that, had he not been in the world, the fatherland would perhaps have been very badly off. The jubilee dinner was marked by toasts, speeches, embraces and tears. In no way had Zhmykhov been expecting his service to be recognized with such an outpouring of heartfelt emotion.

"Ladies and gentlemen!" he said before the dessert. "Two hours ago I was recognized for all the sufferings a man must experience who serves not according to the letter of the law, but from a sense of duty. During all the time of my service I constantly held up before myself the principle: not the public for us, but we for the public. And today I received the highest accolade! My subordinates presented me with an album... Here it is! I was touched."

The celebratory faces stooped to the album and began to examine it.

"Oh, the album is pretty!" said Zhmykhov's daughter Olya. "It must have cost at least fifty roubles. Oh, how delightful it is! Father, give me this album. Do you hear? I shall keep it safe. It's so pretty."

After dinner little Olya took the album away to her room and locked it in a drawer. The next day she took out the pictures of the civil servants and threw them on the floor, and substituted pictures of her school friends. Dress uniforms yielded their place to white pelerines. Kolya, His Excellency's little son, picked up the civil servants and coloured their clothes red. To the whiskerless he added green moustaches – and to the beardless, brown beards. When there was nothing left to colour, he cut the little men out of the photos, pierced their eyes with pins and began to play soldiers. He fixed Titular Councillor Kratyerov to an empty matchbox, and in this way carried him to his father's study.

"Papa, a monument! Look!"

Zhmykhov began to laugh loudly. He rocked back and forth, and, deeply moved, gave Kolya a hearty kiss on the cheek.

"Well, go, naughty child, and show Mama. Let Mama see it too."

The Country Dwellers

A RECENTLY MARRIED COUPLE were strolling back and forth on a station platform in the country. He was holding her around the waist, and she was huddling up to him, and both were happy. From behind scattered clouds the moon gazed down on them and frowned; it was probably envious, and annoyed at the tedium of its enforced solitude. The motionless air was richly saturated with the smell of lilac and bird cherry. Somewhere, on the other side of the rails, a corncrake cried out.

"What a nice night it is, Sasha – how nice!" said the wife. "Really, one might think this is all a dream. Look how peaceful and welcoming the grove looks, and how handsome those solid, silent telegraph poles are! They set off the landscape, Sasha, and say that out here, somewhere, are people... civilization... And don't you like it when the sound of the approaching train comes faintly to your ears on the breeze?"

"Yes... but how hot your hands are! Is it because you are worried about something, Varya? What is there for supper tonight?"

"*Okroshka*,* and chicken... The chicken will be enough for us two. Sardines and *balik* have come from town."

The moon, as if it had taken snuff, hid behind a cloud. Human happiness had reminded it about its loneliness, its solitary bed beyond the forests and valleys...

"The train is coming!" said Varya. "How exciting!"

Three fiery eyes appeared in the distance. The stationmaster came out on the platform. Here and there along the line signal lights began to flash.

"Let's see off the train and go home," said Sasha, yawning. "It's good that we have each other, Varya – so good that it's hard to believe!"

The dark monster crept noiselessly up to the platform and stopped. Through the half-lit carriage windows could be glimpsed sleepy faces, hats, shoulders...

"Ah! Ah!" was heard coming from one carriage. "Varya and her husband have come to meet us! There they are! Varyenka!... Varyechka! Ah!"

Two girls jumped from the carriage and hung on Varya's neck. Behind them appeared a stout, elderly lady and tall, gaunt gentleman with grey side whiskers. Then came two high-school boys, loaded with baggage, followed by a governess; behind the governess came a grandmother.

"Here we are, here we are at last, friend!" said the gentleman with the side whiskers, shaking Sasha's hand. "I dare say you were sick of waiting for us. You were probably cursing your uncle for not coming! Kolya, Kostya, Nina, Fifa... children! Kiss your cousin Sasha! We've come to see you, with all the brood, but just for three or four days. I hope we won't inconvenience you? Please don't stand on ceremony."

Seeing Uncle with the family, the couple were filled with horror. While the old man was speaking and kissing, a picture flashed through Sasha's mind: he saw himself and his wife giving the guests their three rooms, pillows and blankets; he saw the *balik*, sardines and *okroshka* being eaten in an instant, the cousins picking flowers, spilling ink and making a racket, and the aunt talking the whole day about her illnesses (tapeworm and intestinal pain) and about the fact that she was born Baroness von Vinta...

Sasha looked at his young wife with hatred and whispered:

"They've come to see you... the devil take them!"

"No... you!" she replied, growing pale, and also seething with hatred and malice. "They're your relatives, not mine!"

And, turning to the guests, she said with a friendly smile:

"You are welcome."

The moon emerged again from behind the clouds: it seemed to smile – seemed to be pleased that it had no relatives. Sasha turned away in order to conceal from the guests his angry, despairing face, and said, adding a joyous and good-natured tone to his voice:

"You are welcome! You are welcome, dear guests!"

The Intelligent Watchman

IN THE MIDDLE OF THE KITCHEN stood the watchman Filipp, delivering an exhortation. Listening to him were the footman, the coachman, two chambermaids and two cooks – also two kitchen boys, his own children. Each morning he was certain to preach something, and on this particular morning his subject was education.

"You all live like any swinish people," he said, holding in his hands his hat with the buckle. "You all sit here without moving, and it's not possible to see in you anything civilized, just ignorance. Mishka plays draughts, Matryona cracks hazelnuts, Nikifor sneers. Is this really clever? This is not cleverness, but stupidity. You have no mental ability at all! And why?"

"That is so, Filipp Nikandrych," remarked a cook. "It's well known, our intelligence. We are servants. How can we really know anything?"

"And why do you have no mental ability?" continued the watchman. "Because your kind have no ambition. You do not read books, and you know nothing about writing. You should take a book, sit down and read it. I dare say you are literate – you understand the printed word. You, Mishka, should take a book and read it here out loud. It would be useful for you, and enjoyable for the others. All subjects are written about in books. There you will learn about nature, about the Deity, about other countries – what is made from what, and all the languages of other people. And also about idolatry. You would learn about everything from books, if you had the desire. But you just sit by the stove, gorging and drinking. You're just like animals! Foo!"

"It's time for you to go on duty, Nikandrych," remarked a cook.

"I know. It's not your business to tell me. So, take me for example. How do I occupy myself in my old age? What satisfies my

44

Filipp took a tattered book from the cupboard and put it in his
shirt. "This is how I'm going to spend my time. I got into the habit
at an early age. Knowledge is light, ignorance is darkness – you've
probably heard that said? It's so true…"

Filipp put on his hat, grunted and left the kitchen, muttering to
himself. He went through the gate and sat on a bench. A frown
like a black cloud overspread his face.

"They aren't people, but some kind of wretched swine," he
muttered, still thinking about those in the kitchen.

When he had calmed down, he took out the book, sighed con-
tentedly and began to read.

"So well written – it couldn't be better," he thought after reading
the first page. He shook his head. "God does make people wise!"

The book was a good one, a Moscow publication: *The
Cultivation of Root Vegetables: Do We Need Swedes?* After
reading the first two pages, the watchman nodded his head meaningfully and coughed.

"Well written!"

After reading three pages, Filipp fell to thinking. He wanted
to think about education and, for some strange reason, about
Frenchmen. His head sank on his chest, his elbows resting on his
knees. His eyes were half closed.

And Filipp dreamt. Everything, he sees, has changed: the land
is the same, the houses are the same, the gate as before, but the
people have become quite different. All the people are wise – there
is not a single fool, and along the streets is walking Frenchman after
Frenchman. Even the water carrier is capable of reasoning: "I have
to admit, I am very displeased with the climate, and wish to look
at the thermometer." And he too has a thick book in his hands.

"You read the calendar," Filipp says to him.

The cook is stupid, but she interferes in intelligent conversations and shoves her oar in. Filipp goes to the police station, in order to register the lodgers, and strangely, even in this rough place, they speak only about intelligent things, and on all the tables lie books. Now someone goes up to the footman Misha, pushes him and shouts: "Are you sleeping? I ask you: are you sleeping?"

"Do you sleep on duty, you blockhead?" Filipp heard someone's loud voice. "Are you sleeping, you scoundrel, you brute?"

Filipp leapt up and rubbed his eyes. Before him stood the local assistant police constable.

"So, you're sleeping? I shall fine you, you rogue! I shall teach you not to sleep on duty, animal face!"

Two hours later the watchman was summoned to the station.

Then he was again in the kitchen. There, following his instructions, all were sitting around the table and listening to Misha, who was reading something syllable by syllable.

Filipp, frowning and red-faced, went up to Misha, struck the book with his mitten and said in a grim voice:

"Stop it!"

At Christmas Time

I

"WHAT SHALL I WRITE?" asked Yegor, dipping his pen in the ink.

Vasilisa had not seen her daughter for four years. After getting married, her daughter Yefimya had gone with her husband to St Petersburg; she had sent two letters and then disappeared without trace: nothing was seen or heard of her again. And whether the old woman was milking the cow at dawn, stoking the stove or dozing at night, she had just one thought: how was Yefimya – was she still alive? They should have sent a letter, but the old man did not know how to write, and there was no one to ask.

Now it was Christmas time, and Vasilisa could stand it no more. She went to the tavern to see Yegor, the innkeeper's brother-in-law, who, since leaving the service, just sat at home, in the tavern, doing nothing. It was said he could write letters very well, if he was properly paid. Vasilisa had a word in the tavern with the cook, then with the innkeeper's wife, then with Yegor himself. They agreed a fee of fifteen copecks.

And now – this was on the second day of the holiday, in the tavern's kitchen – Yegor was sitting at the table, holding a pen in his hand. Vasilisa was standing in front of him, deep in thought, an expression of care and sadness on her face. With her had come Pyotr, her old man, a very thin, tall man with a brown bald patch; he was standing and looking motionlessly straight ahead, as if blind. In a pan on the stove, pork was being fried; it was sizzling and sputtering, as if saying "Flu-flu-flu". The room was stuffy.

"What shall I write?" Yegor asked again.

"What!" said Vasilisa, looking at him angrily and suspiciously. "Don't rush me! You know you're not writing for free, but for money! Well then, write. To our dear son-in-law Andrei Khrisanfych and our beloved only daughter Yefimya Petrovna with love, a deep bow and undying parental blessings for ever."

"Done. Go on."

"And we also wish you a Happy Christmas. We are alive and well, and we wish you the same, from God… the Heavenly Father."

Vasilisa thought for a moment, and exchanged glances with the old man.

"And we wish you the same, from God… the Heavenly Father…" she repeated, and began to cry.

She could say no more. But earlier, when she had been thinking about it during the night, it had seemed to her that she would not be able to say everything in even ten letters. Since her daughter and son-in-law had left, much water had flowed into the sea, and the old folks had lived like orphans, sighing heavily at night, as if they had buried their daughter. And since then, how many things had happened in the village – how many marriages, deaths! What long winters there had been! What long nights!

"It's hot!" said Yegor, undoing his vest. "It must be about seventy degrees. So what else?" he asked.

The old couple kept silent.

"What does your son-in-law do there?" asked Yegor.

"He is an ex-soldier, you know, my dear fellow," the old man replied in a weak voice. "He left the service at the same time as you. He was a soldier, and now it seems he works at a hydropathic clinic in St Petersburg. The doctor treats patients with water. It seems he's a porter at the doctor's."

"It's written here," said the old woman, taking a letter out of a handkerchief. "We received it from Yefimya, God knows when. Maybe they are no longer in this world."

Yegor thought a little and began to write quickly.

"At the present time," he wrote, "as your fate through your own actions appointed you to Army Servise, then we advise You to look into the Regulations of Dissaplinary Punishments and the

Criminal Laws of the War Office, and you will see in that Law the civelization of the Officials of the War Office."

He wrote and read aloud what he had written, but Vasilisa thought they should have written about how the last year had been so hard, how the bread had run out even before Christmas, and how they had had to sell the cow. They should have asked for money, should have written about how the old man was often unwell and soon would probably have to render his soul to God... But how to express this in words? What to say before, and what after?

"Turn your attention," Yegor continued to write, "to volume 5 of the Milatary Code. Soldier is a generil Name, Well-known. The Very-greatest general and the most-junior Private are called Soldiers..."

The old man moved his lips and quietly said:

"To see the grandchildren, that would be good."

"What grandchildren?" asked the old woman, looking angrily at him. "Maybe there aren't any!"

"Grandchildren? Maybe there are some. Who knows!"

"And therefore You may judge," Yegor hurried on, "which enemy is Foreign and which Domesstic. Our very greatest Domesstic enemy is: Bacchus."

The pen was squeaking, making little flourishes on the paper like fish-hooks. Yegor hurried and read through each line several times. He was sitting on a stool with his legs spread wide under the table, looking well fed and healthy. His face was fleshy, the back of his neck red. He was vulgarity personified – coarse, arrogant, invincible, proud of having been born and raised in a public house. Vasilisa well understood that this was vulgarity, though she could not have expressed it in words, and just looked at Yegor angrily and suspiciously. From his voice, from the incomprehensible words, from the heat and stuffiness, her head began to ache, her thoughts became confused, and now she said nothing: she could not think, and was just waiting for his pen to stop squeaking. But the old man was looking at him full of confidence. He trusted both the old woman, who had brought him there, and Yegor – and when he mentioned the hydropathic clinic, it was clear from his face that he believed in the clinic and in the healing power of water.

Having finished writing, Yegor rose and read the whole letter through from the beginning. The old man did not understand, but nodded his head trustingly.

"It's all right, it reads well," he said. "God grant you health. It's all right."

They put three five-copeck pieces on the table and left the tavern. The old man looked fixedly straight ahead, as if blind. Complete trust was written on his face, but Vasilisa, when she was out of the tavern, threatened to strike the dog and said angrily:

"O-o-o, a plague on you!"

All night the old woman, troubled by her thoughts, did not sleep; in the morning she rose, said her prayers and went to the station to send the letter.

It was eleven versts* to the station.

II

Doctor B.O. Moselweizer's clinic was open on New Year's Day just as on other days, but only the porter Andrei Khrisanfych was wearing a uniform with new braid. There was a special shine to his boots, and he wished all those who arrived a Happy and Prosperous New Year.

It was morning. Andrei Khrisanfych was standing by the door and reading the newspaper. Precisely at ten o'clock a well-known general, one of the regular clients, came in – and, after him, the postman. Andrei Khrisanfych took the general's overcoat and said:

"A Happy New Year – a Prosperous New Year, Your Excellency!"

"Thank you, my good man. And to you too."

Going upstairs, the general nodded towards a door and asked (each day he asked, and then every time forgot):

"What's in that room?"

"It's the massage room, Your Excellency!"

When the general's footsteps had faded, Andrei Khrisanfych looked at the post that had come and found one letter addressed to himself. He opened it, read a few lines and then unhurriedly, looking at the newspaper, went to his room, which was right downstairs at the end of the corridor. His wife Yefimya was sitting on the bed, feeding a child; another child, the eldest, with curly hair, was standing next to her with his head on her knees; a third was sleeping on the bed.

Entering the room, Andrei handed the letter to his wife and said: "It must be from the village."

He went out without raising his eyes from the newspaper, and stopped in the corridor near the door. He could hear how Yefimya was reading the opening lines aloud in a quivering voice. She read and then could read no more: even those lines were enough for her. She burst into tears, and, hugging her eldest child, she kissed him and began to speak, but it was impossible to tell whether she was crying or laughing.

"It's from Granny, from Granddad," she said. "From the village… Queen of Heaven, saints above! The snow is heaped up to the roof there now… the trees are white, so white… The children are on tiny sleighs… And dear bald Granddad is on the stove… and the dear yellow puppy… My own darlings!"

Andrei Khrisanfych, listening to this, recalled that three or four times his wife had given him letters and asked him to send them to the village, but other important jobs had intervened: he had not sent the letters, and they still lay around somewhere.

"And little bunny rabbits run about on the field," continued Yefimya, melting into tears and kissing her boy. "Granddad is gentle and kind, and Granny is also kind, and warm-hearted. They live a simple, God-fearing life in the village… There is a little church in the village, the people sing in the choir. If only the Queen of Heaven, our Holy Mother and Protector, would take us away from here!"

Andrei Khrisanfych went back into the room to smoke until the next client arrived. Yefimya suddenly fell silent and calmed down;

as she wiped her eyes only her lips were trembling. She was afraid of him – oh, so afraid! She shook and trembled in terror at the sound of his footsteps, at the look he gave her, and did not dare say a single word in his presence.

Andrei Khrisanfych lit a cigarette, but just at that moment the bell upstairs rang. He put out the cigarette and, assuming a very serious face, hastened to the front door.

The general was coming downstairs, pink-cheeked, fresh from his bath.

"And what is in that room?" he asked, pointing to a door.

Andrei Khrisanfych came smartly to attention and replied loudly:

"The Charcot shower,* Your Excellency!"

The Decoration

A TEACHER AT A MILITARY high school, Collegiate Registrar Lev Pustyakov, lived next door to a friend, Lieutenant Ledyentsov. To the latter he directed his steps one New Year's morning.

"I'm in a quandary, Grisha," he said to the lieutenant after the usual New Year's greetings. "I wouldn't have disturbed you but for extreme need. Lend me your Stanislav for the day, old man. You see, I'm dining at the merchant Spichkin's today. And you know that rascal Spichkin – he adores decorations, and seems to look on those who do not have something dangling around their neck or affixed to their buttonhole as little more than swine. And what's more, he has two daughters... Nastya, you know, and Zina... I say, as a friend... You understand, my dear man. Give it to me, do me a favour!"

Pustyakov said all this stammeringly, turning red and looking at the door in embarrassment. The lieutenant uttered an oath, but agreed.

At two o'clock in the afternoon Pustyakov took a cab to Spichkin's. Pulling aside his fur coat, he looked down at his chest. There he saw, gleaming with gold and brilliantly coloured enamel, the lieutenant's Stanislav.

"Somehow you feel more self-respect," thought the teacher, holding himself with dignity. "It's just a trinket, worth five roubles, not more, but what a stir it creates!"

Arriving at Spichkin's house, he flung open his fur coat and began slowly to pay off the cabman. The cabman, seeing his shoulder strap, buttons and Stanislav, seemed turned to stone. Pustyakov coughed smugly and entered the house. Taking off his coat in the vestibule, he glanced into the reception room. There, sitting at a long table, some fifteen people were already dining. The sound of voices and the clinking of plates could be heard.

"Who is it who rang?" was heard the voice of the host. "Ah, Lev Nikolaich! Welcome. You're a little late, but it doesn't matter. We have only just sat down."

Pustyakov thrust forward his chest, raised his head and, rubbing his hands, entered the room. But then he saw something appalling. At the table, sitting next to Zina, was his colleague, the French teacher Tremblant. To have the Frenchman see his decoration would be to raise a host of awkward questions – would mean to be humiliated and disgraced for ever... Pustyakov's first impulse was to pull off the decoration or to leave, but the decoration was firmly affixed, and retreat was out of the question. He quickly covered the decoration with his right hand and, stooping awkwardly, bowed to the other guests. Without offering his hand to anyone, he lowered himself heavily onto the free chair just opposite his French colleague.

"He must have been drinking," thought Spichkin, seeing his guest's disconcerted face.

A plate of soup was placed before Pustyakov. He took the spoon in his left hand but, remembering that it was not good manners to eat with the left hand in polite society, said that he had already dined and was not hungry.

"I have already had dinner, sir... *Merci, Monsieur*," he muttered. "I was visiting my uncle, Archpriest Yeleyev, and he prevailed upon me... to... dine."

Pustyakov was oppressed by an irritable feeling of gloom and vexation: the soup was giving off an appealing smell, and from the fresh sturgeon was rising an unusually appetizing cloud of steam. The teacher thought of freeing his right hand and covering the decoration with his left, but did not dare attempt it.

"They will notice. And my arm would be stretched across my chest as if I were about to sing. God, if only this dinner would finish quickly! I could dine later at the tavern!"

After the third course, he glanced timidly at the Frenchman. Tremblant, for some reason highly embarrassed, was looking at him too, and also not eating. Noticing each other's stares, both grew even more disconcerted and lowered their eyes to empty plates.

"He's noticed, the scoundrel," thought Pustyakov. "I can see from his face that he's noticed! And he's a gossip, the swine. Tomorrow he'll doubtless tell the director!"

The host and guests ate the fourth course, and then, inevitably, the fifth too…

A tall gentleman with flared, hairy nostrils, a hooked nose and a natural squint in his eyes rose. He ran his hand over the back of his head and began to speak:

"Ah… ah… I pro… pro… propose that we drink to the health of the ladies present!"

The diners rose noisily and lifted their glasses. A loud hurrah resounded through the rooms. The ladies broke into smiles and stretched out to clink their glasses. Pustyakov rose and took his wineglass in his left hand.

"Lev Nikolaich, be so kind as to pass this glass to Nastasya Timofeyevna," a man appealed to him, offering a glass. "Insist that she drink!"

This time Pustyakov, to his great horror, found he was going to have to use his right hand. The Stanislav, with its by now slightly crumpled red ribbon, was at last revealed and shone in the light of day. The teacher went pale, lowered his head and stole a sideways look at the Frenchman. His colleague looked at him with astonished, enquiring eyes. The Frenchman's lips creased into a sly smile, and the look of discomfort on his face gradually faded…

"Yuli Avgustovich!" the host appealed to the Frenchman. "Pass the bottle along to the other guests!"

Tremblant reluctantly stretched his right hand out towards to the bottle and… oh, what happiness! Pustyakov saw a decoration on his chest. And it was not the Stanislav, but the genuine Anna! So even the Frenchman was a cheat! Pustyakov broke into delighted laughter, sat down and relaxed in relief… Now it was no longer necessary to conceal the Stanislav! Both were guilty of the same offence, so neither could denounce the other…

"Ah-h-h… hmm!" murmured Spichkin, noticing the decorations on the chests of the teachers.

"Yes, sir," said Pustyakov. "Amazing thing, Yuli Avgustovich! How little suspicion we had before the holiday! There are so many people, yet only you and I were honoured. A-maz-ing thing!"

Tremblant happily nodded his head and pushed forward his left lapel, on which gleamed the Anna, third class.

After dinner, Pustyakov strolled through all the rooms showing his decoration to the young ladies. His heart was light and carefree despite a gnawing sensation of hunger in the pit of his stomach.

"If only I had known," he thought, looking enviously at Tremblant, who was conversing with Spichkin about decorations. "I would have put on a Vladimir. Oh, I never thought of it!"

Just this one thought tormented him for a while. But in all other respects he was blissfully happy.

The Comedy Sketch

D INNER HAD FINISHED. The cook was told to clear the table as quietly as possible and not to make a sound with either the crockery or her feet... The children were hurriedly sent off to the woods... The reason was that the master of the dacha, Osip Fyodorych Klochkov – a gaunt, consumptive man with hollow eyes and a hooked nose – had drawn from his pocket a notebook and, self-consciously clearing his throat, was preparing to read a comedy sketch of his own composition. The plot of his sketch was uncomplicated, inoffensive and short. Here it is.

A government official, Yasnosyerdtsev, runs onto the stage and announces to his wife that he has invited his superior, Councillor of State Kleshchov, who had begun to show an interest in their daughter Liza, to visit them. There then follows a long monologue by Yasnosyerdtsev on the theme of how pleasant it would be to be the father-in-law of a general. "He would be all covered in stars, with red stripes down the sides of his trousers, with me sitting next to him, and... it would all seem so natural! As if I am not really the most insignificant creature in the whirling universe!" Dreaming of such a vision, the future father-in-law suddenly notices a strong smell of roasting goose in the room. Because it would be embarrassing to entertain an important guest in a room that stank, Yasnosyerdtsev rebukes his wife. She raises a howl, shouting, "There's no pleasing you!" The future father-in-law clutches his head and demands that she stop crying, as it would not do to meet an important guest with tears. "Fool! Dry your eyes... you corpse, you ignorant Herodias!" Hysterics from the wife. The daughter declares that she is not prepared to live with such wild parents, and dresses to leave the house. Things just get worse and worse. It ends with the important guest finding on the stage a doctor, who is bathing the husband's head with soothing lotion while a police officer writes a report about the breach of the peace. And that is all. Also inserted is a portrait of Liza's betrothed, Granski, a law graduate of distinction and a man of modern outlook, who talks about principles and is presented in the sketch as being good-natured.

As he read, Klochkov kept glancing sideways: were they laughing? To his delight, the guests now and again covered their mouths with their fists and looked at each other.

"Well? What do you say?" Klochkov raised his eyes to the guests, having finished the reading. "How was it?"

In reply to this, the eldest of the guests, Mitrofan Nikolaich Zamazurin, grey-haired and as bald as the moon, rose and, with tears in his eyes, embraced Klochkov.

"Thank you, dear man," he said. "It has been a real treat. You have written this so well that it has even left me in tears. Let me embrace you... once again..."

"Excellent! Wonderful!" Polumrakov leapt up. "Talent, complete talent! Do you know what, brother? Give up your job and be good enough to write! Write and write! It's a sin to hide your light under a bushel!"

There were congratulations and embraces. The guests went into raptures. They sent for Russian champagne.

Klochkov grew very excited. He went red in the face and, overwhelmed with emotion, began to walk around the table.

"For a long time I've sensed this talent developing in me!" he began, coughing and waving his arms. "Right from my very childhood. I write literature, with a dash of wit... I know the stage, because I took part in amateur theatricals for about ten years... What more is needed? Only to do a bit more work in this field, to do a bit of studying... In what way am I worse than others?"

"Indeed, to do a bit of studying," said Zamazurin. "That is certainly true. But this is the thing, dear man... Pardon me, but I believe in speaking the truth... The truth comes before everything... Your depiction of Kleshchov, the councillor of state... It is, my friend, not good... It is nothing, in essence, and somehow, you know, unsubtle... The general is neither one thing nor another. Take

58

him out, brother! What's more, our own general will be angry – will think you are portraying him. The old man will be offended. And he's been very good to us up to now... Take him out!"

"It's true," Klochkov said in a worried voice. "There will have to be a change... I shall call him simply 'Your Honour'... Or no, just 'Kleshchov', without a title..."

"And there's something else," remarked Polumrakov. "It may be a detail, but it's also awkward... it hits you in the eye... You have this here fiancé, Granski, tell Liza that if her parents do not want her to marry him, he'll marry her against their will. Perhaps this is also a small point... perhaps parents really are pigs in their tyranny, but nowadays how can this be mentioned? You might get a lot of criticism!"

"Yes, it's a bit strong," agreed Zamazurin. "Somehow you should gloss over that bit. Also, get rid of the reflection about how pleasant it would be to be the father-in-law of one's superior. It would indeed be pleasant, but you make fun of it. You shouldn't joke about such things, brother... Our boss also married a girl from a poor family, so does it follow that he behaved badly? Did he, in your opinion? Wouldn't he be offended? Well, let's imagine he's sitting in the theatre and seeing this very... Is it something he would find pleas- ant? But wasn't it he who supported you when you and Salaleyev applied for an allowance? 'He is a sick man,' he said. 'He,' he said, 'needs money more than Salaleyev'... Do you see?"

"And you must admit that you were taking him off," said Bulyagin with a wink.

"Certainly not!" said Klochkov. "As God is my witness, I was not thinking of anyone in particular!"

"Yes, well... let's leave it there, shall we? But he certainly loves to run after the fair sex. You've probably noticed that about him. And you should cut out that... police officer. He's unnecessary. And cut out that Granski... he's portrayed as a hero, but God knows what he does. He talks about such strange things. If only you were to criticize him, but on the contrary you sympathize with him... Perhaps he is a good man, but... only the Devil can understand him! You can interpret his words in any way at all..."

"And do you know who that Yasnosyerdtsev is? He's our Yenyakin... He's the one Klochkov is thinking of... The privy councillor, eternally fighting with his wife and daughter... He's the one... Thank you, friend! It serves him right, the scoundrel! Maybe now he'll stop giving himself airs!"

"But even though this Yenyakin, for example, is a wastrel and scoundrel," said Zamazurin, sighing, "all the same he does invite you to his house, and is godfather to your Nastyusha... It's not right, Osip! Take him out! I think it would be better to cut him out. To get involved in these things... truly... Now the talk will go: who, how... why... And you wouldn't be pleased about that!"

"That's true..." confirmed Polumrakov. "It's just a bit of fun, but from such fun may come trouble that you would not set right in even ten years... It would be a mistake to get involved, Osip. It's not your business... It would suit Gogol or Krylov...* They really were scholars – but what education have you had? You're like a worm we can hardly see! Any fly can crush you... Give it up, brother. If our chief finds out, then... Give it up!"

"Tear it up!" whispered Bulyagin. "We won't tell anyone. If they ask, we'll say you read us something, but that we didn't understand..."

"Why say anything? We don't have to talk," said Zamazurin. "If they ask, well, then... we're not going to lie. We have to look after ourselves... But you would cause all this trouble, and we would take the rap! I would suffer worst of all. They wouldn't go for you, a sick man, but we would get it in the neck... I must say, I don't like it!"

"Quiet, gentlemen... Someone's coming... Hide it, Klochkov!"

Klochkov, pale in the face, quickly hid the notebook, scratched his head and fell to thinking.

"Yes, it's true," he sighed. "People will talk... they will misunderstand... Maybe there are even things in my sketch that we can't see but others can... I'll tear it up... And you, my friends, please, talk to no one about... this..."

The Russian champagne was brought in... The guests drank it up and dispersed...

The Civil-Service Exam

"THE GEOGRAPHY TEACHER Galkin has it in for me, and, believe me, I shall not pass his exam today," said Yefim Zakharych Fendrikov, a grey-haired, bearded man with a venerable bald patch and a substantial belly, who was the clerk at the post office in the town of Kh—. He was nervously rubbing his hands and sweating. "I shall not pass... As sure as God is holy... He is angry at me, and only because of a trifle. He came to me once with a registered letter and pushed his way to the head of the queue so that I, do you see, would take his letter before anyone else's. It's not right... Though he is of the educated class, he should, all the same, follow procedure and wait. I gave him a suitable reprimand. 'Wait,' I said, 'your turn, dear sir.' He flared up, and since that time has turned against me like Saul. He gave my son Yegorushka a one,* and called me various names in town. Once, when I was going past Kukhtin's tavern, he leant out of the window holding a billiard cue and drunkenly shouted to all the square: 'Gentlemen, have a look: the used postage stamp is going by!'"

The Russian teacher Pivomedov, who was standing with Fendrikov in the entrance hall of the district school of Kh— and indulgently smoking a cigarette that the other had given him, shrugged and calmly replied:

"Don't worry. There's never been a case of any of you men failing an exam. It's just a formality."

Fendrikov calmed down, but not for long. Through the entrance hall came Galkin, a young man with a straggly, ragged beard, who was wearing rough canvas trousers and a new, dark-blue tailcoat. He looked severely at Fendrikov and walked past.

Then word came that the inspector was on his way. Fendrikov went cold, waiting with the fear so well known to all first-time defendants and examinees. Khamov, the staff supervisor of the

61

district school, strode through the entrance hall to the street. After him the professor of law, Zmiezhalov, wearing the headgear of an Orthodox priest, with a cross on his chest over his cassock, hurried to meet the inspector. Other teachers also came rushing. The inspector of the national schools, Akhakhov, greeted them boisterously, expressed his displeasure about the dust and entered the college. Five minutes later the examinations began.

Two priests' sons were examined for the post of village teacher. One passed, but the other did not. The one who failed blew his nose in a red handkerchief, stood awhile in thought and left. Two military recruits of the third rank were examined. Then came Fendrikov's moment...

"Where do you work?" asked the inspector, turning to him.

"In the local post office, Your Honour, as a clerk," he replied, straightening himself and trying to conceal from the company his trembling hands. "I've served for twenty-one years, Your Honour, but now need certification for promotion to the rank of collegiate registrar, and for that I venture to undergo the examination for the first class."

"Very well, then... Take a dictation."

Pivomedov rose, coughed and began to dictate in a rich, resonant bass voice, trying to catch the examinee on words that are not spelt as they are spoken: "Colt wadder is gud wen yew wan da dring" – and so on.

But however hard the cunning Pivomedov tried, the dictation went well. The would-be collegiate registrar made only a few mistakes, though he paid more attention to his handwriting than to the spelling of the words. The word "emergency" he wrote with two *m*s, the word "better" he wrote "bedder" – and on seeing the words "a new profession" a smile spread over the inspector's face, because Fendrikov had written "a new profeshon" – but after all, these were not serious mistakes.

"The dictation was satisfactory," said the inspector.

"I would like to inform Your Honour," said the encouraged Fendrikov, stealing a sideways glance at his enemy Galkin, "I would like to report that I studied geometry from Davydov's textbook, tutored by Varsonofy's nephew, who had arrived for the holidays from the Trinity Lavra of St Sergius,* the Vifanskaya Seminary. I studied plane and three-dimensional geometry... everything..."

"Three-dimensional geometry is not on the syllabus."

"Not on the syllabus? But I laboured over it for a month... What a shame," sighed Fendrikov.

"But let's leave geometry for the time being. Let's turn to science, which you, as an employee of the post office, probably love. Geography is the study for postmen."

All the teachers smiled deferentially. Fendrikov did not agree that geography is the study for postmen (nowhere had it been written that this was so – neither in postal regulations nor in district orders), but out of respect he said: "Yes, sir." He coughed nervously and awaited the questions in terror. His enemy Galkin leant back in his chair and, without looking at him, asked in a drawl:

"Ah... tell me... what sort of government is there in Turkey?"

"It's well known what... Turkish..."

"Hm!... Turkish... It's a vague reply. Turkey has a constitutional government. And do you know what are the tributaries of the Ganges?"

"I studied Smirnov's geography text, but, excuse me, did not learn it very well... The Ganges, it's the river in India that flows... this river flows to the sea."

"I didn't ask you that. What tributaries does the Ganges have? Do you not know? And where does the Aras River* flow? Do you not know that either? It's strange... In what province is Zhitomir?"

"Route 18, district 121."

A cold sweat broke out on Fendrikov's brow. He began to blink, and gulped so heavily that it seemed as if he had swallowed his tongue.

"As before the true God, Your Honour," he began to mutter. "Even Father Archpriest can confirm... I've served for twenty-one years and now this is the most... which... I shall pray to God for you for the rest of my life..."

"Very well, let's leave geography. What arithmetic have you prepared?"

"I did not learn very much arithmetic either... Even Father Archpriest can confirm... I shall pray to God for you for the rest of my life... I have studied since St Pokrov's Day, I have studied and... have made no sense of it... I am too old to study... Be merciful, Your Honour, and I shall pray to God for you for the rest of my life."

Tears hung from Fendrikov's eyelashes.

"I've served honourably and blamelessly... I fast every year... Even Father Archpriest can confirm... Be lenient with me, Your Honour."

"Have you prepared nothing?"

"I've prepared everything, sir, but can remember nothing, sir... I shall soon be sixty, Your Honour. How on earth can I keep up with studies? Have mercy on me!"

"He has already ordered a cap with a cockade for himself," said Archpriest Zmiezhalov, grinning.

"Very well. Be on your way," said the inspector.

Half an hour later Fendrikov was walking with the teachers to Kukhtin's tavern to have tea and celebrate. His face glowed, his eyes shone with happiness, but by repeatedly scratching the back of his head he showed that some thought was troubling him.

"What a pity!" he muttered. "Be so good as to tell me: was it not complete stupidity on my part?"

"What do you mean?" asked Pivomedov.

"Why did I study three-dimensional geometry, if it's not on the syllabus? You see, I laboured for a whole month over the damn subject. What a pity!"

Truth Will Out

IN A HIRED TROIKA, along back roads, travelling strictly incognito, Pyotr Pavlovich Posudin was hurrying to the little county town of N——, whither he had been summoned by an anonymous letter he had received.

"To catch them... I'll come like a bolt out of the blue," he mused, hiding his face in his collar. "They got up to abominable things and dirty tricks, and are celebrating, probably imagining that no one will be the wiser... Ha-ha... I can imagine their horror and astonishment when at the height of their celebration they hear: 'Bring Tyapkin-Lyapkin here!'* That will really cause an uproar! Ha-ha..."

Having tired of musing, Posudin entered into conversation with his driver. As a man who craved popularity, he first of all asked about himself:

"So do you know Posudin?"

"How can I not know him!" grinned the driver. "I know him."

"Why do you laugh?"

"It would be amazing not to know Posudin when one knows every last clerk! That's why he was sent here, for everyone to know him."

"That's true... Well, what do you think? How is he, in your opinion? A good man?"

"Not bad," yawned the driver. "He's a good gentleman, knows his business... It's not yet two years since he was sent here, but already he's done lots of things."

"What in particular has he done?"

"He's done a lot of good, God give him health. He managed to get a railway, sent Khokhryukov packing from our county town... There was no end to that Khokhryukov... He was a scoundrel, a cunning rogue. He had all the previous ones in the palm of his

65

hand, but Posudin arrived – and away went Khokhryukov to the devil, as if he had never been... There you have it, brother. You'll never bribe Posudin, brother. No-o-o! Offer him even a hundred, even a thousand, and he will not let you burden his soul with sin... No-o-o!"

"Praise God, at least he understands that side of me," thought Posudin, rejoicing. "It's good."

"He's an educated gentleman..." continued the driver. "Not proud... Some of our people went to him with a complaint, and he received them as if they were gentlemen: he shook hands with them all and asked them to sit down... He's energetic and impulsive... He doesn't talk to you calmly, it's always 'Harrumph! Harrumph!' And he never walks anywhere – my God, he does everything on the run, everything on the run! Before our people could say a word to him he shouted 'Horses!' – and came straight here... He came and managed everything... didn't take a copeck. He's much better than the previous man! Of course, even the previous one was good. He was a very distinguished, important-looking man, and no one in the district could shout louder than him. When he was on the road, you could hear him ten versts away – but in any business dealings Posudin is much more cunning! He has a brain a hundred times bigger... There's only one thing wrong... He's a good man in every way, but there's only one thing wrong: he's a drunkard!"

"Well, this is a fine development," thought Posudin.

"Where have you heard," he asked, "that I... that he is a drunkard?"

"Of course, I haven't myself seen him drunk, Your Honour, I shall not lie – but people have said. And those people haven't seen him drunk either, but that's the rumour about him that's going around. In public, or when he goes visiting, or at a ball, or in company, he never drinks. But at home he swills... He gets up in the morning, rubs his eyes and sees to the first business of the day – vodka! When his valet brings him a glass, he is already asking for another... So he spends the whole day getting smashed.

And, believe it or not, he drinks but doesn't at all get drunk. So he knows how to hold his drink. When our Khokhryukov used to drink, not just the people, but the dogs would howl. But that Posudin... his nose doesn't even redden! He locks himself in his study and slurps it up... So that people wouldn't notice, he set up a box with a little pipe on his table. There's always vodka in that box... You just bend down to the pipe, suck and get drunk... There's a briefcase in his carriage..."

"How do they know?" thought Posudin in horror. "Good Lord, even that is known! How utterly appalling..."

"And then in his relations with the fair sex... he's a scoundrel!" The driver shook his head and began to laugh. "It's scandalous, as simple as that! He has about ten of these... floozies... Two of them live in his house. One of them, that's Nastasya Ivanovna, acts as his housekeeper, the other (what the devil's her name?), Lyudmila Semyonovna, is a kind of secretary... Nastasya is the most important of all. Whatever she wants, he does it all for her... She twists him round her little finger, like a fox twisting its tail. She has a lot of influence. And people aren't as afraid of him as of her... Ha-ha... A third wench lives on Kachalnaya Street... Shameful!"

"He even knows their names," thought Posudin, reddening. "And who is it who knows? A peasant, a driver who has never even been in that town!... How abominable... disgusting... vulgar!"

"How on earth do you know all this?" he asked irritably.

"People have said... I haven't myself seen, but have heard from people. Is it hard to learn things? You can't cut off valets' or coach-men's tongues... And maybe even Nastasya herself walks through all the side streets happily boasting to her women friends. You can't hide from people's eyes... And that Posudin also has taken to driving very secretively to inspections... The previous man, when he wanted to go somewhere, let it be known a month before, and when he drove there was noise, thundering hooves, ringing bells and... God preserve us! And people would gallop ahead of him, and gallop behind, and gallop beside him. He would arrive at a place, have a good sleep, eat and drink his fill and then shout himself hoarse about his official business. He would shout, stamp his feet, again have a good sleep and go back in the same way... But nowadays, when Posudin hears about something, he tries to go and come back quietly, quickly, so no one sees or knows... What a joke! He comes out of the house unnoticed, so the officials don't see him, and gets into the train. He gets to whatever station he has to, and then doesn't take post-horses or anything high-class, but tries to engage a peasant to drive him. He wraps himself all up, like a woman, and wheezes all the way, like an old hound, so his voice isn't recognized. You'd just split your sides laughing, when people tell you... He drives along, the fool, and thinks he can't be recognized. But people who understand know him – tfoo! It's as easy as pie..."

"So how do they recognize him?"

"Very easy. Before, when our Khokhryukov used to travel incognito, he could be known from his heavy hands. If the one you were driving hit you in the teeth, it meant it was Khokhryukov. But you can spot Posudin straight away... An ordinary passenger conducts himself ordinarily, but Posudin is not such as to go for simplicity. He arrives, shall we say, at the post-chaise station, and starts in... He says it stinks, and is stuffy, and cold. He demands to be served chicken, and fruit, and all kinds of jams... So at the station they know: if in winter someone asks for chicken and fruit, then it has to be Posudin. If someone calls the superintendent 'my dear man', and then sends people chasing around for various trifles, then you can swear it's Posudin. He doesn't stink like other people, and goes to bed in his own way... He lies at the station on a sofa, sprays scent around him, and demands that three candles be placed by his pillow. He lies there and reads papers... Not just the superintendent, but even a cat can understand who such a man is..."

"True, true," thought Posudin. "Why didn't I know this before?"

"And those who have to know can know him even without the fruit and without the chicken. By telegraph everything is well known… However you cover up your face, however you hide, here they know you're coming. They're expecting you… Posudin has not yet come out of his house, but here already, if you please, everything is ready! He arrives, to catch someone red-handed, to prosecute or dismiss someone, but they're already laughing at him. 'Though you have come unexpectedly, Your Excellency,' they will say, 'look: everything is as it should be!…' He turns around and goes back the way he came… And he praises us all, shakes hands with everyone, asks pardon for the disturbance… There it is! So what do you think? Ho-ho, Your Honour! People here are smart, every last one of them!… Look at any of them, what devils they are! And now, even today, take an example… I'm driving along empty this morning, and the Yid snack-bar assistant comes running to meet me from the station. 'Where,' I ask, 'Your Yiddish Honour, are you going?' And he says: 'I am taking wine and delicacies to the town of N—. They are expecting Posudin there today.' Cunning? Posudin is still, perhaps, only preparing to come, or is muffling up his face so he can't be recognized. Maybe he's already on his way, and thinking that no one has any idea he's coming, but already, for Heaven's sake, wine and salmon and cheese and various delicacies have been prepared for him… So? He's driving along and thinking 'You're done for, lads!' – but the lads couldn't care less! Let him come! They've long ago hidden everything!"

"Turn back!" shouted Posudin hoarsely. "Drive back, swine!"

And the astonished driver turned back.

Ladies

FYODOR PETROVICH, the director of studies for the schools of the province of N—, who considered himself a fair and generous man, one day asked the teacher Vremyensky to see him in the administrative office.

"No, Mr Vremyensky," he said, "you will have to leave. With your voice as it is, you cannot continue in the teaching profession. How did you lose it?"

"I drank cold beer when I was in a sweat..." wheezed the teacher.

"What a shame! A man works for fourteen years, and suddenly such a disaster strikes! The devil knows why your career has to end because of such a trifle. So what do you intend to do now?"

The teacher said nothing.

"Do you have a family?" asked the director.

"A wife and two children, Your Excellency," stuttered the teacher.

A silence set in. The director rose from behind the table and paced nervously back and forth.

"I have no idea what to do with you," he said. "You cannot be a teacher, and you are not yet entitled to a pension... And to release you to the whims of fate, to I don't know what future, is not at all easy. You're one of us – you have served for fourteen years – so it is our responsibility to help you... But how can we help? What can I do for you? Put yourself in my position: what can I do for you?"

A silence set in. The director kept walking and thinking, and Vremyensky, who had suppressed his misery, sat on the edge of the chair and also thought. Suddenly the director brightened, and he even snapped his fingers.

"It's amazing that I didn't think of this before!" He began to speak quickly. "Listen, this is what I propose... Next week a clerk in our hostel is due to retire. If you wish, you can have his job. There you are!"

Vremyensky, not having expected such kindness, also brightened.

"It's an excellent idea," said the director. "Write the application today..."

After dismissing Vremyensky, Fyodor Petrovich felt relief and even pleasure: the bent figure of the wheezing pedagogue was no longer before him, and it was pleasant to think that, having offered Vremyensky the vacant position, he had acted fairly and according to his conscience, like a kind, thoroughly decent man. But this good mood did not last long. When he went home and sat down to dinner, his wife, Nastasya Ivanovna, suddenly recalled:

"Oh yes, I almost forgot! Nina Sergeyevna came to me yesterday to press the case for a young man. They say a vacancy has occurred in our hostel..."

"Yes, but that place has already been promised to another," said the director, frowning. "And you know my rule: I never offer a place through patronage."

"I know, but I suppose it's possible to make an exception for Nina Sergeyevna. She loves us like her relatives, but until now we've never done anything for her. So don't think of refusing, Fedya! With your whims you would offend her, and me too."

"But who does she recommend?"

"Polzukhin."

"What?... Polzukhin? You mean the one who played at Chatsky's New Year's party? That gentleman? Not for anything!"

The director stopped eating.

"Not for anything!" he repeated. "God preserve me!"

"But why?"

"Understand, my dear, that if a young man acts indirectly, through a woman, then he is worthless! Why doesn't he come to see me himself?"

After dinner, the director lay down on the sofa in his study and began to read the newspapers and letters that had come.

"Dear Fyodor Petrovich," the wife of the district council chairman wrote to him. "You once said that I am a student of human nature and a good judge of people. Now there is an opportunity for you to verify this in practice. One of these days a certain K.N. Polzukhin, whom I know to be a fine young man, will come to you to ask to be appointed to the position of clerk in our hostel. He is a very pleasant young man. If you give him a chance, you will be satisfied…" Etc.

"Not for anything!" said the director. "God help me!"

After this, not a day passed when the director did not receive letters recommending Polzukhin. One fine day Polzukhin himself even arrived. He was a young man, stout, with the clean-shaven face of a jockey, wearing a new black suit…

"I do not deal with business affairs here, but in the office," the director said drily after listening to his request.

"Forgive me, Your Excellency, but our mutual acquaintances advised me to come directly to you."

"Hm!…" mumbled the director, casting a look of distaste at the young man's pointed shoes. "As far as I know," he said, "your father is well off, and you are not in need. How is it that you need this position? The salary is really a pittance!"

"It's not for the salary, but so that… It's nevertheless an entry to the civil service…"

"All the same… I think that after a month or so the work will bore you and you'll give it up. Meanwhile there are candidates for whom the position would be a career for life. There are needy people for whom—"

"I shall not be bored, Your Excellency," interrupted Polzukhin. "On my word of honour, I shall apply myself!"

The director was boiling with anger.

"Listen," he said, smiling disdainfully, "why didn't you come straight to me, but think it necessary to trouble the ladies?"

"I didn't know you would find it disagreeable," replied Polzukhin in embarrassment. "But, Your Excellency, if you attach no importance to letters of recommendation, I can supply you with testimonials…"

He drew from his pocket a piece of paper and gave it to the director. At the bottom of the testimonial, which was written in official language and handwriting, lay the signature of the governor. It seemed likely that the governor had signed it without reading it, if only to get rid of some importunate lady.

"There is no more to be done – I relent... I'll do as I'm told..." said the director with a sigh after reading through the testimonial. "Send in your application tomorrow... There is no more to be done..."

When Polzukhin left, the director was overcome by a feeling of disgust.

"Worthless boy!" he hissed, pacing back and forth. "So you got your own way, devious operator. Ladies' man! Swine! Vermin!"

The director swore loudly at the door by which Polzukhin had gone out, and felt suddenly embarrassed, because just then there came into his study a lady, the wife of the financial director...

"If I may trouble you for a moment, just a moment..." began the lady. "Sit down, my friend, and listen carefully to me... Now then, they say you have a position available... Tomorrow or today a young man will come to see you, a certain Polzukhin..."

The lady chattered on, while the director gazed at her with lacklustre, dazed eyes, like a man about to faint; he looked at her and smiled politely.

The next day, after calling Vremyensky into his office, it was a long time before the director could bring himself to tell the man the truth. He hesitated, got confused and could not decide where to begin or what to say. He wanted to apologize to the teacher, to tell him the whole truth, but his speech was indistinct, like a drunk's, and his ears were burning. It became suddenly painful and annoying that he had to play such a ridiculous role – in his own office, before a subordinate. Suddenly, he struck the table, leapt up and angrily shouted:

"I have no position for you! None whatsoever! Leave me now in peace. Don't torment me! Leave me. Do me a favour!"

And he walked out of the office.

Small Fry

"HONOURED SIR, FATHER AND BENEFACTOR!" wrote the clerk Nevyrazimov in the rough draft of a congratulatory letter. "I wish you good health and prosperity – not just on this Easter Day, but on many more to come. And I also wish your fami—"

The lamp, in which the kerosene was already running low, was smoking and giving off a smell of burning. On the table near Nevyrazimov's writing hand a cockroach that had lost its way was frantically running. Two rooms away from the duty room, the porter Paramon was cleaning his ceremonial boots for already the third time, and doing it so energetically that his spitting and the noise of the blacking brush could be heard through all the rooms.

"What more can I write to him, the scoundrel?" thought Nevyrazimov, raising his eyes to the blackened ceiling.

On the ceiling he saw a dark circle – the shadow from the lamp shade. Beneath this were dusty cornices and, lower still, walls painted in bygone days a shade of dark blue-brown. The duty room looked so desolate that it seemed wretched not just to him, but even to the cockroach...

"Even I will come off duty and leave here, but it'll be on duty all its cockroachy life," he thought, stretching. "I'm depressed! Maybe I should clean my boots."

And, stretching once more, Nevyrazimov lazily sauntered along to the porter's room. Paramon was no longer cleaning his boots... Holding in one hand a brush, and with the other hand making the sign of the cross, he was standing by the open little swing window and listening...

"They're ringing, sir!" he whispered to Nevyrazimov, looking at him with intent, wide-open eyes. "Already, sir!"

74

Nevyrazimov placed his ear to the little window and listened. Through the window, together with the fresh spring air, the sound of Easter bells was wafting into the room. The pealing of the bells mixed with the sound of carriages, and above the resulting din only the high-pitched sound of ringing from the nearest church and someone's loud, shrill laughter could be distinguished.

"How many people there are!" sighed Nevyrazimov, looking down at the street, where, one after another, human shadows could be seen flitting around lampions that had been lit. "They are all hurrying to midnight Mass... Our colleagues now have probably been drinking and are reeling around town. How much laughter and talking there is! I'm the only one so unfortunate as to have to sit here on such a day. And every year I have to do the same!"

"But who forced you to take on this job? You're not supposed to be on duty today, but Zastupov got you to stand in for him. When other people are enjoying themselves, you decide to work... Greed!"

"What the devil do you mean, 'greed'? It's not greed: only two roubles and a tie thrown in... It's poverty, not greed! But it would be good now, you know, to be going with some companions to Mass and then to break the fast... I wish I could drink, have something to eat and then fall into bed... You sit at a table, and there's an Easter cake, and the samovar is hissing, and by your side is some little charmer... You drink a glass of wine and chuck her under the chin, and you feel good... you feel like a man... Ahh... I've wasted my life! Over there some floozy is driving by in a carriage, while I sit here and think my thoughts..."

"Each to his own, Ivan Danilych. God willing, you too will have your reward: you will drive in a carriage."

"Even I? Well, no, brother, you're joking. I'll never get further than titular councillor – not for the life of me... I have no education."

"But our general has no education either..."

"Well, the general, before he attained that rank, embezzled a hundred thousand. And his appearance, brother, is not like mine.

With an appearance like mine you'll not get far! And my surname is common: Nevyrazimov! In a word, brother, my situation is hopeless. If you wish, live like that – if you don't, go hang yourself..."

Nevyrazimov moved away from the little window and began to pace sadly through the rooms. The pealing of the bells became louder and louder. To hear them it was no longer necessary to stand by the window. And the more distinctly the ringing of the bells and the loud clattering of the carriages could be heard, the darker appeared the brown walls and the blackened cornices, and the more heavily the lamp smoked.

"Is it possible to slip away from being on duty?" thought Nevyrazimov.

But such an escape did not promise anything better... After coming out of the office and making his way through town, Nevyrazimov would have returned to his flat, but his flat was even greyer and more depressing than the duty room... He could have spent the day well, in comfort, but what about after that? All those grey walls, all those days on duty, standing in for others and writing letters of congratulation...

Nevyrazimov stopped in the middle of the duty room and fell to thinking.

The need for a new, better life made his heart ache with unbearable pain. He wanted terribly to find himself on the street, to mingle with the lively crowd, to participate in the festivities for which all those bells were pealing and carriages clattering. He longed for the things he had known in childhood: a family gathering, the cheerful faces of those near to him, a white tablecloth, light, warmth... He remembered the carriage in which the lady had just passed; the coat in which the director strutted around, showing off; the gold chain adorning the chest of the secretary... He thought of a warm bed, the Order of St Stanislav, new boots, a uniform jacket without worn elbows... He thought of all these things because he did not have them...

"Shall I steal?" he thought. "It may not be hard to steal, but to get away with it would be harder... They say that thieves escape to America with stolen goods, but the devil knows where that America is! It seems one must have education even to steal."

The sound of the bells died away. All that could be heard was the distant noise of carriages and Paramon's cough, but Nevyrazimov's sadness and anger grew all the stronger and more unbearable. In the office, the clock struck half-past midnight.

"Shall I write a denunciation? Proshkin was an informer, and he prospered…"

Nevyrazimov sat down at the table and fell to thinking. The lamp, in which the kerosene was almost used up, was smoking heavily and threatening to go out. The cockroach that had got lost was still scurrying along the table without finding a refuge…

"I could send in a denunciation, but how could it be written? It would all have to be done with ambiguities and subtlety, the way Proshkin did it… But I'll never do it! Whatever I write would get me into trouble. I'm so muddle-headed, let the devil take me!"

And Nevyrazimov, racking his brains over how to escape from his desperate position, stared at the draft of the letter he had written. This letter was written to a man whom he detested and feared with all his soul, from whom for already ten years now he had tried to get a transfer from a position paying sixteen roubles to one paying eighteen…

"Ah… so you're still running around here, you devil!" He maliciously slapped his palm over the cockroach, which had the misfortune to catch his eye. "What a disgusting thing!"

The cockroach fell on its back and desperately began to wiggle its legs. Nevyrazimov picked it up by one leg and threw it into the lamp. The lamp blazed up and began to crackle.

And Nevyrazimov felt better.

Zakuska

A Pleasant Memory

I T WAS EASTER EVE. An hour before midnight Mass my
friends came to call for me. They were in tails and white ties.

"You've come at the right moment, gentlemen," I said. "You
can help me lay the table.* As a bachelor, I have no woman in the
house, and so... friendly help is needed. Plumbov, let's move the
table to one side."

My friends moved to the table, and five minutes later it presented
a most appetizing sight – ham, sausage, a selection of vodkas
and wines, jellied piglet... Having prepared the table, we put on
our top hats: it was time to go! Nothing of the kind... Someone
rang the bell...

"Are you at home?" We heard someone's hoarse voice. "Come
in, Ilya, don't be afraid!"

Prekrasnovkusov entered. After him shyly stepped a sickly-
looking little man... Both were carrying briefcases under their
arms...

"Shhh!" I said to my friends. "Hold your tongues!"

"May I introduce," said Prekrasnovkusov, indicating the sickly
man, "Ilya Drobiskulov! He came to us the other day, joined the
force... Now, don't be embarrassed, Ilyusha! It's time to get accustomed! We, you know, were just walking around and decided to
drop in. Let's, I thought, call in and collect our little something,
so as not to disturb them tomorrow..."

I thrust a five-rouble note into the hand of each. Drobiskulov
was embarrassed.

"Well, sir," continued Prekrasnovkusov after looking in his fist.
Are you already leaving? Isn't it too early? Why don't we stay a
minute... relax. Sit down, Ilya, don't be afraid! Get accustomed!

Good Lord, so many *zakuski*...* *zakuski*! Eh, what *zakuski*! The ham reminds me of an anecdote..."

And Prekrasnovkusov, devouring with his eyes my *zakuski*, told us a smutty story. A quarter of an hour passed. In order to get rid of the guests, I sent my Andryushka into the street to shout "help". Andryushka went out and shouted for about five minutes, but my guests didn't react. They paid no attention, as if a cry for help had nothing to do with them...

"It's still so long to wait before the feasting can begin," said Prekrasnovkusov. It would still be a sin, otherwise we would, Ilyusha, ah... maybe just a sip each... What about it, gentlemen, why don't we have a little shot each? Surely vodka is a Lenten drink! What do you think? Let's have some!"

My friends liked the idea. They went to the table, poured and drank. They helped themselves to a little herring, but only looked at the forbidden foods. Prekrasnovkusov praised the vodka, and, wishing to know what make it was, drank another glassful. Ilyusha was embarrassed, but also wanted to know... They drank, but didn't discover.

"Wonderful vodka!" said Prekrasnovkusov. "My uncle had his own distillery. So he had, my uncle had, so to speak..."

And the guest told us how he had a rendezvous with his uncle's floozy in the fire-station watchtower. My friends surrounded him and asked him to tell them something else... They had another drink. Drobiskulov very deftly covered a piece of sausage with his sleeve, took it in his handkerchief and, blowing his nose, slipped it into his mouth. Prekrasnovkusov ate a piece of cottage-cheese *paskha*.*

"Oh, I forgot, it's forbidden!" he said as he swallowed it. "I shall have to wash it down..."

They say the bells were ringing at midnight for matins, but we did not hear them. At midnight we were walking around the table and asking ourselves what else we could drink... what else? Drobiskulov sat in the corner and, looking embarrassed, was chewing some jellied piglet. Prekrasnovkusov was beating his briefcase with his fist and saying:

"You doan love me, but I... l-l-love you! Honestly and truf-fully, I l-l-love you! I'm a hen poacher, a wolf, a kite, bird of prey, but I still have enough brain and feeling to understand that I shouldn't be loved. For example, I took here a holiday tip... Din I? But tomorrow I shall come and say I hadn't taken one... Is it really possible to love me after that?"

Drobiskulov, having finished off the piglet, overcame his timidity and said:

"What about me? I can still be loved... I'm an educated man... I'm really not suited to this job. It's not my line! I have no vocation for it... It's only *pour manger*.* I... am a poet... ye-e-es... When I'm drunk I write reports in verse. I love openness too. I don't like newspapers only because they're too biased. I couldn't work out from them who is a conservative and who a liberal. Impartiality is the main thing! If a conservative plays dirty tricks, beat his ugly mug – if a liberal does the same, thrash him! Thrash them all! My dream is to publish a newspaper. Hee-hee... I would sit in my editorial office, would puff up my mug and open envelopes. There would be all kinds of things in the envelopes... all kinds of things... Hee-hee-hee... I would open them, would read and... would arrest him, the contributor! Wouldn't that be interesting?"

At three o'clock the guests took their briefcases and left for the tavern, to look for disorderly behaviour. On my table only knives, forks and two spoons remained. The other six spoons had disappeared...

The Mesmeric Seance

THE BIG HALL was brightly lit and swarming with people. In it, a mesmerist was holding sway. He was lean and slightly built, and was dressed in a costume that glittered and sparkled. The people smiled and applauded as they watched him. They did exactly what he told them to do, and were captivated.

He was literally performing miracles. One person he put to sleep, another he stiffened and made numb, a third he placed lying with the back of the head on one chair and the heels on another... He bent one tall, thin journalist into a spiral. In short, he did the devil knows what. He had an especially strong effect on women.

They fell at his glance like flies. Oh, the susceptibilities of women! But without them, how dull a place the world would be!

Having tested his devilish art on all, the mesmerist came up to me.

"You seem to have a very receptive, compliant nature," he said to me. "But you are nervous and anxious... Would you like to go to sleep?"

Why not go to sleep? Be kind, and obligingly go along with it. I sat on a chair in the middle of the hall. The mesmerist sat on a chair opposite, took me by the hands and with his terrible serpent's eyes fixed his gaze on my poor eyes.

The public surrounded us.

"Sh-h-h... Ladies and gentlemen! Sh-h-h... Silence!"

They calmed down... We sat – we looked into each other's pupils... A minute passed, two... I felt as if insects were crawling up my back, but I didn't feel sleepy...

We sat... Five minutes went by, seven...

"He's not yielding!" said someone. "Bravo! Good man!"

We sat, we looked... I didn't want to sleep or even doze. Had I been reading the minutes of a government or council meeting, I

81

would already long ago have fallen asleep... The public began to whisper, to snigger. The mesmerist was embarrassed and began to blink... Poor devil! Who could be pleased with such a failure? Come to his aid, you spirits, send Morpheus to my eyelids!

"He's not yielding!" said the same voice. "Enough, give it up! Didn't I tell you this is all a hoax?"

But then, just when I, heeding the suggestion of that voice, made a movement to rise, I felt something being pressed into the palm of my hand... By touch, I identified this object as a banknote. My papa was a doctor, and doctors can identify the value of a banknote by touch alone. In keeping with Darwin's theory, I inherited this ability, along with many others, from Papa. I identified the object as a five-rouble banknote. Having identified it, I instantly fell asleep.

"Bravo, mesmerist!"

The doctors who were in the room came up to me, looked at me this way and that, inspected me closely and said:

"Y-e-s-s... He's asleep..."

The mesmerist, pleased with his success, waved his hands over my head and I, still asleep, began to plod around the hall.

"Make his arm go numb!" suggested someone. "Can you do that? See if you can freeze his arm..."

The mesmerist (not a hesitant man!) took my right arm and began to give it his treatment. He rubbed it, blew on it, slapped it. My hand didn't respond. It hung down like a rag, and refused to stiffen.

"It's not working! Wake him up, otherwise you'll harm him... He's weak, nervous..."

Then, in the palm of my left hand, I felt another five-rouble banknote... By a reflex action the feeling passed from left to right, and a moment later the arm stiffened.

"Bravo! Look how hard and cold it is! Like a corpse's!"

"Full anaesthesia, lowered temperature and weakened pulse," declared the mesmerist.

The doctors began to prod my arm.

"Yes, the pulse is weaker," one of them remarked. "Complete paralysis. The temperature is much lower…"

"How can this be explained?" asked one of the ladies.

The doctor shrugged meaningfully, sighed and said:

"We have only the facts! Explanations – alas! – no…"

You had facts, but I had two five-rouble banknotes. Mine were more valuable. I thanked mesmerism for that, and didn't need any explanations.

Poor mesmerist! But why did you get involved with me, a snake in the grass?

P.S. Well, was it not damnable? Not a swinish trick? Only later did I learn that the five-rouble notes were not put into my hand by the mesmerist, but by Pyotr Fyodorych, my boss…

"I did that," he said, "to test your honesty…"

Oh, to the devil with it!

"Shame on you, brother… It's not good… I did not expect…"

"But you know I have children, Your Excellency… A wife… A mother… At a time of high prices…"

"It's not good… And you even want to publish your own newspaper… You cry when you speak at official dinners… Shame on you… I thought you were an honest man, but it turns out that you… *hapyen zee gevezyen.*"*

I had to give him back the two five-rouble notes. What else could I do? A reputation is dearer than money.

"I am not angry with you!" said my boss. "To hell with you, it's just in your nature… But she! She! It's a-ston-ish-ing! She! Meek, innocent, refined and so on! Well? You see, even she was tempted by money! She also fell asleep!"

By the word "she", my boss meant his wife, Matryona Nikolayevna…

At the Council Meeting

A Play in Two Acts

ACT ONE

The municipal office. A meeting.

COUNCIL CHAIRMAN (*having chewed his lips awhile and poked a finger in his ear*): At this time would you not like, gentlemen, to hear the opinion of fire chief Semyon Vavilych, who is a specialist in this field? Let him explain, and then we'll decide.

FIRE CHIEF: As I understand it... (*He blows his nose in a checked handkerchief.*) Ten thousand, assigned to the fire department, is perhaps a lot of money, but... (*wiping his bald patch*) it only seems a lot. It's not the money, but a dream, a vision. Of course it's possible to have a fire brigade for even ten thousand, but what kind? It would just be a joke! You see... The most important thing for human life is... the watchtower, and any expert will tell you this. Our own municipal watchtower, frankly speaking, is not at all suitable, because it's too small. The houses are tall (*raising his hands*), and block the view from the watchtower, so it's not just fires, but God knows you can't even see the sky. I hold the firemen responsible, but are they really at fault if they can't see anything? Then, with respect to the horses, and concerning the barrels... (*He undoes his waistcoat, sighs and continues his speech in the same manner.*)

COUNCILLORS (*unanimously*): Add another two thousand to the budget!

(*The* COUNCIL CHAIRMAN *calls for a short break while the conference correspondents are escorted from the hall.*)

FIRE CHIEF: Very well. Now, so you discuss whether the watch-tower should be raised by two *arshins*...* Very well. But if you consider the matter bearing in mind the interests of the public – government interests, so to speak – then I must say, gentlemen of the council, that if a contractor undertakes this business, you have to consider that this will cost the town twice as much, because the contractor, and not the public, will have an interest. If you build in an economical way, not rushing, and if bricks, let's assume, are fifteen roubles a thousand and the delivery is by the fire horses – and if (*raising his eyes to the ceiling as if doing a mental calculation*), and if fifty beams, twelve *arshins* by five *vershoks*...* (*He calculates.*)

COUNCILLORS (*in an overwhelming majority of voices*): Assign the repairs of the watchtower to Semyon Vavilych, and allocate for this purpose, as a first instalment, one thousand, five hundred and twenty-three roubles, forty-four copecks!

FIRE CHIEF'S WIFE (*who is sitting among the public and whispers to her companion*): I don't know why my Senya takes on himself so much trouble. Is it good for his health to undertake such building repairs? Also, is it fun to fight with workers all day? He gets for the repair some trifle, about five hundred roubles, but damages his health by a thousand. His kindness ruins him, the fool!

FIRE CHIEF: Very well. Now, let's talk about the office staff. Of course I, it's possible to say, as an interested party (*embarrassed*), I may only mention, that to me... to me it's all the same... I am no longer a young man... I am not well, and may die any day. The doctor said that I have a hardening in my intestines, and that if I do not look after my health, then a vein will burst inside me and I shall die without confession...

A WHISPER IN THE PUBLIC: A dog's death for a dog.

FIRE CHIEF: But I'm not thinking of myself. I've lived my life, and thank God for that. I don't need anything... It's just surprising to me and... and even a shame... (*He waves a hand hopelessly.*) You work for just a salary, honestly, blamelessly...

knowing no peace either by day or by night, not sparing your health and... and you don't know what it's all for. Why do you take the trouble? What's the point of it? I am not talking about myself, but in general... No one else would live like that... A drunkard may accept this job, but a solid, business-like man would rather die of hunger than have the trouble of dealing with horses and firemen for such a salary... (*He shrugs.*) What's the point? If foreigners were to see how we order these matters, I think we would be ridiculed in all their newspapers. In Western Europe – take, if you like, Paris for example – there is a watchtower on every street, and each year they give the fire chief an allowance equal to his annual salary. That's the place to work!

COUNCILLORS: Give Semyon Vavilych a one-off payment of two hundred roubles for his long years of service!

FIRE CHIEF'S WIFE (*whispers to her companion*): It's good that he asked... Clever man. The other day we lost a hundred roubles playing *stukolka** with Father Archpriest, and now, you know, well... it's such a pity! (*She yawns.*) Ah, such a pity! I think it's time to go home, have tea.

ACT TWO

A scene at the watchtower. The guard.

SENTRY ON THE WATCHTOWER (*shouts down*): Oy! There's a fire in the sawmill yard! Raise the alarm!

SENTRY BELOW: And you've only just now seen it? People have been running around for half an hour, but you, you clown, have only just noticed? (*To himself:*) Whether you put a fool above or below, it's all the same. (*He sounds the alarm.*)

(*Three minutes later, at the window of his flat, located opposite the watchtower, the fire chief appears,* en déshabillé *and with sleepy eyes.*)

86

FIRE CHIEF: Where's the fire, Denis?

SENTRY BELOW (*coming to attention and saluting*): In the sawmill yard, Your Honour!

FIRE CHIEF (*shaking his head*): God save us! There's a wind... it's so dry... (*He waves his hand.*) Good Lord! Nothing but grief from these calamities!... (*He rubs his face.*) Look here, Denis... Tell them, brother, to harness the horses and go... I'll come a little later... I have to dress, and so on...

SENTRY BELOW: But there's no one to go, Your Honour! They've all gone off, only Andrei is at home.

FIRE CHIEF (*frightened*): Where have they gone, the swine?

SENTRY BELOW: Makar was putting on new soles – has now taken the boots out of town, to the deacon. Mikhail, Your Honour, you yourself sent to sell oats... Yegor took the fire horses to drive the supervisor's sister-in-law across the river. Nikita is drunk.

FIRE CHIEF: And Alexei?

SENTRY BELOW: Alexei went to catch crayfish. He said you told him to go, because you said you're having guests for dinner tomorrow.

FIRE CHIEF (*contemptuously shaking his head*): How can you work with such people? Ignorant, uneducated... drunk... If foreigners were to see, we would be a laughing stock in their magazines. Over there – take Paris, for example – the fire brigade is constantly galloping along the street, running over people – whether there's a fire or not, they just keep galloping! But here, the sawmill yard is on fire, it's dangerous, but no one's at home... The devil has eaten them up! No, we are still a long way from Europe! (*He turns around to the room, speaks tenderly.*) Mashenka, lay out my full-dress uniform.

The Zealot

FOR TWENTY YEARS the director of the ZBK railway had been intending to sit down at his writing table. Finally, two days before, he managed to do so. The thoughts of half a lifetime – burning, intense, relentless – had been going through his head, taking form, being rounded out with detail and finally growing into a grand project... He sat down at his table, took pen in hand and... embarked upon the arduous path of authorship.

The morning was quiet, bright, frosty... It was warm and cosy in the room... On the table stood a faintly steaming glass of tea... There was no knocking, no shouting, no interruptions of talk... How delightful to write under such conditions! Take a pen in hand and go at it!

The director did not have to think for long before starting... In his head all had already long ago been started and finished: press on and transfer from brain to paper!

He frowned, pursed his lips, took a deep breath and wrote the title: 'A Few Words in Defence of the Press'. The director loved the press. He was devoted to it with all his soul, with all his heart and with all his thought. To write his own words in defence of it, to proclaim those words loudly for all to hear, was his dearest twenty-year dream. He owed a lot to the press: for his personal development, the exposing of corruption, his position... A lot! He had to show his gratitude towards it... And so he wanted to be an author, if only for a day... Though writers are abused, they are respected all the same... Especially by women... Hmm...

Having written the title, the director emitted a deep breath, and a minute later had written fourteen lines. It came out well, smoothly... He began about the press in general and, after writing half a page, began to elaborate on the freedom of the press... He demanded this and that... Protests, historical data, quotations, sayings, reproaches, mockery simply rained down from under his sharp pen.

"We are liberals," he wrote. "You may laugh at this term! Smile at it! But we are proud and will continue to be proud of this name, as long as—"

"They have brought the newspapers!" announced the footman.

At ten o'clock the director usually read the newspapers. And today he did not alter his routine. Leaving his writing, he rose, stretched, lay down on the couch and got down to the newspapers. Picking up *Novoye Vremya*,* he smirked scornfully, ran his eyes over the editorial and, without reading to the end, threw down the paper.

"What a rag!" he muttered. "I shall remember this."

Having thrown *Novoye Vremya* on the armchair, the director took up *Golos*.* His eyes began to glow with pleasure, and the colour rose to his cheeks. He loved *Golos*, and himself had at one time occasionally written for it.

He read the editorial and some brief news items... He ran his eyes over a satirical article... The more he read, the more his eyes sparkled with satisfaction. He read through 'In the Newspapers and Magazines'... He turned to the third page...

"Yes, yes. That's true. I mentioned that too... Correct, absolutely correct! Hmm. But what's this about?"

The director screwed up his eyes...

"A rather strange development has recently been happening on the ZBK railway," he began to read. "This development was initiated by the director of the railway himself, formerly..."

After half an hour of reading *Golos*, the director, red in the face, sweating, trembling, was sitting at his writing table and writing. He was writing 'A General Order to All the Employees of the Railway'... In this order was the instruction not to subscribe to "some" newspapers and magazines.

Near the angry director lay torn scraps of paper. Half an hour before, these scraps had formed his 'A Few Words in Defence of the Press'.

*Sic transit gloria mundi!**

The Discovery

Digging through a pile of manure,
A cockerel found a pearl…

Krylov*

STATE COUNCILLOR BAKHROMKIN, an engineer, was sitting at his writing table, and, having nothing to do, had fallen into a reflective mood. Just that evening, at a ball given by some friends, he had unexpectedly met a lady with whom he had been in love some twenty-odd years before. Then, she had been a remarkable beauty, with whom it was just as easy to fall in love as to step on your neighbour's corn. Bakhromkin especially remembered her big deep eyes, which seemed laid in soft blue velvet, and her long chestnut-golden hair, which resembled a field of ripening rye when it is agitated by the wind before a thunderstorm… The beauty was unapproachable, looked severe, rarely smiled – but then, when she did smile, "the flames of dying candles with a smile she revived"…* Now she was a shrivelled-up, garrulous old woman with watery eyes and yellow teeth… Ugh!

"Disgraceful!" thought Bakhromkin, running a pencil mechanically over a piece of paper. "No evil fate whatever plays such dirty tricks on people as does nature. If the beauty had known that in time she would turn into such a gargoyle, she would have died from horror…"

Bakhromkin had been reflecting thus for some time when suddenly he leapt up as if stung…

"Lord Jesus!" he cried in amazement. "What's this? I can draw?!"

On the sheet of paper on which he had been doodling had emerged, from behind the casually fashioned strokes and scribbling, the head of an attractive woman, the very one with whom he had formerly been in love. In overall presentation it was poor, but the languid, distracted look, the softness of features

90

and the dishevelled wave of the thick hair were conveyed to perfection...

"How odd," said Bakhromkin, astonished. "I can draw! For fifty-two years I've lived in the world and not suspected I had any talent whatsoever, and suddenly in old age – I never expected anything of the kind – talent appeared! It's unbelievable!"

Not believing in himself, Bakhromkin seized a pencil and near the beautiful head drew the head of an old woman... This was as good as the other...

"Wonderful!" He shook himself. "Not at all bad, damn it! What does it mean? I'm an artist! It means I have a calling! So why did I not know it before? How strange!"

Had Bakhromkin found money in his old waistcoat pocket, or received news that he had been promoted to full state councillor, he would not have been so pleasantly surprised as he was now, discovering in himself a talent to create. He spent a whole hour at his table, drawing heads, trees, fires, horses...

"Superb! Bravo!" He was carried away. "If only I studied technique, it would be absolutely excellent."

He was stopped from drawing any longer and getting carried away when his valet brought into the study a little table with dinner. After eating hazel grouse and drinking two glasses of Burgundy, Bakhromkin relaxed and fell to thinking... He recalled that, in all his fifty-two years, he had not once suspected the existence in himself of any talent. It was true that all his life he had had a taste for the arts. In his youth he had engaged in amateur theatricals, played, sang and painted scenery... And into old age he never stopped reading, loving the theatre and copying good poetry from memory. He was agreeably witty, spoke well, criticized fairly. His little talent, evidently, had in every way possible been deadened by common task.

"We can but see what will happen," thought Bakhromkin. "Perhaps I am yet able to write poetry and novels? Indeed, had I discovered a talent in myself when young, when it was not too late, would I have become an artist or poet? Well, would I?"

And in his imagination was opened a life unlike millions of other lives. To have compared it with the lives of ordinary mortals would have been quite impossible.

"Society is right not to give artists ranks and decorations," he thought. "They stand above class and title... And only a select few can really judge their achievements..."

Just then, appropriately, Bakhromkin recalled an incident from his distant past... His mother – a nervous, eccentric woman – walking with him one day, met on the stairs a certain drunken, dissolute man, and kissed his hand. "Mama, why did you do that?" he asked in surprise. "He is a poet," she replied. And he felt that she had been right... Had she kissed the hand of a general or senator, it would have been servility, self-abasement, a gesture worse than any that could be imagined for a mature woman to contemplate – but to kiss the hand of a poet, artist or composer... it was natural...

"A free life, not a humdrum existence," thought Bakhromkin as he went to bed. "But what about fame, notoriety? However big a step I take in the service, to whatever grade I climb, my name will not be known further than my own anthill...* But poets and artists are quite different... While they are peacefully sleeping or getting drunk, they will be unaware that people in towns or villages are memorizing their verses or scrutinizing their pictures... Not to know their names is considered ill-bred, ignorant... uncultivated..."

Having finally relaxed, Bakhromkin lowered himself onto the bed and nodded to his valet... The valet went up to him and carefully began to undress him.

"Ye-s-s... Life is strange... Railways will one day be forgotten, but Phidias and Homer will always be remembered... Bad as Trediakovsky* was, even he will be remembered... B-r-r-r... it's cold!... But what if now I were an artist? How would I feel?"

While his valet removed his outer garments and put on his nightshirt, he painted a picture to himself... There he is, an artist or poet, trudging home on a dark night... There are no horses for the talented: like it or not, they go on foot… He walks pitifully, in a faded coat, perhaps even without galoshes… At the entrance to his furnished room dozes a porter – this crude swine opens the door without looking at him… Out there, somewhere in the crowd, the name of the poet or artist is honoured, but from this honour he derives no benefit: the porter is not more courteous, the servants not more solicitous, the members of the household not kinder… The name is honoured, but the person is neglected… So he, weary and hungry, finally enters his dark and stuffy room… He is hungry and thirsty, but – alas! – there is no hazel grouse and Burgundy… He is dreadfully tired, to the point where he cannot keep his eyes open and his head falls on his chest, but the bed is as hard and cold as in a hotel room… He pours out the water himself, undresses himself… goes barefoot on the cold floor… At last, shivering, he manages to fall asleep knowing he has no cigars, no horses… that in the middle drawer there is no Order of St Anna or Stanislav, and in the lower… no cheque-book…

Bakhromkin shook his head, collapsed onto the spring mattress and quickly drew the downy blanket over himself.

"To hell with it," he thought, snuggling down and falling into a sweet sleep. "To hell… with… it… It's just as well that I… in youth… did not… did not discover…"

His valet extinguished the lamp and went out on tiptoe.

Longing for Sleep

NIGHT-TIME. The childminder Varka, a girl of thirteen, is rocking the cradle in which a baby lies, and is very faintly humming:

> Lullaby baby, what shall I do?...
> I shall sing a song for you...

A little green lamp burns in front of the icon; across the room from corner to corner stretches a cord, on which hang baby clothes and big black trousers. The icon lamp projects a big green spot on the ceiling, and the baby clothes and trousers cast long shadows on the stove, the cradle and Varka... When the lamp begins to flicker, the spot and shadows come to life and start to move, as if agitated by a wind. It is stuffy in the room. There is a smell of *shchi* and the paraphernalia of a cobbler.

The baby cries. He long ago went hoarse and became exhausted from crying, but still he yells, and it is not clear when he will calm down. But Varka longs to sleep. Her eyes feel heavy, her head hangs down, her neck aches. She cannot move either her eyelids or her lips, and she feels as if her face has dried up and grown numb, and that her head has become as small as a pinhead.

"Lullaby baby, what shall I do?" she hums. "*Kasha** I shall cook for you..."

A cricket chirrups in the stove. In the adjacent room, behind a closed door, the master and his apprentice, Afanasy, are gently snoring. The cradle squeaks plaintively, Varka herself hums – and all this blends into soothing night-time music, which is so sweet to listen to when you lie in bed. But now this music only irritates and oppresses, because Varka is driven to drowsiness yet is not allowed to sleep – if, God forbid, she were to fall asleep, her employers would beat her.

The lamp flickers. The green spot and shadows start to move, creeping into Varka's half-open, motionless eyes, forming up into vague reveries in her half-asleep brain. She sees dark clouds, which chase each other across the sky and yell like a baby. But now a wind begins to blow, the clouds vanish, and Varka sees a wide, muddy road – along the road stretch convoys of carts, people trudge with knapsacks on their backs, shadows flit back and forth... on both sides, through the cold, thick fog, forests can be seen. Suddenly the shadows and the people with knapsacks fall to the ground, into the mud. "Why is this?" asks Varka. "To sleep, to sleep!" they reply to her. And they fall soundly asleep, sleep sweetly, while on the telegraph wires crows and magpies sit screaming like babies, trying to awaken them.

"Lullaby baby, what shall I do?... I shall sing a song for you..." hums Varka, and now sees herself in a dark, stuffy hut.

Her deceased father, Yefim Stepanov, is moving on the floor. She does not see him, but hears how he rolls in pain on the floor, moaning. He has what he calls a "racing hernia". The pain is so bad that he cannot utter a single word, and only breathes in and out through his teeth making a sound like a drumroll:

"Boo-boo-boo-boo..."

Her mother Pelageya has run to the manor house to tell the master that Yefim is dying. She left already long ago, and should by now have returned. Varka lies on the stove, not sleeping, and listening to her father's "boo-boo-boo". But now there is the sound of someone driving up to the hut. It is the mistress of the grand house, bringing a young doctor who has come from town to visit them. The doctor enters the hut – he cannot be seen in the dark, but can be heard coughing and rattling the door.

"Light a lamp," he says.

"Boo-boo-boo..." replies Yefim.

Pelageya rushes to the stove and starts to look for the broken pot with matches. A minute passes in silence. The doctor, who has been rummaging in his pockets, lights his own match.

"Just a moment, dear man, just a moment," says Pelageya. She rushes from the hut and a little later returns with the ends of some candles.

Yefim's cheeks are pink, and his eyes are shining, and the look on his face is somehow especially penetrating, as if he is looking right through the hut and the doctor.

"Now then, what's the matter? What do you think?" says the doctor, bending down to him. "So! Have you had this for long?"

"What does it matter? The time has come to die, Your Honour... Soon I shall not be among the living..."

"Enough of that nonsense... We'll set you right!"

"Just as you like, Your Honour, thank you very much, but I'm the only one who knows. If death comes, it's all right with me."

The doctor fusses over Yefim for a quarter of an hour, then rises and says:

"I can do nothing... You'll have to go to the hospital. They will operate on you there. Go immediately... Go without fail! It's rather late... everyone in the hospital is already asleep... but that doesn't matter. I shall give you a note. Do you hear?"

"How can he go, dear man?" says Pelageya. "We have no horse."

"It's all right, I'll ask at the manor house, they'll give you a horse."

The doctor leaves, the candle goes out, and again there is the sound of "boo-boo-boo"... Half an hour later someone drives up to the hut. The people at the grand house have sent a cart to take Yefim to the hospital. He gets ready and goes...

Now dawns a fine, clear morning. Pelageya is not at home: she has gone to the hospital to discover what is happening to Yefim. Somewhere a baby is crying, and Varka hears how someone with her own voice is singing:

"Lullaby baby, what shall I do?... I shall sing a song for you..."

Pelageya returns; she makes the sign of the cross and whispers:

"They treated him during the night, but towards morning he rendered his soul to God... The kingdom of heaven be his, eternal peace... They say it was too late to do anything... He should have gone sooner..."

Varka goes to the forest and cries there, but suddenly someone hits her on the back of the head with such force that she strikes her forehead against a birch tree. She raises her eyes and sees her master, the cobbler, standing in front of her.

"What's all this, you good-for-nothing girl?" he says. "The child cries, and you're asleep?"

He slaps her heavily behind the ear, and she shakes her head, rocks the cradle and hums her song. The green spot and shadows of the baby clothes and trousers sway and wink at her, and soon again overwhelm her brain. Again she sees the road, covered in mud. Shadows, and people with knapsacks on their backs, sprawl out and sleep soundly. Looking at them, Varka has a terrible longing for sleep – she would lie down with pleasure, but her mother Pelageya walks alongside and hastens her on. They are hurrying to town together to get jobs.

"Give alms, for Christ's sake!" begs her mother of the passers-by. "Show charity, for the love of God, merciful people!"

"Give me the baby!" someone's familiar voice replies to her. "Give me the baby!" repeats the same voice, this time angrily and abruptly. "Are you asleep, worthless child?"

Varka leaps up and, looking around, understands what is happening: there is no road, no Pelageya, no passers-by, but standing in the middle of the room there is only the mistress, who has come to feed her baby. While the fat, broad-shouldered mistress nurses and calms the baby, Varka stands looking at her, waiting for her to finish. Outside, it is already growing light; the shadows and green spot on the ceiling are turning noticeably pale. Soon it will be morning.

"Take him!" says the mistress, doing up the nightdress over her breast. "He is crying. Someone must have placed the evil eye on him."

Varka takes the baby, puts him in the cradle and begins to rock it again. The green spot and shadows little by little disappear, and by now there is no one to creep into her head and cloud her brain. But, as before, she wants to sleep, wants terribly to sleep!

Varka lays her head on the edge of the cradle and rocks her whole body to overcome her tiredness, but still her eyes close and her head feels heavy.

"Varka, light the stove!" bawls the master's voice from behind the door.

It means it is already time to rise and get down to work. Varka leaves the cradle and runs to the shed for firewood. She is glad of this. When you run and walk, you no longer want to sleep so much as when you are sitting down. As she brings wood and lights the stove, the feeling starts to return to her numb face, and her thoughts become clearer.

"Varka, put on the samovar!" cries the mistress.

Varka splits some kindling and only just manages to light it and thrust it into the samovar when she hears a new order:

"Varka, clean the master's galoshes!"

She sits on the floor, cleans the galoshes and thinks that it would be good to thrust her head into a big, deep galosh and doze there for a while... And suddenly the galosh begins to grow – it swells and fills the whole room. Varka lets the brush fall, but immediately shakes her head; she opens her eyes wide and stares so that the objects around don't grow and move around in her sight.

"Varka, wash the steps outside: it would be shameful to let the customers see them!"

Varka washes the steps, tidies up the rooms, then lights another stove and runs to the shop. There is much work to be done, and not a single free minute.

But nothing is so hard as to stand in one place before the kitchen table and peel potatoes. Her head droops towards the table, the potatoes waver in her eyes, the knife drops from her hand, and nearby walks the fat, angry mistress with her sleeves rolled up, talking so loudly that Varka's ears start to ring. Agonizing also is it to serve at dinner, to do the laundry, to sew. There are times when she wants to ignore it all, to fall on the floor and sleep.

The day passes. Seeing how the windows darken, Varka presses her hands to her numb temples and smiles, not knowing herself why she is glad. The gloom of evening caresses her heavy eyes, promising quick, sound sleep. In the evening, guests arrive.

"Varka, light the samovar!" cries the mistress.

The samovar is small, and she has to heat it up five times before the guests have had all the tea they want. After tea, Varka stands for a whole hour in one spot, looking at the guests and waiting for orders.

"Varka, run and buy three bottles of beer!"

She darts off, trying to run quickly in order to banish sleep.

"Varka, run for vodka! Varka, where's the corkscrew? Varka, clean a herring!"

But now at last the guests leave – the lights are extinguished: her master and mistress go to bed.

"Varka, rock the baby!" is the last order to be heard.

A cricket chirrups in the stove; the green spot on the ceiling and the shadows of the trousers and baby clothes again steal into Varka's half-open eyes, flickering and clouding her mind.

"Lullaby baby, what shall I do?…" she hums. "I shall sing a song for you…"

But the baby cries and does not tire of crying. Varka sees again the muddy road, people with knapsacks, Pelageya, her father Yefim. She understands everything, recognizes everyone – but, half-asleep, she can in no way understand the force that binds her hand and foot and prevents her from living. She looks around, seeking that force in order to escape from it, but cannot find it. Finally, tired out, she strains every nerve and both eyes, looks up at the flickering green spot and, listening to the screaming, finds the enemy that will not let her live.

The enemy is the baby.

She laughs. She is astonished: how is it that she was unable to understand such a simple thing before? The green spot, the shadows and the cricket also seem to be laughing, and are astonished.

The false notion seizes Varka. She rises from the stool and, smiling broadly, not blinking her eyes, starts to pace back and forth in the room. She feels pleased, and tickled by the thought that she will now be saved from the baby that is binding her hand and foot... Kill the baby, and then sleep, sleep, sleep...

Laughing, winking and threatening the green spot with her fingers, Varka steals up to the cradle and bends over the baby. Smothering him, she quickly lies down on the floor, laughing with delight at being able to sleep, and a minute later is sleeping as soundly as the dead...

The Idler and the Young Lady

Episode from the Life of a Gentleman

O N THE WELL-FED, shining face of the gentleman was written the most deadly boredom. He had only just emerged from the arms of the postprandial Morpheus and did not know what to do. He did not want either to think or sit staring... He had long ago grown sick of reading... it was too early for the theatre, and he was too lazy to go for a drive... What could he do? How could he amuse himself?

"A young lady has arrived!" announced Yegor. "Asks for you!"

"Young lady? Hm... Who could it be? But it doesn't matter... Invite her in..."

An attractive, dark-haired young woman entered the study. She was dressed plainly... even very plainly. She came in and bowed.

"Excuse me," she began in a quivering treble. "I, you know... I was told that you... you could be found only at six o'clock... I... I... am the daughter of Court Councillor Paltsev..."

"Pleased to meet you! S-s-sit down! What can I do for you? Sit down, don't be shy!"

"I have come to you with a request..." continued the young lady, sitting awkwardly and tugging with trembling hands at her buttons. "I have come... to ask you for a ticket for a free trip to my home. You, I heard, give... I want to go, but I have... I am not rich... I want to go from Petersburg to Kursk..."

"Hm... Well, then... And why do you want to go to Kursk? Do you not like it here?"

"No, I like it here, but, you know... my parents. I'd like to see my parents. I haven't seen them for a long time... Mama, they write, is ill..."

"Hm... Do you work here, or study?"

The young lady told him where and for whom she worked, how much she was paid and whether there was a lot of work...

"So... you work... Yes indeed, it can't be said that you earn very much... It can't be said... It would be inhumane not to give you a free ticket... Hm... So you say you are going to see your parents. But I suppose you have a lover in Kursk, do you? A young lover? Hee-hee-ho... A fiancé? Are you blushing? Well, all right then! It's a good thing... Go ahead. It's about time you married... But who is he?"

"A civil servant..."

"That's good... Go to Kursk...They say that a hundred versts from Kursk it already smells of *shchi* and crawls with cockroaches... Hee-hee-ho... It's probably boring in this Kursk, is it? But take off your hat! Don't be shy, then! Yegor, bring us tea! I dare say it's boring in this... what's it called... Kursk?"

The young lady, not expecting such a warm reception, beamed and described to the kind gentleman all the entertainments on offer in Kursk... She told him she had a brother who was in the civil service, an uncle who was a teacher, and cousins who were high-school pupils... Yegor served tea... The young lady shyly reached for the glass and, fearing to mumble, drank in silence... The kind gentleman looked at her and smirked... He no longer felt bored...

"Is your fiancé handsome?" he asked. "And how did you meet him?"

The young lady shyly replied to both questions. She trustingly moved a little closer to the kind gentleman and, smiling, told him how, here in Petersburg, several suitors had courted her, and how she had refused them all... She spoke for a long time. She finished by drawing from her pocket a letter from her parents and reading it to the kind gentleman. The clock struck eight.

"Your father's handwriting isn't bad... With what flourishes he writes! Hee-hee... However, I must go... The theatre has already started... Goodbye Marya Yefimovna!"

"So may I hope?" asked the young lady, rising.

"For what, my dear?"

"That you will give me a free ticket..."

"Ticket? Hm... I have no tickets! You must be mistaken, madam... Hee-hee-hee... You have come to the wrong place. You came in at the wrong entrance... Next door indeed lives a man who works on the railway, but I work in a bank, my dear! Yegor, have the horses harnessed! Goodbye, *ma chère** Marya Semyonovna! Delighted to have met you... Delighted..."

The young lady put on her coat and left... Next door she was told that *he* had left for Moscow at seven-thirty.

Up the Staircase

PROVINCIAL COUNCILLOR DOLBONOSOV, being once on business in St Petersburg, was invited to a party at Prince Fingalov's. At this party, to his surprise, he happened to meet Shchepotkin, a law student who some five years before had been tutor to his children. Knowing no one else at the party, he went up to Shchepotkin out of boredom.

"So you… then… how did you come to be here?" he asked, yawning into his fist.

"Just as you yourself did…"

"Well, I dare say, not as I did…" frowned Dolbonosov, looking at Shchepotkin. "Hm… So… how are things with you?"

"All right… I finished my course at the university and am working as a civil servant on special assignments for Podokonnikov."

"Really? It's not bad for a start… But… ah… forgive the indiscreet question, how much does he pay you?"

"Eight hundred roubles…"

"P-f-f!… It's barely enough for tobacco," muttered Dolbonosov, again adopting a patronizing tone.

"Of course, for a comfortable life in St Petersburg it's not enough, but I'm also secretary to the board of the Ugaro-Deboshirskaya Railway… That gives me one and a half thousand—"

"Ye-s-s, in that case, of course…" Dolbonosov interrupted, a radiant look spreading over his face. "By the way, dear boy, how did you come to know the host of this house?"

"Very simple," replied Shchepotkin indifferently. "We met at State Secretary Lodkin's…"

"You… go to Lodkin's?" Dolbonosov goggled…

"Quite often… I am married to his niece…"

"To… his… niece? Hm… Tell me… I, you know… ah… always wished you… predicted a brilliant future for you, Ivan Petrovich…"

"Pyotr Ivanych…"

"Yes, Pyotr Ivanych… You know, when I looked just now, and saw your familiar face… I recognized you at once… Let me, I thought, invite him to have dinner with me… Hee-hee… Surely he wouldn't refuse an old man! Come to the Hotel Europa, room 33… from one to six."

The Holiday Obligation

...cunning simpletons,
Sinister old women and men,
Senile from nonsense and imaginings.
Griboyedov, *Woe from Wit**

I T WAS NOON ON NEW YEAR'S DAY. The widow of former
Vice Governor Lyagavoi-Gryslov, Lyudmila Semyonovna, a
little sixty-year-old woman, was sitting in her living room and
receiving callers. Judging by the quantity of *zakuski* and drinks
that was ready in the hall, she was expecting a huge number of visitors, but at present only one had arrived to offer New Year's wishes
– senior adviser to the provincial government Okurkin, a decrepit
man with a lemon-coloured face and crooked mouth. He was sitting in the corner next to an oleander plant, and, while carefully
taking snuff, was telling the "benefactress" the news of the town.

"Yesterday, dear lady, a drunken soldier almost fell from the fire
brigade's watchtower," he said. "He leant, don't you know, over
the railing, and the railing... crash! It broke, don't you know...
Fortunately, his wife had just then arrived at the tower with his
lunch, and held on to him by his coat-tails. Had it not been for
his wife, he would have fallen, the rascal... Anyway... Day before
yesterday, dear lady, Your Excellency, there was a meeting at bank
inspector Pertsev's place... All the employees gathered and discussed today's visits. They unanimously decided, the fools, not
to make calls today."

"Well, that can't be true, dear man," smiled the old woman.
"How can they manage without visits?"

"Really, Your Excellency. It's astonishing, but true... They all
agreed, instead of making visits, to gather today at the club, offer
best wishes to each other and contribute a rouble each for the
relief of the poor."

"I don't understand..." said the hostess, shrugging her shoulders. "You are telling me something strange..."

"Such, dear lady, is now being done in many towns. They are not going around offering congratulations. They donate a rouble each, and that's all! Hee-hee-hee. It's not necessary to drive around, or to congratulate people – not necessary to spend money on a cab... You go to the club, and then go home."

"It's much better," sighed the old woman. "Let them not have to go out. It's easier for us..."

Okurkin heaved a loud, hoarse sigh, shook his head and continued:

"They consider it humbug... But being too lazy to respect the old, to congratulate them on holidays, that is what's humbug. Nowadays, you know, they do not treat the elderly with respect. Before it was different."

"What can be done?" sighed the hostess again. "Let them not come! If they don't want to... they don't have to."

"In the past, dear lady, when there was not this liberalism, visiting was not considered humbug. Visits were made not under compulsion, but with a sense of pleasure... They used to come out from all the houses, stop on the pavement and think: 'Who else could we show respect to?' We loved, dear lady, older people... We loved them so much! I remember, the deceased Pantelei Stepanych, God grant him the kingdom of heaven, he liked us to be respectful... God preserve us, if it ever happened that someone did not make a visit, he would gnash his teeth! One Christmas, I recall, I was sick with typhus. And what do you think, dear lady? I got out of bed, gathered all my remaining strength and went to call on Pantelei Stepanych... I arrived. How I was burning with fever, just burning with fever! I wanted to say 'Happy New Year', but what came out was 'Win with a trump!' Hee-hee... I was delirious, you see... And another thing I remember... Zmeishchev had smallpox. The doctors, of course, had forbidden us to go to him, but we ignored the doctors: we went and congratulated him. We didn't consider it humbug. I'll have a drink, dear lady, Your Excellency..."

"Drink, drink… It's all the same: no one else will come – there is no one else to drink… Perhaps your colleagues will come."

Okurkin waved his hand hopelessly and twisted his mouth into a scornful grin.

"They're louts… all cut from the same cloth."

"Is that how it is, Yefim Yefimych?" exclaimed the old woman in surprise. "So even Verkhushkin will not come?"

"He will not come… He is at the club…"

"Do you know, I am godmother to that scoundrel! It was my influence that got him his position!"

"He doesn't seem grateful… Yesterday he was the first to arrive at Pertsev's."

"Well, they are as they are… They have forgotten an old woman, so let them, but it's a sin for the directors. And Vanka Trukhin? Will not even he come?"

Okurkin waved his hand hopelessly.

"And Podsilkin? Also? You know, I dragged that rascal by the ears out of the gutter! And Proryekhin?"

The old woman mentioned a dozen more names, and each name brought a bitter smile to Okurkin's lips.

"All, dear lady! They have no respect!"

"Thank you…" Lyagavaya-Gryslova sighed and nervously began to pace back and forth in the living room. "Thank you… If their benefactress… an old woman… has become repulsive to them… if I am so horrible, disgusting… very well…"

The old woman sank into an armchair. Her wrinkled eyes began to blink.

"I see I am no longer needed by them. But it doesn't matter… You go too, Yefim Yefimych… I'm not keeping you. Just go."

The hostess pressed a handkerchief to her face and began to whimper. Okurkin looked at her, scratched his head in fright and shyly went to her…

"Dear lady…" he said in a tearful voice. "Your Excellency! Benefactress!"

"You go too… Leave… Just leave…"

"Dear lady, my angel... Please don't cry... My dear! I was joking... For Heaven's sake, I was joking! Spit in my face, my old mug, if I was not joking... They will all come! Dear lady!"

Okurkin knelt before the old woman, took her blue-veined hand and struck his bald patch with it.

"Beat me, dear lady, my angel! 'Don't joke, you scum! Don't joke!' On the cheek! On the cheek! 'That's for you, damned liar!'"

"No, you were not joking, Yefim Yefimych! I feel it in my heart!"

"Burst open... break the earth under me! So that I live no longer if... You'll see now! But for the time being goodbye, dear lady... Because of my cruel jokes I don't deserve your kindness. I shall cut myself off... I shall leave, and you imagine that you drove me away, wretched infidel. Your dear hand... I shall kiss..."

Okurkin gave the old woman's hand a lingering kiss and left quickly.

Five minutes later he was at the club. His colleagues had already exchanged best wishes, had given a rouble each and were leaving the club.

"Stop! You!" Okurkin waved at them. "What are you doing, clever oafs? Why are you not going to Lyudmila Semyonovna's?"

"Don't you know? We are not making visits any more..."

"I know, I know... *Merci** to you all... Now look here, civilized men... If you don't go now to visit the witch, you'll be sorry... She's crying her eyes out! She is praying like a Tatar for you to come."

His colleagues exchanged looks and scratched their heads...

"Hm... But if we go to her, surely we'll have to go to everyone..."

"So why not do it, dear men? Go even to everyone... You won't fall off your feet... But do as you like – it doesn't matter to me even if you don't go... You are the only ones who will suffer!"

"Damn it! You know, we've already paid a rouble each!" groaned Yashkin, a teacher at the district school.

"A rouble... But you still have your job?"

The officials scratched their heads once again, and, grumbling, set off to Lyagavaya-Gryslova's place.

A Somebody

"A VACANCY EXISTS for the position of junior clerk in the administrative department of the tax inspector, at a salary of 250 roubles a month. Those who have finished at least primary school, or three years of the high school, must apply in writing with their biographical details, addressing the application to the tax inspector on Gusiniy Street in the village of Podzhilkin."

Having read through this notice for the twentieth time, Misha Nabaldashnikov, a young man in coffee-coloured trousers with a spotty forehead and a nose red from a chronic head cold, walked around, thought for a while and said, addressing his mother:

"I didn't finish three years of the high school, but four. I have the most excellent handwriting, and could even be a writer or government minister. As for the salary, you see for yourself, it's wonderful – twenty roubles a month! With our poverty I would even go for five! Say what you like, but the position is very suitable. I don't need anything better… Only one thing worries me, Mama: I have to write a biography."

"Well, so what? Just go and write…"

"It's easy to say 'write'! In order to compose a biography, one has to have talent. How can one write without talent? You yourself know it's embarrassing to write to no purpose, any nonsense at all. After all, this is not work to be given to the teacher, but sent with an application, to the administrative office, with documents! It's not enough that it should be written on good paper, and neatly. It also has to be in good style… Of course! Otherwise, what do you think? If you look at the tax inspector, Ivan Andreich, in one way, then he is not an important person… a provincial secretary who went six years without a position and was in debt to all the local shops. But if you look more closely, then, no-o-o, Mama, he is a somebody, an important person! Didn't you hear what it said in the notice? 'Addressing the application'... Ap-pli-ca-tion! And applications are only sent to important people! They don't send applications to you or me or Uncle Nil Kuzmich!"

"That is so," agreed Mama. "But why does he need your biography?"

"I can't tell you that... It must be necessary!"

Misha once more read through the notice, paced from corner to corner and gave himself up to dreams... Those who even once in life have been without a job, tormented by idleness, know how advertisements excite the soul like higher writing. Misha, who since his time in school had not eaten a single crust without being reproached as a parasite, who had worn Uncle Nil Kuzmich's old trousers, going out only in the evenings when his torn boots and shabby jacket could not be seen, was excited by the possibility of getting a job. Twenty roubles a month... it was not a small sum. True, it would not get you horses, or let you put on a wedding, but then it would be quite enough, in the first month, Misha dreamt, to buy himself new trousers, boots, a peak cap and accordion, and to give his mother five or six roubles for provisions. At any rate, a little salary was better than big poverty. But for Misha the twenty roubles were not as important as the thought of the blissful time when his mother would stop reproaching him for being a sponger, while at the same time crying her eyes out, and Uncle Nil Kuzmich would put an end to his lectures and his threats to thrash his parasite-nephew.

"Instead of pacing back and forth in the room," Mama said, interrupting his daydreams, "it would be better to sit down and write."

"I don't know how to write, Mama," sighed Misha. "To tell the truth, I've already about five times sat down to write, but not a damn thing comes out. I want to write in an intelligent way, but it comes out in simple language, the way you write to Auntie in Kremenchuk..."

"It doesn't matter that it's simple... The inspector will not be hard on you... With my maternal prayers and patience God will soften his heart: he won't be angry, if what... God knows how educated even he probably was at your age!"

"Perhaps I shall try again, but you should know that nothing will come out... All right, I shall try..."

Misha sat down at the table, placed a sheet of paper in front of himself and fell to thinking. After staring for a long time at the ceiling, he took up a pen and, shaking his dangling hand the way all admirers of their own handwriting do, began: "Honoured sir! I was born in 1867 in the town of K—, from my father Kiril Nikanorovich Nabaldashnikov and my mother Natalya Ivanovna. My father worked in the sugar factory of merchant Podgoiski as a clerk and received 600 roubles a year. Then he resigned and lived for a long time without a job. Then..."

Later, his father had taken to drink and died of drunkenness, but this was really a family secret, which Misha did not want to impart to the honoured gentleman. Misha thought for a while, crossed out everything he had written and, after more thought, wrote again the very same things...

"Then he passed away," he continued, "in poverty, mourned by a wife and a dearly loving only son, which was I, Mikhail. When I had reached the age of nine, I was sent to the preparatory school; Podgoiski paid for me, but when Father resigned from him he stopped paying for me, and I left in the fourth year. I was not a good pupil, and had to repeat years 1 and 3, but in calligraphy and behaviour I always received a five."* Etc.

Misha filled the whole page. He wrote sincerely, but incoherently, without any plan or chronological order, repeating himself and getting muddled. What came out was padded, overlong and childishly naive... Misha finished thus: "But now I live supported by my mother, who has no means for living, and that is why I most humbly beg Your Honour to give me a position, so that I may live and feed my sick mother, who also begs You. And excuse me for disturbing You." (Signed.)

The next day, after much doubt and timid indecision, a fair copy of this résumé was made and sent to its destination together with some documents. Two weeks later Misha, who was exhausted from waiting, stood, his whole body trembling, in the corridor of the tax inspector's office expecting an honorarium for his composition.

"May I ask, where is the clerical office?" he said, looking from the corridor into a big, poorly furnished room where a red-haired man was lying on a sofa wearing dress shoes and a summer cloak instead of official attire.

"What do you want?" asked the red-haired man.

"Here I… two weeks ago sent an application… about a position as a clerk… May I see Mr Inspector?"

"It's simply outrageous…" muttered the red-haired man, adding an expression of suffering to his face and pulling his cloak more tightly about him. "A hundred people a day! They just keep coming and coming! Is it possible, sir, that you have nothing else to do but disturb me?"

The red-haired man jumped up, stood with his legs apart and said, articulating every word:

"I have already said a thousand times, to everyone, that I have a clerk! I have, I have and I have! It's now time to stop coming! I already have a clerk! So tell everyone!"

"I'm sorry, sir," muttered Misha. "I did not know, sir…"

And, bowing awkwardly, Misha went out. As for the honorarium… alas and alack!

A Blunder

"I'M TIRED!" I thought, sitting in the bank. "I shall go home and get some sleep."

"What bliss!" I whispered, standing by my bed after hastily dining. "It's good to live in this world! Wonderful!"

With a fixed smile on my face, stretching and luxuriating on the bed like a tomcat in the sun, I closed my eyes and started to fall asleep. In my closed eyes I could see little ants running about. A mist began to swirl in my head… wings began to wave as some sort of fur flew up to the sky from my head… something like cotton wool seemed to be creeping into my head from the sky… It was all big, soft, fluffy, vague. Little people started running around in the mist. They ran, whirled and hid in the mist… When the last person disappeared and Morpheus was triumphing, I gave a sudden start.

"Ivan Osipych, come here!" bawled a voice somewhere.

I opened my eyes. In the next room there was a pop as someone opened a bottle. I turned on my other side and covered my head with the blanket.

"I loved you, love is still perhaps…"* sang out a baritone in the next room.

"Why don't you get yourself a piano?" asked another voice.

"The devils," I muttered. "They won't let me sleep!"

Another bottle was uncorked, and I heard the clattering of dishes. Someone began to pace back and forth, spurs jangling. Doors slammed.

"Timofei, can you get the samovar ready quickly? Look lively, brother! More plates! Well, gentlemen? In keeping with Christian values, let's each drink a little something… Mademoiselle Christabel, lamb's legs, *je vous prie*!"*

A drinking bout started in the next room. I buried my head under the pillow.

"Timofei! If a tall, fair-haired man in a bearskin coat arrives, tell him we're here."

I swore, leapt up and knocked on the wall. It went quiet in the next room. I closed my eyes again. The ants began to run, and there was the fur and the cotton wool... But – alas! – a minute later they started bawling again.

"Gentlemen!" I cried in a pleading voice. "This really is the limit of swinish behaviour! I must beg you! I am ill and want to sleep."

"Are you talking to us?"

"Yes."

"What do you want?"

"Be so good as not to shout! I want to sleep!"

"So sleep. No one's stopping you. And if you're sick, go to the doctor! 'The knights have love and honour...'"* sang the baritone.

"How stupid this is," I said. "Very stupid! Even despicable."

"I would ask you not to complain!" An old man's voice was heard from behind the wall.

"Wonderful! Someone in there is now giving orders! A real bigwig! And who are you?"

"Don't com–plain!!!"

"Peasants! Stuffed with vodka and shouting!"

"Don't com–plain!!!" The old man's voice repeated about ten times.

I kept turning over on the bed. The thought that I couldn't sleep because of these idle loafers drove me little by little into a rage... They started to dance...

"If you don't be quiet," I shouted, choking with fury, "I shall go for the police! Where's the porter? Timofei!"

"Don't complain!!!" cried the old man's voice once again.

I leapt up and ran next door like a madman. I was determined at all costs to have it my own way.

There, they were partying. Bottles stood on a table, where several people, their bulging eyes goggling like lobsters', were sitting. Deeper in the room, on a sofa, reclined a bald old man... On his chest lay the head of a notorious courtesan. He was looking at the wall of my room and shouting:

"Don't complain!!"

I opened my mouth wide to start cursing him, and... oh, horror!!!

I recognized the old man as the director of the bank where I worked. In an instant sleep, anger and contempt all deserted me... I ran from the room.

For a whole month the director did not look at me and said not a single word to me... We avoided each other. After a month he sidled up to my desk and, bending his head and looking at the floor, muttered:

"I thought... hoped, that you yourself would guess... But I see that you do not intend. Hm... Don't worry. You may even sit down... I thought that... We two could not work together... Your behaviour in Bultykhin's rooms... You gave my niece such a fright... You understand... Hand over your work to Ivan Nikitich..."

Then, raising his head, he walked away from me.

And I lost my job.

A Tale Hard to Entitle

IT WAS NOON ON A HOLIDAY. Twenty of us colleagues were sitting at a big table, enjoying life. Our drunken eyes were resting on the enticing caviar, fresh lobster and wonderful salmon, and on the many bottles that were standing in a row along almost the whole length of the table. In our stomachs the warmth was spreading – or, as an Arab would say, the sun was rising. We ate and drank. We conversed freely. We talked about... May I, reader, rely on your discretion? We did not talk about strawberries, or about horses... no! We discussed important matters. We talked about a man, the village constable, and about the rouble... (don't tell anyone, my dear!) A colleague drew out of his pocket a scrap of paper and read some verses in which humorous advice was given to tax residents: ten roubles if they use both eyes, five roubles if they use only one, and nothing at all if they are blind. A light-fingered man (Fyodor Andreich), usually a quiet and respectful person, on this occasion succumbed to the spirit of the gathering. He said: "His Excellency, Ivan Prokhorych, is such a swine... such a swine!" After each phrase we all cried: "*Pereat!*"* We even led the waiters astray from the path of virtue by making them drink to fraternity... The toasts were sparkling, racy, quite outrageous! I, for example, proposed a toast to the flourishing of the natur... – may I rely on your discretion? – the natural sciences.

When they served the champagne, we asked provincial secretary Ottyagayev, our Renan and Spinoza,* to make a speech. After a half-hearted protest he agreed, and, with a backward glance at the door, said:

"Comrades! Among us are neither superiors nor inferiors! I, for example, a provincial secretary, do not feel the slightest urge to show my power over those collegiate registrars who are sitting here, while at the same time I hope those titular and court councillors

117

sitting here do not look on me as on a spot of dirt. Do allow me... M-mm... No, allow me... Look around! What do we see?"

We looked around and saw a collection of deferentially smiling, servile physiognomies.

"We see," continued the orator, having glanced again at the door, "torment, suffering... All around is theft, embezzlement, pilfering, robbery, extortion... Widespread drunkenness... Oppression at every step... How many tears! How many sufferers! We pity them, we... we shall weep for them..." Tears began to flow from the orator's eyes. "We shall weep and shall drink to..."

At this moment the door creaked open. Someone came in. We looked and saw a little old man with a big bald patch and with a benevolent smile on his lips. This man was very well known to us. He came in and stopped, in order to listen to the end of the toast.

"...We shall weep and shall drink to," continued the orator, having raised his voice, "to the health of our boss, patron and benefactor, Ivan Prokhorych Khalchadayev! Hurrah!"

"Hurrah!" came bawling from all twenty throats, as sweet streams of champagne flowed into twenty mouths...

The old man came up to the table and graciously nodded his head at us. He, clearly, was delighted.

The Delegate

A Story about How Desdemonov's
Twenty-Five Roubles Were Lost

*Dedicated to L.I. Palmin**

"SHHH... LET'S GO TO THE PORTER'S LODGE. It's awkward here... We can be heard..."

They set off to the porter's lodge. The porter Makar was hastily sent to the treasury, so that he wouldn't eavesdrop and inform on them. Makar took the delivery book and put on his hat. He didn't go to the treasury, but hid under the staircase: he knew there would be a rebellion... Kashalotov was the first to speak, then Desdemonov, and after Desdemonov Zrachkov... Dangerous passions began to rage. Red faces were convulsed with anger, fists began to beat on chests...

"We live in the second half of the nineteenth century, not the devil knows when, not in prehistoric times!" Kashalotov began. "What those pot-bellies were allowed before, they are not allowed now! We've had enough at last! The time has already passed when..." And so on.

Desdemonov thundered in much the same way. Zrachkov even swore indecently. All began to make a din. One sensible person came forward, however. This sensible person pulled a worried face, wiped his nose with a snotty handkerchief and said:

"Well, is it worth it? Ah... Well, let's assume, even if... it's true – but why? As you measure, so it will be measured unto you:* when you are the bosses, they will rebel against you. Believe me. You are destroying only yourselves."

But no one listened to the sensible person. They did not let him finish speaking, but pushed him aside towards the door. Realizing that he would get nowhere with his sensible talk, he became like the rest, and also began to rage.

"It's time to make him understand that we are the same people as he is!" said Desdemonov. "We, I repeat, are not lackeys, not plebeians! We are not gladiators! We shall not allow ourselves to be ridiculed! He accuses us, does not acknowledge our bows, makes a face when we give a report, criticizes us... Nowadays you're not even allowed to treat lackeys like that, let alone sensible people! So we should tell him!"

"The other day," said Kashalotov, "he turns to me and asks, 'What's that on your snout? Go to Makar, let him clean you with his mop!' What a clown! And also, one day—"

"One day I'm walking with my wife," interrupted Zrachkov. "I meet him... 'And you,' he says, 'Thick-Lips, you're always hanging around with loose women! Even in broad daylight!' This, I say, is my wife, Your Excellency... But he does not apologize – just smacks his lips. After this insult, my wife raged for three days. She is not a loose woman, but on the contrary... as you know..."

"In a word, gentlemen, we cannot live like this any longer. It's either us or him, but in any case it's impossible to work with him any longer. Either he goes or we go! It's better to live without a position than to have your self-respect destroyed. It's the nineteenth century now. We all have our pride. Though I am a little man, I am not just anyone, and my soul is my own. I shall not allow it! So he should be told. One of us should tell him that it's not acceptable. On our behalf. Go! Who will go? Go straight to him and tell him! Don't be afraid, nothing will happen. Who will go? Tfoo, damn it... I have become quite hoarse..."

They began to choose a delegate. After long argument and discussion, Desdemonov was chosen as the cleverest, most eloquent and bravest of them. He belonged to the library, wrote beautifully and was acquainted with educated ladies – which meant he was clever: he would know what to say and how to say it. As for his bravery, that was unquestionable. Everyone knew how, at the club, he once demanded an apology from a policeman who mistook him for "some man": the policeman wasn't able to correct his mistake before gossip about Desdemonov's bravery spread through the world and became imprinted on everyone's memory.

"Go, Senya! Don't be afraid! Just tell him! You should say, 'We've had enough.' Say, 'We're not putting up with this any more, Your Excellency. You're mistreating us! Look for other lackeys. We weren't born yesterday, Your Excellency, we know how to behave. There's no point in covering things up!' That's it... Go, Senya... friend... Only, comb your hair... Just tell him."

"I'm too short-tempered, gentlemen... I might easily say something I shouldn't. It would be better if Zrachkov goes."

"No, Senya, you go... Zrachkov is brave only when confronting sheep, and then only when drunk... He's a fool, but you still... Go, dear man..."

Desdemonov combed his hair, adjusted his waistcoat, coughed in his fist and went... The others all held their breath. Entering the office, Desdemonov stopped at the door and passed a shaking hand over his lips: how should he begin? The pit of his stomach went cold and tightened, as if with a belt, when he saw the bald head with the familiar black wart... A cold draught seemed to run up his spine... It didn't matter, though – it could happen to anyone inexperienced, one just shouldn't be shy... Be brave!

"Ah... what do you want?"

Desdemonov made a step forward, moved his tongue, but did not emit a single sound: something seemed to have become entangled in his mouth. At the same time, the delegate sensed that there was confusion not only in his mouth, but also in his intestines... From his heart his courage went to his belly, rumbled there, went along his thighs down to his heels and got stuck in his boots... And his boots were torn... Horror!

"Ah... what do you want? Do you hear?"

"Hm... It's nothing... I just... I heard, Your Excellency... I heard..."

Desdemonov held his tongue, but his tongue wouldn't obey, and he continued:

"I heard that they say Her Excellency has entered her carriage in the lottery... A ticket, Your Excellency... Hm... Your Excellency..."

"A ticket? All right... I only have five tickets left... Will you take all five?"

"Na... na... no, Your Excellency... One ticket... it's enough..."

"I'm asking if you'll take all five?"

"Very well, then, Your Excellency."

"They are six roubles each... But you can give me five for each... Sign here... With all my heart I hope you win..."

"Hee-hee-hee... *Merci, Monsieur*, Your Excellency... Ah, most delighted..."

"Go, now!"

Five minutes later Desdemonov was standing by the porter's lodge, and, red as a lobster, with tears in his eyes, was asking his friends for a loan of twenty-five roubles.

"I gave him twenty-five roubles, brothers, but it was not my money! My mother-in-law gave it to me to pay the rent... Give it to me, gentlemen, I beg you!"

"But why are you crying? You'll get to drive in a carriage..."

"In a carriage... a carriage... I would frighten people in a carriage, wouldn't I? I'm not a priest. And where would I put it, if I win? What would I do with it?"

They talked for a long time, and while they were talking, Makar (who was literate) was making notes, writing it all down... It's a long story, ladies and gentlemen! But anyway, the lesson that springs from this is: don't rebel!

Without Work

LAW GRADUATE PEREPYELKIN was sitting in his room and writing:

Dear Uncle Ivan Nikolayevich,
    The devil take you for your letters of recommendation and practical advice! It's a thousand times better, more noble and decent to sit without work and to live on hope in a vague future than to have to bathe in the cold, stinking mud which you pushed me into with your letters and advice. I feel unbearably sick, as if poisoned by fish. The sickness is the worst kind – mental – which is impossible to dispel with either vodka, sleep or edifying thoughts. You know, Uncle, even though you are an old man, you are a real swine. Why did you not warn me that I would have to experience such vileness? Shame on you!
    I shall relate to you, one by one, all my ordeals. Read and blame yourself. First of all, I set off with your letter of recommendation to Babkov. I found him in the office of the railway company N—. He is a small, entirely bald old man with a yellow-grey, clean-shaven face and crooked mouth. His upper lip pulls to the right, the lower to the left. He sits behind his own table and reads the newspaper.
    Around him, as around Apollo on Parnassus, sit women on commercial stools behind fat books. These women are dressed stylishly, with bustles, fans, massive bracelets. How they can afford to appear like that on beggarly women's salaries is hard to understand. Either they work there because they have nothing else to do, being well off from the support of their fathers and uncles, or the bookkeeper is just a puppet who fulfils both those roles for them. Then I realized they don't do a damn thing: their work falls on the shoulders of various supernumeraries – silent

men who receive 10–15 roubles a month. I gave Babkov your letter. Without inviting me to sit down, he slowly took off his antediluvian pince-nez, even more slowly unsealed the envelope and started to read.

"Your uncle asks me to give you a job," he said, scratching his bald pate. "We have no vacancies, and probably won't have any time soon, but in any case, I shall try for your uncle's sake. I shall talk to the director of the company. Maybe we'll find something."

I almost jumped with joy, and was preparing to thank him profusely when suddenly, dear Uncle, I heard him say this:

"But, young man, were this to be a place for your uncle personally, I would expect nothing from him, but as it's for you, then, how shall I put it... I'm sure, that you will want to thank... me appropriately... Do you understand?..."

You warned me that I would not get a place for nothing, that I would have to pay, but you did not say that these nasty sales and purchases are carried out so openly, publicly, shamelessly... in the presence of women! Oh, Uncle, Uncle! Babkov's last words so took me aback that I almost died from nausea. I was so ashamed, as if I myself had taken a bribe. I grew red, began to babble some nonsense and, under the gaze of the smiling eyes of twenty women, staggered back to the exit. In the hall, a gloomy, haggard individual accosted me and whispered that even without Babkov's help it would be possible to get me a job.

"Give me five roubles and I shall take you to Sakhar Myodovich. He doesn't work, but he finds work for others. And he charges a little something for this service: half the salary for the first year."

I should have spat at him and laughed, but I thanked him, felt embarrassed and set off down the stairs as if scalded. From Babkov I went to Shmakovich. He is a mild, chubby little fat man with a red, good-humoured face and greasy little eyes. His eyes glistened with such sickly sweetness that they seemed smeared with castor oil. Learning that I was your nephew, he rejoiced wholeheartedly, and even began to neigh with delight.

He put aside his work and went about getting me tea. What a kind man! All the time he was looking me in the face, trying to find a likeness to you. He remembered you with tears in his eyes. When I reminded him about the point of my visit, he slapped me on the shoulder and said:

"There will be plenty of time to talk about business... Business is not a bear – it will not run off to the forest.* Where are you dining? If it's all the same to you, let's go to Palkin's.* We'll have a chat there."

With this letter I enclose Palkin's bill. Seventy-six roubles for food and drink for your friend Shmakovich, who turned out to be quite a gourmand. Of course it was I who paid the bill. From Palkin's, Shmakovich took me to the theatre. I bought the tickets. What then? After the theatre your scoundrel of a friend suggested we go for a drive out of town, but I refused, as my money had almost run out. Bidding me farewell, Shmakovich asked me to convey his greetings to you and tell you that it will take him at least five months to find me a job.

"I will not give you a job on principle," he joked, kindly slapping my stomach. "In any case, why do you, a university man, so want to work for our company? For Heaven's sake, you should go into the civil service."

"I know about civil-service jobs even without your telling me. But give me a job!"

With your third letter I set off to your cousin Khalatov on the board of the Zhivodyer–Khamski railway. Here something disgusting happened, something even surpassing both Babkov and Shmakovich. I say once more: go to the devil! I feel sick and outraged, and it's all your fault. I did not find your Khalatov. I was received by a certain Odekolonov – a gaunt, sinewy figure with a pockmarked, Jesuitical phiz. Learning that I sought a job, he sat me down and read me a whole lecture about the difficulties of finding a position nowadays. After the lecture he promised to talk to someone, to do his best, put in a word and so on. Remembering your advice, to offer money wherever possible, and seeing that the pockmarked face was not averse to taking a bribe, when saying goodbye I shoved into his fist... His extended hand squeezed my finger, the phiz grinned, and more promises rained down, but... Odekolonov glanced back and saw behind him some of his colleagues, who could not but have seen the handshake. The Jesuit was embarrassed and muttered:

"I promise to find you a position, but.... I don't accept gratitude... No, no! Take it back! No, no! You are offending..."

He unclenched his fist and gave me back the money – not the twenty-five-rouble note I had given him, but a three-rouble note. What kind of conjuring trick was that? These devils must have a whole system of springs and threads up their sleeves, otherwise I don't understand how my poor twenty-five-rouble note could have been transformed into a wretched three-rouble one.

The subject of your fourth letter of recommendation – Grysodubov – seemed the cleanest and most honest of them all.

He was a handsome man, still young, with a noble bearing, foppishly dressed. He received me, although languidly, with evident reluctance, but kindly. From conversations with him I learnt that, despite finishing university, he had had to struggle in the past to keep body and soul together. He treated my request very sympathetically, the more so because it was his long-standing dream to have an educated workforce... I've seen him already three times, and on none of the occasions has he told me anything definite. He somehow prevaricated, seemed to avoid giving straight answers, as if he were embarrassed, or couldn't make up his mind... I gave you my word not to be emotional. You assured me that all cheats are of noble bearing and most knightly behaviour. Perhaps this is true, but you just try and separate the cheats from the honest ones. You will get into a mess beyond belief. Today I was with Grysodubov a fourth time... As before, he prevaricated and said nothing definite... I was exasperated... I don't know why I suddenly remembered that I had given you my word to offer money to everyone without exception, so now I felt as if someone was pushing my elbow... As some bring themselves to plunge into cold water, or to climb to a height, so I brought myself to risk slipping some paper currency...

"Oh, what will be will be," I decided. "For once in my life I can try..."

I decided to try it not so much for the sake of securing a position as for the sake of the novelty of the experience. I thought I would see at least once in my life how decent people react to the offer of "gratitude"! But the "experience" went horribly wrong. I carried it out clumsily, crudely... I drew from my pocket a banknote and, reddening, shaking all over, seized a moment when Grysodubov was not looking at me and placed it on the table. Unfortunately just then Grysodubov put some books on the table, covering the banknote... So my experiment didn't succeed... Grysodubov didn't see the banknote... Either it will be lost among the papers or the watchmen will steal it... But if he sees it, he may be offended... That's it, *mon oncle...** The money is gone and it's a shame... a great shame! And it's all because of you with your damned practical advice! You corrupted me... I'm breaking off this letter, because someone is knocking... I'm going to open the door...

I've just received a letter from Grysodubov. He writes that there is a vacancy in the department for goods duty at sixty roubles a month. He must have found my banknote.

Conversation of a Man with a Dog

I T WAS A FROSTY, MOONLIT NIGHT. Alexei Ivanych Romansov brushed a little green devil off his sleeve, carefully opened the gate and entered the yard.

"Man," he philosophized, steadying himself as he went around a cesspit, "is dust, a mirage, ash... Pavel Nikolaich is the governor, but even he is ash. His seeming greatness is a dream, smoke... Blow once, and he's gone!"

"Rrrr..." reached the ears of the philosopher.

Romansov looked to the side, and two paces away saw a huge black steppe sheepdog, the size of a big wolf. It was sitting near the caretaker's hut and rattling its chain. Romansov looked at it and thought for a moment. A look of surprise came over his face. Then he shrugged, shook his head and smiled sadly.

"Rrrr..." repeated the dog.

"I doan unnerstand!" slurred Romansov, throwing wide his arms. "And you... can you growl at a man? Well? Firs time in my life I hear this. God strike me dead... Doan you know man is the summit of creation? Just you look... I'll come up to you... Look here... Am I not a man? What do you think? Am I a man or not a man? Explain!"

"Rrrr... Gaff!"

"Give me your paw." Romansov stretched out his hand to the dog. "Your p-paw! You won't give it? You doan want to? Well, so be it. We'll remember that. But meanwhile, allow me to caress your muzzle... I like..."

"Gaff! Gaff! Rrrr... gaff! Afaff!"

"Ah... do you bite? Very well, awright. We'll remember. Does that mean you doan give a damn about man being the summit of creation... the king of the beasts? Does it follow that you would even bite Pavel Nikolaich? Yes? All prostrate themselves before

Pavel Nikolaich, but what is he to you, jus another object – the same as the others? Do I unnerstand you correctly? Ah... So does it mean you're a socialist? Well, answer me... Are you a socialist?"

"Rrrr... gaff! Gaff!"

"Stop, doan bite... What was I saying?... Ah yes, about ashes. Blow and it's gone! Pfff! And why do we live, you ask? We are born of a mother's pain – we eat, drink, learn, die... And what is all that for? Ashes! Man is worth nothing! You are a dog and unnerstand nothing, but if you were able... to get into my soul! If only you were able to unnerstand psychology!"

Romansov turned his head and spat.

"Filth... You think that I, Romansov, a collegiate secretary... am the lord of nature... You are wrong! I am a parasite, bribe-taker, hypocrite!... I'm a rat!"

Alexei Ivanych struck his chest with his fist and burst into tears.

"I'm a slanderer, informer... Do you think Yegor Kornyushkin was not sacked because of me? Well? And who, may I ask, stole two hunnerd roubles from the committee and blamed Surguchov? Was it not I? I'm a rat, a Pharisee... A Judas! A toady, swindler... scum!"

Romansov wiped his tears with his sleeve and sobbed.

"Bite me! Eat me! No one in my life ever tole me the truth... Deep down, everyone thought me a scoundrel, but to my face there was nothing but praise and smiles – oh no! If only someone would beat me in the face or swear at me! Eat me, dog! Bite me! Rrrip the damned one to pieces! Devour the traitor!"

Romansov tottered and fell on the dog.

"So, exactly so! Tear the lickspittle! Show no pity! Even if it's painful, show no mercy. Here are my hands, bite them! Aha, blood is flowing! I deserve it, odious wretch! So! *Merci*, Zhuchka, or whatever your name is... *Merci*... Tear my fur coat too. It was just a bribe... I denounced my neighbour and bought the coat with the money I got... And also a peak cap with a cockade... But what am I talking about?... I have to go... Goodbye little dog... little rascal..."

"Rrrr."

Romansov stroked the dog and, allowing it to bite his leg one more time, drew his coat about him and tottered home...

Waking up the next day at noon, Romansov noticed something strange. His head, arms and legs were in bandages. Around the bed were standing his weeping wife and an anxious doctor.

Two in One

D ON'T BELIEVE THESE JUDASES, these chameleons! In our time it's easier to lose faith than an old glove – and I lost it!

It was evening. I was travelling in a horse-drawn tram. It is inappropriate for me, as a high-ranking official, to be going by tram, but I was wearing a heavy fur coat and was able to hide my face behind a marten collar. And it was cheap, you know... Although the hour was late, and it was cold, the carriage was crowded. No one recognized me. The marten collar made me incognito. I was going along, dozing and studying my fellow passengers.

"No, it's not him," I thought, looking at a little man in a rabbit-fur coat. "It's not him! Yes, it's him! It's him!"

I was thinking, and at the same time believing and not believing my eyes...

The man in the rabbit-fur coat bore a strong resemblance to Ivan Kapitonych, one of my clerks... Ivan Kapitonych is a small, crushed, flattened creature, who lives only to pick up fallen handkerchiefs and offer congratulations on holidays. He is young, but his back is bent in an arc and his knees sag; his hands are dirty and hang limply at his sides. His face, which is sour and pitiful, looks as if it has been crushed in a door or beaten with a wet rag: seeing it, one has the urge to sing 'Luchinushka'* and pine with sadness. At the sight of me he always trembles, grows pale and reddens, as if he thinks I want to eat him or cut his throat – and when I tell him off, he goes cold and starts to shake all over.

I know of no one more downtrodden, more silent or insignificant than him. I don't even know of any animals more unassuming than him...

The little man in the rabbit-fur coat reminded me strongly of Ivan Kapitonych: it was him to a T! Only he was not so bent as the other, did not seem so crushed: he was behaving more expansively

– and, most astonishingly of all, was talking to the passenger next to him about politics. The whole carriage was listening to him.

"Gambetta* is dead," he said, turning from side to side and waving his arms. "This suits Bismarck's purposes.* You see, Gambetta played his cards close to his chest. He would have gone to war with the Germans, and demanded reparations, Ivan Matveich! Because he was a genius. He was French, but he had a Russian spirit. He was a gifted man!"

Oh, what rubbish!

When the conductor came to him with tickets, he abandoned the subject of Bismarck.

"Why is it so dark in this carriage?" he asked the conductor aggressively. "Don't you have any candles? What kind of organization is this? There's no one in charge. Abroad, they would know how to deal with you! The public isn't here for you: you're here for the public! The devil take it! I don't understand what the authorities are playing at!"

A minute later he demanded that we all rise.

"Get up! I'm telling you! Give the lady a seat. Be more polite! Conductor! Come here, conductor. If you take our money, you should give us a seat. It's disgraceful!"

"Smoking is not permitted in here," the conductor shouted at him.

"Who doesn't permit it? Who has the right? It's an infringement of liberty! I'm a free man!"

Oh, what a swine! I looked at his face and could not believe my eyes. No, it wasn't him. It couldn't be! He wouldn't know such words as "liberty" and "Gambetta".

"There is nothing to be said. Fine customs these are!" he said, stubbing out his cigarette. "We have to live with such people! They are wedded to form, to the letter of the law! They are formalists, philistines! They stink!"

I could stand it no longer, and burst out laughing. Hearing my laughter, he stole a glance at me. His voice faltered. He recognized my laugh, and must have recognized my fur coat. His back bent at once, his face froze in an instant, his voice faded, his hands dropped to the sides, his legs gave way. He changed in a moment! I was no longer in doubt: this was Ivan Kapitonych, my clerk. He sat down and hid his face behind his rabbit-fur collar.

Then I looked at his face.

"Is it possible," I thought, "that this crushed, flattened creature is able to use such words as 'philistine' and 'liberty'? Well? Is it possible? Yes, he can. It seems incredible, but it's true. Oh, what a scoundrel!"

After this, if you wish, you may believe in the pitiable faces of these chameleons.

But I no longer believe. That was enough: I'll not be deceived!

Joy

I T WAS MIDNIGHT.

Excited and dishevelled, Mitya Kuldarov rushed into his parents' flat and began to pace restlessly from room to room. His parents had already gone to bed. His sister lay in bed reading the last page of a novel. His schoolboy brothers were asleep.

"Where have you come from?" his parents asked in astonishment. "What's the matter with you?"

"Oh, don't ask! I couldn't wait! I just couldn't wait! This is… this is quite incredible!"

Mitya burst out laughing, and, from sheer happiness, lacking the strength to stay on his feet, collapsed into an armchair.

"It's unbelievable! You cannot imagine! Take a look at this!"

His sister leapt out of bed and, throwing on a blanket, went up to him. The schoolboys awoke.

"What's the matter with you? You look strange!"

"I'm filled with joy, Mama! Because now everyone in Russia knows about me! Everyone! Before, only you knew that there exists in the world Collegiate Registrar Dmitry Kuldarov, but now all of Russia knows about him! Mama! Oh, God!"

Mitya jumped up, ran through all the rooms and again sat down.

"So, what's happened? Talk sense!"

"You live like wild animals, don't read newspapers, don't know what goes on, but there are so many wonderful things in newspapers! Nowadays, if something happens, everyone knows about it. Nothing is covered up. How happy I am! Oh, God! You see, they print things only about famous people in the newspapers, but now they've gone and printed something about me!"

"What do you mean? Where?"

His father went pale. His mother looked at the icon and made the sign of the cross. The schoolboys jumped out of bed and, still in their short nightshirts, went up to their elder brother.

"Yes! They have published something about me. Now all of Russia knows about me! Keep this edition as a souvenir, Mama! Read it from time to time. Look at it now and again!"

Mitya drew from his pocket a copy of a newspaper and handed it to his father, pointing at a place encircled with a blue pencil.

"Read!"

His father put on his spectacles.

"Go on and read!"

His mother looked at the icon and crossed herself again. His father coughed and began to read:

"On 29th December, at eleven o'clock at night, Collegiate Registrar Dmitry Kuldarov—"

"You see, you see? Go on!"

"...Collegiate Registrar Dmitry Kuldarov, coming out of the porter's lodge in the Kozikhin residence on Malaya Bronnaya, and being in a state of drunkenness—"

"That was me, with Semyon Petrovich... All described to a nicety! Continue! Go on! Listen!"

"...and being in a state of drunkenness, slipped and fell under the horse of a cabman, a peasant from Durykina, in Yukhnovsky Province, Ivan Drotov, which was standing there. The frightened horse stepped over Kuldarov and, pulling the sleigh – in which was seated the Moscow merchant of the second guild, Stepan Lukov – over Kuldarov, tore off down the street until it was stopped by some nightwatchmen. Kuldarov was taken unconscious to the police station and was examined by a doctor. The blow, which he received on the back of the head—"

"That was from the shaft, Papa. Read on! Keep reading!"

"...which he received on the back of the head, was deemed to be light. A report was made about the incident. The injured man was given medical aid."

"They advised applying cold water to the back of my head. Now you've read it? Well? What did I tell you? Now it will spread through all Russia! Here, give it to me!"

Mitya grabbed the newspaper, folded it up and put it in his pocket.

"I shall run to the Makarovs and show them... I have yet to show it to the Ivanitskis, Natalya Ivanovna, Anisim Vasilich... I must run! Goodbye!"

Mitya put on his peak cap with the cockade and, radiant and happy, ran out into the street.

The Naive Wood Goblin

A Fairy Tale

O NE BEAUTIFUL MORNING, in the forest, on the bank of a
river guarded day and night by a tall rush, stood an attractive young wood goblin. Near him on the grass sat a mermaid,
very young and so pretty that had I known her exact address I
would have abandoned everything – literature, a wife, studies –
and rushed to her... The little mermaid was frowning and pulling
angrily at a tuft of green grass.

"I ask you to understand me," said the wood goblin, stammer-
ing and shyly blinking. "If you understood, you would not be
so severe with me. Allow me to explain everything to you from
the very beginning... Twenty years ago, at this very spot, when I
asked for your hand, you said you would only marry me if I got
rid of the stupid expression on my face, and for this you advised
me to go out into the world and learn some sense. As you know, I
obeyed you and set off into the world. Excellent... Arriving among
people, I first of all asked what professions and trades there were.
One lawyer told me that the best and most harmless profession
would be to lie on a sofa with my feet up and spit at the ceiling
– but I, an honest, stupid wood goblin, did not believe him. First
of all, through patronage, I got the job of a postmaster. It was a
horrible job, *ma chère*! The people's letters were so boring that
the job became complete drudgery."

"But why did you read the letters, if they were so boring?"

"It was the accepted practice... What's more, it had to be
done... The letters were of various kinds... Some of them were
signed 'lieutenant' or suchlike, and under the title of lieutenant
the names Lassalle* or Spinoza... Well, then through patronage
I got a job as the chief of a fire brigade... Also a horrible job!

There were constant fires... You would sit down to dine, or to play vint – and there would be a fire. You'd go to bed – a fire. But how can you go to a fire if it's known from experience that fire horses can't be fed with oats?* I once ordered the horses to be given oats and – what do you think? – the inspector was so amazed that I felt ashamed... I gave it up...

"There are, *ma chère*, people in the world whose job it is to ensure that there is nothing unnecessary in the heads or pockets of their fellow citizens. This job is very like that of a fire chief. I joined them. In the beginning all my work consisted of accepting gratitude from people. At first I liked this a lot... In our practical age such feelings as gratitude cannot be expected from stones, and have to be encouraged... But then I was quite disappointed. People were terribly devious... They thanked me with post-dated cheques and even counterfeit banknotes. And besides that, they thanked me, but without any sign of a warm feeling in their eyes. Let me continue! Teaching was very much like that job. I became a pedagogue. At first I had luck, and the director even shook my hand several times. He really liked my stupid face. But alas! One day I read in the *Vyestnik Yevropi** an article about the harm done by the destruction of forests, and felt pangs of conscience. Even before that, frankly speaking, I had thought it a shame to use the branches of our dear, green birch trees for such vile aims as pedagogical ones.

"I conveyed my doubts to the director, and he realized the stupid expression on my face was not genuine. I took flight! Then I got a job as a doctor. At first I was lucky. Diphtheria, you know, and typhus... Though I did not increase the mortality rate, I was nevertheless noticed. I was promoted to be a doctor in the Moscow foundling hospital. Here, besides prescriptions and ward visits, I was required to bow and grovel and show the ability to travel *na zapyatka.** The senior doctor, Solovyov – the one who, at a conference in Odessa, felt himself to be like a god – demanded that I treat him with reverence. When I said that bowing and reverence were not taught in the medical faculty, he decided I was a freethinker and a person of no breeding...

"After my unsuccessful efforts as a doctor, I went into business. I opened a bakery and started to bake rolls. But, *ma chère*, it's simply terrible how many insects there are in the world! Whatever *kalatches** you break into, there are cockroaches and woodlice in all of them."

"Oh, enough of your nonsense!" exclaimed the mermaid, losing patience. "What devil asked you, you fool, to become a fire chief, or bake rolls? Were you really, you peasant, unable to find anything in the world more intelligent or uplifting? Do people really not have learning, literature?"

"I wanted to enter university, but one official told me there was nothing but trouble there... I did indeed become a man of letters. The devil took me to that literature! I wrote well and even had hope – but, *ma chère*, it's so cold and there are so many bedbugs in jail that when I think about it I can smell the bedbugs in the air even now. I was finished with the literary life... I died in hospital... The literary fund buried me at its expense. Reporters spent ten roubles drinking vodka at my funeral. My dear! Don't send me again among the people! I assure you, I would not bear the ordeal!"

"It's terrible! I pity you, but look in the river! Your face has become stupider than before! No, go out again! Take up science, art... travel, at last! Don't you want to? Well then, go and take the advice the lawyer gave you!"

The wood goblin began to entreat her... He gave all the reasons he could to avoid going on that unpleasant journey. He said he had no passport, that he was on the register of the proscribed, that in his present situation it would be hard to undertake any trips at all, but nothing helped... The mermaid insisted on having it her own way. And the wood goblin went again among the people. Now he did well, rose to the rank of state councillor, but the expression on his face did not change at all: it was as stupid as before.

The Wicked Boy

I VAN IVANYCH LAPKIN, a young man of pleasing appearance, and Anna Semyonovna Zamblitskaya, a young girl with a turned-up nose, went down a steep bank and sat on a small bench. The bench stood by the water's edge among thick clumps of young willows. A wonderful spot! Sitting there, you were hidden from the world, seen only by the fish and the water spiders skimming like lightning on the water. The young people were equipped with rods, nets, jars of worms and other fishing paraphernalia. Having sat down, they at once set about fishing.

"I am glad that finally we are alone," began Lapkin, looking around. "I have much to say to you, Anna Semyonovna... Very much... When I saw you for the first time... You have a bite... I understood then why I live, understood what my idol is, to whom I have to devote my honest working life... This, surely, is a big bite... Having seen you, I fell in love for the first time – fell passionately in love! Wait before pulling... Let it get firmly on the hook... Tell me, my dear, I plead with you, may I hope – not for mutual feeling, no!... I am unworthy of that, do not dare even to think about it – may I hope for... Pull!"

Anna Semyonovna lifted the rod, pulled it and cried out. In the air flashed a silver-green fish.

"Good Heavens, a perch! Oh, oh... Quickly. It's come off!"

The perch came off the hook, flopped on the grass towards its natural environment and... plop! fell into the water.

In pursuit of the fish, Lapkin, instead of catching it, somehow unintentionally caught Anna Semyonovna's hand and pressed it impulsively to his lips... She drew back, but was too late: their lips met suddenly in a kiss. This was quite unintentional. After the kiss came another kiss, then vows, assurances... Happy moments! However, in this earthly life there is no such thing as absolute happiness. Happiness usually carries poison with it, or is poisoned by something else. So it was this time. While the young people were kissing, laughter was suddenly heard. They looked at the river and froze: up to the waist in the water stood a naked boy. It was Kolya, a schoolboy, Anna Semyonovna's brother. He was standing in the water, looking at the young people and smiling maliciously.

"Ah-h-h! Are you kissing?" he said. "All right, then. I shall tell Mama."

"I would hope that you, as a man of honour..." muttered Lapkin, reddening. "To spy is mean, and to tell is low, vile and disgusting... I expect that you, as an honourable man and a gentleman..."

"Give me a rouble, then I shan't tell!" said the honourable man. "Otherwise, I'll tell."

Lapkin drew a rouble from his pocket and gave it to Kolya. The boy squeezed the rouble in his wet fist, whistled and swam away. And the young people did not kiss again.

The next day Lapkin brought paints and a ball from town for Kolya; his sister gave him her collection of pillboxes. Then he had to give his cufflinks with the face of the dog. The wicked boy obviously liked these things very much: in order to get even more, he began to watch the young couple. Wherever Lapkin and Anna Semyonovna went, he followed. He did not leave them alone for a moment.

"Scoundrel!" cursed Lapkin, grinding his teeth. "So young, and yet already such a great scoundrel! What will become of him?"

All June Kolya gave the poor lovers no peace. He threatened denunciations, watched them and demanded gifts. To him, nothing was enough – finally he began to talk about a pocket watch. So what happened? He was promised a watch.

One evening, during supper, when waffles were served, he suddenly began to laugh, winked an eye and asked Lapkin:

"Shall I tell? Shall I?"

Lapkin reddened terribly and began to chew the napkin instead of the waffle. Anna Semyonovna leapt from the table and ran into the next room.

The young couple found themselves in this situation until the end of August, until the day when, at last, Lapkin proposed to Anna Semyonovna. Oh, what a happy day that was! Having spoken with her parents and received their consent, Lapkin straight away ran to the garden and began to look for Kolya. Finding him, he almost wept with pleasure: he seized the wicked boy by the ear. Anna Semyonovna came running, also looking for Kolya, and took him by the other ear. And it had to be seen what pleasure was written on the faces of the lovers when Kolya began to cry and implore them:

"Dear ones, sweet ones, kind ones, I'll never do it again! Ai, ai, forgive me!"

Later, they both admitted that, during all the time they were courting, not once did they experience such happiness, such overwhelming bliss, as at that moment, when they were pulling the wicked boy by the ears.

The Chameleon

POLICE INSPECTOR OCHUMYELOV is going through the market square; he is wearing a new overcoat and carrying a small parcel in his hand. Behind him follows a red-haired constable with a sieve, full to the brim with confiscated gooseberries. All around is quiet… There is not a soul in the square… The open doors of the shops and taverns look out cheerlessly on God's world, like hungry mouths. Not even beggars are around.

"So you bite, you devil!" Ochumyelov hears suddenly. "Don't let her go, lads! Nowadays there is a law against biting! Hold her! Oh… ah!"

A dog's yelp is heard. Ochumyelov looks around and sees a dog hobbling on three legs and looking back, running from the wood-yard of the merchant Pichugin. A man in a starched cotton shirt and unbuttoned waistcoat is chasing it. From behind, he throws himself forward, falls on the ground and catches the dog by its hind legs. A second yelp from the animal is heard, and the cry "Don't let go!" Sleepy faces look out from the shops, and soon a crowd, rising up as if from the ground, gathers around the woodyard.

"Some disturbance, Your Honour!" says the constable.

Ochumyelov makes a left turn and marches towards the crowd. Near the gate to the yard he sees the aforementioned man in the unbuttoned waistcoat, who is standing and holding up his right hand to show the crowd a bleeding finger. On his half-drunk face seem to be written the words: "I'm really going to deal with you, you brute!" The very finger seems to be a sign of his intent. In this man Ochumyelov recognizes the goldsmith Khryukin. On the ground in the centre of the crowd, with front legs spread and its whole body trembling, sits the cause of the disturbance – a white borzoi pup with a pointed muzzle and a brown spot on its back. In its watering eyes is a look of sadness and fear.

SMALL FRY AND OTHER STORIES

"What's going on here?" asks Ochumyelov, forcing his way through the crowd. "What's the reason for this? Why the finger?... Who shouted?"

"I'm walking along, Your Honour, minding my own business," begins Khryukin, coughing into his fist, "to see Mitry Mitrich about some firewood, when suddenly this base creature, for no reason at all, bites my finger... You know, I am a working man... My work is delicate. They should pay me, because... I shall not be able to use this finger for a week. Even the law, Your Honour, does not say we have to suffer such treatment from animals... If they all go around biting, the world would not be fit to live in..."

"Hm!... All right..." says Ochumyelov sternly, coughing and raising his eyebrows. "All right... Whose dog is this? I'll not let the matter rest! I'll teach people not to let dogs loose! It's time to deal with those who refuse to obey the law! If they are fined, the scoundrels will learn not to let dogs and other stray animals wander the streets. I'll teach them a lesson!... Yeldyrin," the inspector addresses the constable, "find out whose dog this is and make a report! And the dog must be destroyed. No delaying! It may be rabid... Whose dog is this, I ask."

"I think it's General Zhigalov's," someone says from the crowd.

"General Zhigalov's? Hm! Can you help me take off my coat, Yeldyrin? It's terrible how hot it is! It's probably going to rain... There is just one thing I don't understand: how was she able to bite you?" Ochumyelov addresses Khryukin. "How was she able to get at your finger? She is small, but you are a really well-built man! I think you pierced your finger with a nail, and then had the idea of blaming the dog. I suspect you have a reputation around here! I know your type – you're devils!"

"He poked a cigarette in her face for a laugh, Your Honour, and she, being no fool, bit him. He's a stupid man, Your Honour!"

"You're lying, One-Eye! You didn't see, so why do you lie? His Honour is a clever gentleman, and understands who is lying and who is honest in the sight of God... But if I'm lying, let the judge decide. He knows what the law says... Nowadays everyone's equal... My own brother is in the police... if you want to know..."

"Don't argue!"

"No, this dog is not the general's," remarks the constable thoughtfully. "The general has no such dogs. He has mostly setters..."

"Do you know this for a fact?" asks Ochumyelov.

"I do, Your Honour..."

"I know it too. The general has valuable dogs, pure-bred, but this one is... the devil knows what! It has no distinguishing features... it's just a mongrel... And you're saying this is his dog? Where's your sense? If this dog were found in St Petersburg or Moscow, do you know what would happen? They would not consider the law there, but in an instant... snuff it out! You, Khryukin, have suffered, so don't let the matter drop... A lesson must be taught! It's time..."

"But perhaps it's the general's after all," says the constable reflectively. "Nothing is written on its face... Such a dog was seen outside his house recently."

"Of course it's the general's," says a voice from the crowd.

"Hm!... Can you help me put on my coat, brother Yeldyrin... It's getting windy... I feel chilly... Take the dog to the general's and make enquiries. Say that I found her and sent... And say they shouldn't let her out on the street... She may be valuable, and if every swine pokes a cigarette in her face it wouldn't take long to spoil her appearance. The dog's a gentle creature... And you, you blockhead, lower your hand! There's no need to display your stupid finger! It's your own fault!"

"The general's cook is coming, let's ask him... Hey, Prokhor! Can you come here, my friend? Take a look at this dog... Is it yours?"

"Certainly not! We've never in our born days kept such dogs."

"There is nothing more to know," says Ochumyelov. "It's a stray! There is no more to discuss now... If I say it's a stray, then it's a stray. Have it destroyed – that's all there is to it."

"She's not ours," continues Prokhor. "She belongs to the general's brother, who arrived recently. Our general doesn't like borzois. His brother does."

"Is his brother really here? Vladimir Ivanych?" asks Ochumyelov, a tender smile spreading over his face. "Good Heavens! And I didn't even know! Has he come to visit?"

"Yes, he has."

"Good Heavens!... The general missed his brother... And I really didn't know! So this is his brother's dog? I'm so glad... take her... The doggie's all right... She's clever... She bit this fellow's finger! Ha-ha-ha... Well, why are you shivering? Rrr... Rrr... She's angry, the rascal... such a puppy..."

Prokhor calls the dog and leaves the woodyard with it. The crowd laughs at Khryukin.

"I'll deal with you later!" Ochumyelov threatens. He tightly buttons up his overcoat and continues on his way through the market square.

The Tutor

SEVENTH-YEAR STUDENT YEGOR ZIBEROV kindly offers Petya Udodov his hand. Petya, a twelve-year-old lad in a grey uniform, chubby and red-cheeked, with a small forehead and bristly hair, greets him very politely and reaches into the cupboard for his copybook. The lesson begins.

According to the agreement reached with Udodov's father, Ziberov must study with Petya for two hours every day, and receive for that six roubles a month. He is preparing him for the second year of high school. (Last year he prepared him for the first year, but Petya failed.)

"Well, sir," begins Ziberov, lighting a cigarette. "You were given the fourth declension. Decline *fructus*!"*

Petya starts to decline.

"Again you haven't learnt it!" says Ziberov, rising. "I set you the fourth declension for the sixth time and you still don't know a damn thing about it! When on earth will you finally start to learn your lessons?"

"Did he not learn it again?" A voice and a cough are heard behind the door, and into the room enters Petya's father, retired Provincial Secretary Udodov. "Again? So why haven't you learnt it? Oh, you pig, you pig! Would you believe it, Yegor Alexeich? Only yesterday I thrashed him!"

Sighing heavily, Udodov sits near his son and starts looking into a tattered copy of Kühner's grammar.* Ziberov begins to examine Petya in the presence of his father. Let a stupid father see how stupid his son is! The student gets into an examiner's passion. He hates and holds in contempt the little rosy-cheeked dunce, and longs to beat him. So sick is he of this Petya that he even finds it annoying when the boy answers correctly.

147

"You don't even know the second declension! You don't know the first, either! This is how you study! Well, tell me, what is the vocative of *meus filius*?"*

"Of *meus filius*? *Meus filius* would be... it would be..."

Petya looks at the ceiling for a long time, and for a long time moves his lips, but does not give an answer.

"And what is the dative plural of *dea*?"*

"*Deabus... filiabus!*" blurts out Petya.

Udodov senior nods his head approvingly. The tutor, not having expected a correct response, feels annoyed.

"And what other noun has the ending *-abus* in the dative?" he asks.

It turns out that *anima* – the soul – also has *-abus* in the dative, but it's not in Kühner.

"Sonorous language, Latin!" remarks Udodov. "*Alon... tron... bonus...* antropos...*" Baffling! And it's all so necessary!" he says with a sigh.

"This swine is interfering with my teaching," thinks Ziberov. "He hovers over us, supervising. I can't bear this surveillance!"

"Well, sir," he says, addressing Petya. "For the next time your task in Latin will be the same. Now, to arithmetic... Take the blackboard. What is the solution to the following problem?"

Petya spits on the blackboard and wipes it with his sleeve. The tutor takes up a book of problems and dictates:

"A merchant bought 138 *arshins* of black and blue fabric for 540 roubles. The question is: how many *arshins* did he buy of one and the other if the blue cost 5 roubles per *arshin* and the black 3 roubles? Repeat the problem."

Petya repeats the problem, and without saying a word straight away begins to divide 540 by 138.

"Why in Heaven's name are you dividing? Wait! But... so... continue. What is the remainder? There may be no remainder. Let me do the dividing!"

Ziberov divides, gets the answer 3 plus a remainder and quickly wipes the board.

"It's strange," he thinks, ruffling his hair and reddening. "I wonder how it's solved? Hm!... This problem requires equations with unknowns... it's not really arithmetical..."

The tutor looks up the answers and sees that they are 75 and 63.

"Hm!... It's strange... Add 5 and 3 and then divide 540 by 8? So is that it? No, that's not right..." Then he says to Petya: "Solve it!"

"Well, why are you thinking? That problem is really simple!" Udodov says to Petya. "What a fool you are, boy! You solve it for him, Yegor Alexeich."

Yegor Alexeich picks up the chalk and tries to solve it. He stammers and reddens, and then grows pale.

"This problem, properly speaking, is algebraic," he says. "It can be solved with x and y. However, it can also be solved like this. I, like so, divided... understand? Now, you see, you have to subtract... understand? Or, here is what... Solve this problem for me yourself by tomorrow... Think about it..."

Petya smiles maliciously. Udodov also smiles. They both recognize the teacher's confusion. The seventh-year student grows even more embarrassed. He rises and begins to pace back and forth.

"It can be solved even without algebra," says Udodov, reaching for the abacus and sighing. "Here, kindly observe..."

He flicks the beads on the abacus, and gets the correct answers, 75 and 63.

"There it is, sir. That's how we do it, in a unscientific way."

The teacher becomes very uneasy. His heart seems to stand still as he looks at the clock and sees that there is still an hour and a quarter to go until the end of the lesson – a whole eternity!

"Now, dictation."

After dictation, geography – after geography, religious instruction, then Russian language. So many subjects in this world! But then, at last, the two-hour lesson finishes. Ziberov takes up his hat, politely offers his hand to Petya and says goodbye to Udodov.

"Would it be possible to give me a little money today?" he asks shyly. "Tomorrow I have to pay the fees for my studies. You owe me for six months."

"I? Ah, yes, yes," mutters Udodov, not looking at Ziberov. "With pleasure! Only I have nothing just now. I'll pay you in a week... or two..."

Ziberov acquiesces. He puts on his heavy, muddy galoshes and goes to another lesson.

Sergeant Prishibeyev

"SERGEANT PRISHIBEYEV! You are charged with the following offences: that on the third of this instant September you
insulted with words and actions village constable Zhigin, rural
elder Alyapov, assistant constable Yefimov, witnesses Ivanov and
Gavrilov, and also six peasants; moreover, that the first three were
subjected to your insults while in the performance of their official
duties. Do you plead guilty?"

Prishibeyev, a wrinkled non-commissioned officer with a trucu-
lent face, comes to attention and answers hoarsely in a strangulated voice, pronouncing each word distinctly, as if giving orders.

"Your Honour, Mr District Magistrate! By all articles of the
law, we must first consider the circumstances of this case from
both sides. It's not I who's guilty, but all the others. This all
happened because of a dead body – may the kingdom of heaven
be his. I am going along quietly and with dignity on the third
of this month with my wife Anfisa when I see, standing on the
shore, a crowd of all sorts of people. What right, I ask myself, do
people have to gather here? Why? Is it said in the law that people
should follow the herd? I shout: 'Go away!' I start to push away
the people, to make them go home. I order the constable to pull
them away by force…"

"Allow me to say, you surely are not the constable, nor the village
elder. Is it really your business to send people away?"

"It's not! It's not!" Voices are heard from various corners of the
room. "We can't live with him, Your Honour! We've put up with
him for fifteen years! Ever since he left the service people have
been leaving the village. He persecutes everyone!"

"Precisely so, Your Honour," says the chief witness. "Everyone
complains about him. It's impossible to live with him! Whether
there is a church procession with the icons, or a wedding, or, let's

say, something else is happening, he is always there, shouting, making a scene, insisting on order. He pulls the children's ears and spies on the women to make sure they behave, as if he's their father-in-law. The other day he went through the village telling people they mustn't sing songs or have lights burning. There's no law, he says, that allows you to sing."

"Wait, you'll have the chance to give evidence," says the magistrate, "but now let Prishibeyev continue. Continue, Prishibeyev!"

"Listen to me, sir," wheezes the sergeant. "You, Your Honour, are pleased to say it's not my business to send people away... Very well, sir... But what if there is a disturbance? How can we allow people to misbehave? Where is it written in the law that people must be given such freedom? I can't allow it, sir. If I don't tell them to go, and call them to account, then who would? No one in the village knows the proper rules. I may say, Your Honour, that I alone know how to treat people of low rank. And, Your Honour, I am able to understand everything. I'm not a peasant, but a non-commissioned officer, a retired quartermaster sergeant. I served in Warsaw, at headquarters, sir. After that, you should know, when I retired I served in the fire brigade. I left the fire brigade because of ill health, and served for two years as the doorman at a boys' classical prep school... I know all the rules, sir. But a peasant is a simple man. He understands nothing and should obey me, because... it's for his own good. Take this matter, for example... I am dispersing the crowd, and see on the sand along the shore the body of a drowned man. For what reason, I ask, is he lying here? Is this really acceptable? What is the village constable doing? Why do you, I say, constable, not make a report to the authorities? Maybe this drowned corpse drowned himself, but maybe this business smells to Siberia. Maybe this here is a criminal murder... But Constable Zhigin takes no notice, just smokes a cigarette. Who is this, he says, giving such an order? Where, he says, does he get such authority? Don't we know how to behave, he says, without him interfering? Then I say, you don't know, you are such a fool if you stand here without paying attention. I, he says, reported it yesterday to the district policeman. But why, I ask, to the district policeman? By what article of the legal code? How, in such cases, like drowning and strangling and so forth – how in such cases can the district policeman help? This, I say, is a criminal case, a civil case... What you have to do, I say, is immediately send a messenger to Their Honours the investigator and magistrate, sir. First and foremost you must, I say, make a report and send it to His Honour the magistrate. But he, the constable, just listens and laughs. And the peasants do too. They all laugh, Your Honour. I can testify to this under oath. One of them laughs, and then another, and Zhigin laughs. What, I ask, is so funny? And the constable says, such matters, he says, are not the concern of the magistrate. When I heard those words, I became upset... Constable," the sergeant says, addressing village policeman Zhigin, "you said this, didn't you?"

"I did."

"Everyone heard you say this very thing in the presence of all those simple people: such matters are not the concern of the magistrate. Everyone heard you say this very... I, Your Honour, became upset. I was horrified. Repeat, I say, repeat, you so-and-so, what you said! And he again said those very words... I say to him, how, I say, can you say this about His Honour the local magistrate. You are a police constable, and you dare to oppose authority? Well? And do you know, I say, that His Honour the magistrate may, if he wishes, report you for such words to the governor's police administration as being proof of unreliable conduct? And do you know, I say, where His Honour the magistrate has the power to send you for uttering such political sentiments? But the village elder says: the magistrate, he says, can't do anything. It's outside his jurisdiction. He only deals with minor matters. He really said that – everybody heard... How, I say, do you dare to disparage authority? Don't crack jokes with me, brother, or it'll be bad for you. When I was serving in Warsaw, or as a doorman at a boys' classical prep school, if I heard such inappropriate words, I would look in the street to see if there was a policeman around. Come here, officer, I would say, and I would report the matter to him. But here in the village, who is there to report to?... I was angry. I was offended that the people there had forgotten the rules through wilfulness and disobedience. I swung my fist... not, of course, with all my strength, but just gently, lightly, so that he wouldn't again dare say such words about Your Honour. The constable came to the aid of the elder. So I hit him too... And so it went. I got overheated, Your Honour, and... well, surely it's not possible to settle such matters without a beating. If you don't beat a stupid man, you will carry sin in your soul. Especially if you have a reason for it... if there is disorder..."

"Allow me to speak! There are people to go to if there is a disturbance. There is the village constable, the headman, the assistant constable—"

"The constable can't see everything, and doesn't know what I know..."

"But you must understand, it's not your business!"

"What, sir? How is it not my business? It's strange, sir... People misbehave, and it's not my business! I should praise them, should I? So they complain to you that I forbid them to sing songs. And what's the good of songs? Instead of doing something useful, they sing... And more, they've also taken to sitting in the evening with the lights on. They should go to bed, but they have conversation and laughter. I have written it down, sir!"

"What have you written down?"

"The names of the ones who sit with the lights on."

Prishibeyev takes a greasy piece of paper from his pocket, puts on his glasses and reads:

"The peasants who sit with the lights on: Ivan Prokhorov, Savva Nikiforov, Pyotr Petrov. Soldier's widow Shustrova lives in unlawful promiscuity with Semyon Kislov. Ignat Svyerchok practises magic, and his wife Mavra is a witch, who goes out at night to milk other people's cows."

"Enough!" says the magistrate, and begins to interrogate the witnesses.

Sergeant Prishibeyev raises his glasses to his forehead and looks with surprise at the magistrate, who is clearly not on his side. His wide-open eyes are shining, his nose becoming bright red. He looks at the magistrate and the witnesses, and in no way can he understand why the magistrate is so overwrought and why from all corners of the room are heard either murmurs or suppressed laughter. Likewise incomprehensible to him is the sentence "One month in jail!"

"For what?" he asks, raising his hands in bewilderment. "By what law?"

Now it is clear to him that the world has changed, and that it is in no way possible for him to live on this earth. Gloomy, depressing thoughts seize him. But leaving the chamber and seeing the peasants crowding around and talking about something, he, out of a habit he can no longer control, comes to attention and cries hoarsely in an angry voice:

"You people, break it up! Don't crowd around! Go home!"

Vanka

VANKA ZHUKOV, a nine-year-old boy who three months before
had been apprenticed to the shoemaker Alyakhin, did not
go to bed on Christmas Eve. Having waited until his master and
mistress had gone with the other apprentices to midnight Mass,
he got from his master's cupboard a pot of ink and a pen with
a rusty nib, and, having spread out a crumpled sheet of paper,
prepared to write. Before forming the first letter, he looked fear-
fully several times at the doors and windows, cast a sidelong look
at the dark icon, along either side of which stretched shelves of
lasts, and sighed despondently. The paper lay on a bench, and he
knelt before the bench.

"Dear Granddad Konstantin Makarych," he wrote. "I am
writing you a letter. I send you Christmas greetings and wish you
everything good from the Lord God. I have no father or mother:
you alone are left to me."

Vanka shifted his gaze to the dark window, in which twinkled
the reflection of his candle, and vividly imagined his grandfather
Konstantin Makarych, who worked as a nightwatchman on the
Zhivaryevs' estate. He was a small, gaunt, but unusually brisk
and lively old man of sixty-five with a perpetually smiling face
and the eyes of a drinker. By day he slept in the servants' kitchen
or joked with the cooks, but at night, wrapped in a loose-fitting
sheepskin cloak, he walked around the estate, shaking his rattle.*
Behind him, their heads lowered, plodded the old bitch Chestnut
and the hound Bindweed, who was nicknamed thus for his black
colouring and long, weasel-like body. This Bindweed was unusually
respectful and affectionate, and looked equally ingratiatingly on
his masters as on strangers, but had acquired little credit. Behind
his meekness and respect was hidden the most Jesuitical malice. No
one knew better than he how to steal up and grab someone's leg,

how to get into the ice house or steal a hen from a peasant. More than once he had had his hind legs broken, had twice been hung, and each week was thrashed half dead – but he always recovered.

Now, probably, Granddad would be standing by the gate, screwing up his eyes at the bright-red windows of the village church, stamping his feet in his felt boots and joking with the servants. His rattle would be tied to his belt. He would beat his arms, huddle up from the cold and, with a senile giggle, pinch now the maid, now the cook.

"A little pinch of snuff for us to take?" he would say, holding out his snuffbox to the women.

The women would sniff and sneeze. Grandfather would go into raptures, burst into happy laughter and cry:

"Wipe it off! It'll freeze!"

The dogs too would be given a pinch of snuff. Chestnut would sneeze, wrinkle her nose and, offended, move away. But Bindweed, out of respect, would not sneeze – just wag his tail. And the weather would be wonderful, the air calm, clear and fresh. The nights would be dark, but you would be able to see the whole village, with its white roofs and the columns of smoke rising from the chimneys, the trees silver-plated with hoar frost, the snowdrifts. All the sky would be strewn with gaily twinkling stars, and the Milky Way would stand out as clearly as if it had been washed and rubbed with snow for the holiday...

Vanka sighed, dipped his pen in the ink and continued writing:

"Yesterday I got a dressing-down. The master dragged me by the hair out to the yard and beat me with a stirrup for having accidentally fallen asleep while I was rocking his child in the cradle. And during the week the mistress ordered me to clean a herring, and I started at the tail, but she took the herring and poked me in the face with its head. The apprentices laugh at me, send me to the tavern for vodka, and order me to steal the owner's cucumbers, and the master beats me with whatever comes to hand. And there is nothing at all to eat. In the morning they give me bread, for dinner *kasha*, and in the evening bread again, but as for tea or *shchi*, those are kept for the master and mistress. They make me sleep in the hall, and when the baby cries I don't sleep at all, but have to rock the cradle. Dear Granddad, for God's sake, take me home from here, to the village... there is no future at all for me here... I beg you on bended knees and will pray eternally to God for you: take me away from here or I shall die..."

Vanka's lips began to tremble; he wiped his eyes with a black fist and let out a sob.

"I shall grate your tobacco for you," he continued. "I shall pray to God for you, and if I cause any trouble, then beat me black and blue. And if you think there's no job for me, then I shall ask the steward for Christ's sake to let me clean boots or serve as a shepherd boy instead of Fedka. Dear Granddad, there is no future for me at all – only death. I would have gone back to the village on foot, but I have no boots, and am afraid of the frost. And when I grow to be big, for having helped me I shall look after you and give offence to no one, and when you die I shall pray for the peace of your soul just as I do for my mother Pelageya.

"Moscow is a big city. The houses are all very grand, and there are many horses, but there are no sheep, and the dogs are not vicious. Here the children don't walk out carrying a star* and no one is allowed to sing in church, and once I saw in a shop window hooks for sale complete with fishing lines, for all kinds of fish, very valuable ones – there was even one hook that would hold a catfish weighing a *pood*.* And I saw some shops where there were all kinds of guns like the ones used by the master, so they probably cost a hundred roubles each... And in the butchers' shops there is grouse, partridge and rabbit, but where they shoot them the shop assistants won't say. Dear Granddad, when the master has a Christmas tree with presents under it, get me a gilded nut and hide it in the green box. Ask the master's daughter, Olga Ignatyevna for it: say it's for Vanka."

Vanka sighed despairingly and again gazed at the window. He remembered how Granddad always went to the forest to get a Christmas tree for the master, and took his grandson with him. It was a happy time! Granddad was joyful, the frost seemed joyful, and, looking at them, Vanka was also joyful. Before cutting down the fir tree, Granddad would smoke his pipe, spend a long time taking snuff, chuckle at the frozen Vanyusha... Young fir trees, wrapped in hoar frost, stood motionless, waiting. Which of them was to die? As if from nowhere, a rabbit would come flying like an arrow over the snowdrifts... Granddad could not help but cry:

"Catch him, catch him... catch him! Ah, the bob-tailed devil!"

Granddad would drag the felled fir tree to the master's house, and there they would begin to decorate it. Busiest of all would be Olga Ignatyevna, Vanka's favourite. When Vanka's mother Pelageya was still alive and serving as a maid in the master's house, Olga Ignatyevna used to give him fruit drops, and, having nothing better to do, would teach him to read, write, count to a hundred and even dance the quadrille. But when Pelageya died, the orphan Vanka was sent to Granddad in the servants' kitchen, and from the kitchen to the shoemaker Alyakhin in Moscow...

"Do come, dear Granddad," continued Vanka. "I beg you for Christ's sake, take me away from here. Pity me, an unfortunate orphan, because they keep beating me, and I am terribly hungry, and so unhappy that it is impossible even to tell you. I keep crying. And the other day my master hit me on the head with a boot tree, so that I fell down and woke up only with difficulty. My life is hopeless, worse than any dog's... And finally I send my greetings to Alyona, one-eyed Yegorka and the coachman, but don't give my harmonica to anyone. I remain your grandson Ivan Zhukov – dear Granddad, do come."

Vanka folded in four the sheet that was now covered in writing and put it in an envelope he had bought the day before for a copeck. After a moment's thought, he dipped the pen in the ink and wrote the address:

To Granddad in the village

Then he scratched his head, thought awhile and added: "To Konstantin Makarych". Pleased that he had not been interrupted in his writing, he put on his cap and, not bothering with his jacket, straight away ran out to the street in his shirt...

The assistants at the butcher's shop whom he had questioned the day before had told him that letters were dropped into a postbox, and from the box were conveyed to all lands in postal troikas with drunken coachmen and ringing bells. Vanka ran up to the nearest postbox and thrust the precious letter into the slot...

An hour later, lulled with sweet hopes, he was soundly asleep. He dreamt of a stove. On the stove sat Granddad, his bare feet dangling, reading the letter to the cooks... Around the stove padded Bindweed, wagging his tail...

From the Diary
of an Assistant Bookkeeper

11th May 1863. Our sixty-year-old bookkeeper Glotkin drank some milk with brandy to relieve a cough, and as a result had an attack of delirium tremens. The doctors, with characteristic self-assurance, assert that tomorrow he'll die. So at last I shall be bookkeeper! The position was already long ago promised to me.

Secretary Kleshchev is to go on trial for having beaten a petitioner who called him a bureaucrat. This, evidently, has been decided.

I took a decoction for catarrh of the stomach.

3rd August 1865. The bookkeeper Glotkin's chest has again been giving him trouble. He started to cough, and has taken milk with brandy. If he dies, I shall get his position. I nourish the hope, though slight, because evidently delirium tremens is not always fatal!

Kleshchev grabbed an Armenian's promissory note and tore it up. Perhaps this matter will go to court.

An old woman (Guryevna) said yesterday that I don't have catarrh, but latent haemorrhoids. Very likely!

30th June 1867. In Arabia, they write, there's cholera. Perhaps it will spread to Russia and open up many vacancies. Maybe old man Glotkin will die and I'll get the position of bookkeeper. Tenacious man! To live so long, I believe, is reprehensible.

What should be taken for catarrh? Shouldn't I try wormwood seeds?

2nd January 1870. A dog was howling all night in Glotkin's yard. My cook Pelageya says this was a sure omen, and we talked till two in the morning about how I, when I have become bookkeeper, shall buy myself a raccoon coat and smoking jacket. And perhaps I shall marry. Not to a young girl, of course – I am too old for that – but to a widow.

Yesterday Kleshchev was expelled from the club for telling an improper story aloud and laughing at the patriotism of a member of the trade deputation, Ponyukhov. It's thought that the latter will bring an action.

I want to go to Doctor Botkin for my catarrh. They say he's very good.

4th June 1878. They say there's the plague in Vetlyanka. They say people are just falling down dead. Because of this, Glotkin has taken to drinking pepper vodka. Well, pepper vodka will hardly help such an old man. If the plague comes, then for sure I shall be the bookkeeper.

4th June 1883. Glotkin is dying. With tears in my eyes I asked his forgiveness for having awaited his death with such impatience. Also with tears, he magnanimously forgave me and advised me to take acorn coffee for my catarrh.

And Kleshchev is again about to go on trial. He had pawned to a Jew a piano he had hired. Yet despite all this he already has the St Stanislav and the rank of collegiate assessor. It's surprising what goes on in this world!

Ten grams of saffron extract, 6 grams of ginger, 4 grams of strong vodka, 20 grams of coral powder – all mixed and infused in a one-litre vodka bottle and taken by the small glass on an empty stomach for catarrh.

7th June, the same year. They buried Glotkin yesterday. Alas! The death of this distinguished old man will be of no benefit to me! I dream at night that he appears to me wearing a white gown and wagging his finger. And woe, woe is me, a sinner: the new bookkeeper is not I, but Chalikov. It was not I who got the job, but a young man who has the patronage of a general's aunt. All my hopes are dashed!

10th June 1886. Chalikov's wife has run off. He is miserable, the poor man. Perhaps out of grief he'll do away with himself. If he does, then I shall be the bookkeeper. There is already talk of this. It means hope is not yet lost. I'll wait, and maybe it won't be long before I get that raccoon coat. As for marriage, I have nothing against it. Why not marry, if a good opportunity arises? But it will be necessary to talk to someone: it's a serious step.

Kleshchev walked off with with Privy Councillor Lirmans's galoshes. Scandal!

The porter Paisy advises taking a solution of powdered mercury chloride for catarrh. I'll try it.

Vint

ONE FOUL AUTUMN NIGHT, Andrei Stepanovich Peresolin was being driven home from the theatre. Going along, he was reflecting on the benefit theatres might bring if they presented plays of moral content. As he passed the government offices, he stopped thinking such thoughts and directed his gaze at the windows of the department of which, applying the language of poets and skippers, he was at the helm. Two windows, which looked out from the duty room, were ablaze with light.

"Are they really still busy with the accounts at this time of night?" Peresolin thought. "Four fools are up there, and still not finished! For all I know people might think I give them no rest even at night. I shall go up and send them home…"

"Stop, Gury!"

Peresolin climbed down from the carriage and walked up to the building. The front door was locked, but the back door, which had only one bolt, and that one out of order, was wide open. Peresolin went through; moments later he was standing by the door of the duty room. The door was slightly open: looking through it, Peresolin saw something extraordinary. At a table, which was piled with large sheets of accounts, four officials were sitting and playing cards by the light of two lamps. Concentrated, motionless, their faces tinged with the green light of the lampshade, they put him in mind of fairy-tale gnomes or, Heaven forbid, currency counterfeiters… Even greater mystery was added by their game. Judging by their manner and the card terms which from time to time they called out, it was vint, but judging by everything else that Peresolin heard, the game could not be called either vint or even a game of cards at all. It was something unheard of, strange and mysterious… Among the words they called out, Peresolin recognized the names of the officials Serafim Zvizdulin, Stepan Kulakevich, Yeremei Nedoyekhov and Ivan Pisulin.

"How on earth can you lead like that, you Dutch devil?" Zvizdulin was saying angrily, looking with frenzy at his partner opposite. "How is it possible to lead like that? I had in my hand Dorofeyev and another, Shepyelev, and his wife, and Styopka Yerlakov, and you lead with Kofeikin. So now we're two down! You should have led with Pogankin, cabbage-head!"

"Well, and so what then would have happened?" snapped his partner. "I could have led with Pogankin, but Ivan Andreich holds Peresolin in his hand."

"They are mentioning my name for some reason," thought Peresolin, shrugging. "I don't understand."

Pisulin dealt again, and the officials continued:

"The State Bank…"

"Two… the Provincial Treasury…"

"No trumps…"

"You go no trumps? Hm!… Provincial Administration – two… If it's lost, it's lost, the devil take it! Last time I was one down in the Education Department, now I'm up against the Provincial Administration. Damn it!"

"A small slam in the Education Department!"

"I don't understand!" whispered Peresolin.

"I am leading with a state advisor… Put down, Vanya, some titular councillor or provincial secretary."

"Why bother with a titular councillor? We'll get you with Peresolin…"

"We don't care about your Peresolin… don't care… We have Rybnikov. You'll be three down! Bring out Peresolin's other half! It's no good hiding the bitch behind your cuff!"

"They are talking about my wife," thought Peresolin. "I don't understand."

And, not wanting to remain any longer in puzzlement, Peresolin opened the door and entered the duty room. If the Devil himself, with horns and tail, had appeared before the officials, he would not have astonished or frightened them as much as their chief frightened and astonished them. Had their departmental supervisor, who had died the previous year, appeared before them and said in a sepulchral voice "Get thee behind me, Satan,* to the place prepared for sinners" and breathed on them the cold air of the grave, they would not have blanched as they blanched when they recognized Peresolin. Nedoyekhov was so frightened that his nose began to bleed; Kulakevich felt a drumming in his right ear, and his tie loosened of its own accord. The officials threw down the cards, slowly rose and, having exchanged glances, directed their gaze at the floor. Silence reigned for a minute in the duty room...

"You really are doing the accounts well!" began Peresolin. "Now I understand why you love to spend so much time on them. What were you doing just now?"

"We, only for a minute, Your Excellency," whispered Zvizdulin, "were looking at some photographs... Taking a break..."

Peresolin went to the table and slowly shrugged his shoulders. On the table lay not playing cards, but ordinary photographs that had been removed from their backing and stuck on playing cards. There were a lot of photographs. Examining them, Peresolin saw himself, his wife, many of his subordinates, acquaintances...

"What nonsense... How on earth do you play this game?"

"It's not we who devised it, Your Excellency... God forbid... We only borrowed the idea..."

"Kindly explain, Zvizdulin! How do you play? I saw everything, and heard how you trumped me with Rybnikov... Well, what have you got to say? I really won't eat you. Tell me!"

For a long while Zvizdulin felt ashamed, and was too nervous to speak. Only when Peresolin began to get angry and snort and redden with impatience, did he obey. After gathering up the cards and shuffling them, he laid them on the table and started to explain:

"Each portrait, Your Excellency, just like each card, has its significance... its value. As in a pack, so here too there are fifty-two cards and four suits... Officials of the Provincial Treasury are hearts, those of the Provincial Administration are clubs, employees of the Ministry of Public Education are diamonds, and those of the State Bank are spades. Then, sir... the higher

166

state councillors are our aces, state councillors are kings, wives of those in the fourth and fifth class of councillors are queens, collegiate councillors are jacks, court councillors are tens, and so on. I, for example – here is my photograph – am a three, by virtue of being a provincial secretary…"

"Well, well… I, therefore, am an ace?"

"Of clubs, sir. And Her Excellency your wife is the queen, sir…"

"Hm! It's original… Well, all right then. Let's play. I'll see how it goes."

Peresolin took off his coat and, smiling warily, sat down at the table. He told the officials to sit down too, and the game began…

The watchman Nazar, arriving at seven the next morning to sweep the duty room, was thunderstruck. The scene that greeted him when he entered with his broom was so striking that he can recall it to this day, even when lying in a drunken stupor. Peresolin – pale, sleepy, his hair dishevelled – was standing before Nedoyekhov and, holding him by a button, was saying:

"You must understand that you couldn't lead with Shepyelev if you knew that I had in my hand myself and three other clubs. Zvizdulin had Rybnikov and his wife, three high-school teachers and my wife. Nedoyekhov had bankers and three clerks from the Provincial Office. You should have led with Kryshkin! You should have ignored it when they led with the Provincial Treasury. They're very crafty!"

"I opened with a titular councillor, Your Excellency, because I thought they had a state councillor."

"Oh, my dear fellow, you really shouldn't have thought so! That's not the game! Only cobblers play like that. Think about it!… When Kulakevich opened with the court councillor at the state department, you should have played Ivan Ivanovich Grenlandski, because you knew that he had Natalya Dmitryevna, two others in that suit and Yegor Yegorych… You've spoilt everything! I'll show you now. Sit down, gentlemen, let's play one more rubber!"

And, having sent away the amazed Nazar, the officials settled down to continue the game.

The Cat

VARVARA PETROVNA woke up and listened. She went pale; her big black eyes grew even bigger, and glinted with fear when she realized it was not a dream... She covered her face with her hands in horror, raised herself on one elbow and started to awaken her husband. Her husband, who was curled up like a bread roll, was gently snoring and breathing on her shoulder.

"Alyosha, dear... Wake up, dearest!... Oh... it's awful!"

Alyosha stopped snoring and stretched his legs. Varvara Petrovna pinched his cheek. He stretched, sighed deeply and awoke.

"Alyosha, dear... Wake up. Someone is crying..."

"Who's crying? What are you imagining?"

"Listen carefully. Do you hear? Someone's moaning... It must be a child that's been put on our doorstep... Oh, I can't bear it!"

Alyosha raised himself and began to listen. Through the wide-open window he could see the dark night. Along with the smell of the lilac and the quiet whispers of the delicate lime trees, strange sounds were being carried to the bed... It was impossible to make out straight away what these sounds were: it was either a child crying or someone moaning or wailing... You could not make them out. Only one thing was clear: the sounds were being made beneath the window, and not by one voice, but several... There were trebles, altos, tenors...

"Well, Varya, they're cats," said Alyosha. "Silly one!"

"Cats? It can't be! Whose is the bass voice?"

"It's a pig grunting. After all, don't forget we're in the country... Do you hear? Just as I thought, it's cats... Well, calm down – you better go back to sleep."

Varya and Alyosha lay down and drew the blanket over themselves. A morning freshness set in through the window, and it began to feel slightly cool. The couple curled up like bread rolls and closed their eyes.

Five minutes later Alyosha began to toss, and turned on his other side.

"I can't sleep, the devil take it!... They're so loud..."

The cats' singing, meanwhile, reached a crescendo. Fresh singers, fresh forces, had evidently joined the group, and the light rustle beneath the window gradually turned to noise, din, uproar... Piano, as tender as aspic, reached the power of fortissimo, and soon the air was filled with outrageous sounds. Some cats were emitting staccato sounds, others were giving voice to joyous trills, as if from a musical score, in quavers and semiquavers – a third group were drawing out long, sustained notes... But one cat, probably the eldest and most ardent, was singing in some unnatural voice, quite unlike a cat, now like a bass, now like a tenor.

"Miaow... miaow... Rrr-yow... Rrr-yow... karr-yow..."

If it had not been for the hissing, it would have been impossible to think the noise was being made by cats... Varya turned on her other side and muttered something... Alyosha leapt up and, shouting a curse, closed the window. But the glass was not thick, and let in sounds and electric light.

"I have to get up at eight o'clock to go to work," muttered Alyosha, "but they howl, and don't let me sleep, the devils... At least you be quiet, please, woman! Whining right in my ear! Whimpering! Am I to blame? After all, they're not mine."

"Chase them away, dear!"

Her husband swore, jumped out of bed and went to the window... Night was easing into morning.

Looking at the sky, Alyosha saw only one star, and even that was barely glimmering, as if in a haze... Sparrows, frightened by the sound of the opening window, were cheeping in the lime tree. Alyosha looked down and saw about ten cats on the ground. With extended tails, hissing and delicately padding on the grass, they were walking like dromedaries around a pretty kitten that was sitting on an overturned, upside-down washtub and miaowing. It was hard to tell what was more important to them: the attraction of the kitten or their dignity. Had they come out of love, or only to display their dignity? Their attitudes to one another showed the most exquisite disdain. On the other side of the small front garden a pig with piglets was rubbing against the railing, trying to get in.

"Psssh!" hissed Alyosha. "Ksssh! You devils! Psssh!... Ffwitt!"

But the cats paid no attention. Only the kitten looked in his direction, and even then coolly, reluctantly. She was happy, and not at all interested in Alyosha...

"Pssh... pssh... cursed things! Tfoo, the devil take you all! Varya, why don't you bring me the decanter? We'll pour water over them. The devils!"

Varya leapt out of bed and brought him not the decanter, but the jug from the washstand. Alyosha leant with his chest on the window sill and tilted the jug...

"Oh, you people!" He heard someone's voice over his head. "Youngsters, youngsters! How can you do that, eh? Ah-ah-ahh... Young people!"

A long sigh followed this. Alyosha looked up and saw a pair of shoulders in a cotton dressing gown decorated with big flowers, and lean, veined fingers. On the shoulders was placed a little grey-haired head in a nightcap, while the fingers were making a threatening gesture... An old man was sitting at the window, watching the cats. His eyes were gleaming with pleasure and full of delight, as if watching ballet.

Alyosha gaped, grew pale and smiled...

"Were you sleeping, Your Excellency?" he asked unnecessarily.

"It's not right, sir. You are going against nature, young man. You are undermining... ahh... so to speak, the laws of nature. It's not right, sir! What business is it of yours? Aren't they... ahh... living beings? What do you think? Living beings? You have to understand. I'm not happy with you, sir!"

Alyosha was frightened, went on tiptoe to the bed and meekly lay down. Varya curled up next to him and suppressed a sigh.

"It's our..." whispered Alyosha. "Himself... And he's not asleep. He's admiring the cats. The devil take him. It's awkward to live near your boss."

"Y-y-young man!" A minute later Alyosha heard the old man's voice. "Where are you? Come here!"

Alyosha went to the window and turned to look at the old man.

"Do you see that white cat? What do you think of him? It's mine. Look what he does, what he does! At how he walks! Just look! Miaow, miaow... Vaska! Vasyushka, you rascal! What whiskers the creature has! Siberian, the rascal. From a distant land... Hee-hee-hee... But the pussy-cat... she'll be... she'll be in trouble! Hee-hee. My cat always has his own way. You'll see it now! Watch what he does, what he does!"

Alyosha said he liked the cat's coat very much. The old man began to tell him about the cat's life and habits. He got carried away and talked until daybreak. He spoke in great detail, smacking his lips and licking his veined fingers... There wasn't even time for Alyosha to doze off.

At one o'clock the following night the cats again broke into song and again woke Varya. Alyosha did not dare to chase the cats away: among them was the cat belonging to His Excellency, his boss. Alyosha and Varya listened to the feline concert till morning.

Reading

A Tale of a Wise Old Bird

O NE DAY the impresario of our theatre, Galamidov, was sitting in the office of our boss Ivan Petrovich Semipalatov and
talking to him about the performances and beauty of our actresses.

"But I don't agree with you," said Ivan Petrovich, signing a
request for a grant. "Sofya Yuryevna is a strong, original talent.
Such a dear, so graceful... So charming..."

Ivan Petrovich wanted to go on, but from rapture was unable to
say a single word more, and smiled so broadly and sweetly that the
impresario, looking at him, could taste the sweetness in his mouth.

"What I like in her... ah... is the excited trembling of her young
breast when she delivers a monologue. She just exudes passion –
just exudes it! At that moment, tell her, I'm ready... for anything!"

"Your Excellency, be good enough to sign the response to the
Kherson police governing body, concerning..."

Semipalatov raised his smiling face and saw the clerk Merdyayev.
Merdyayev was standing in front of him and, his eyes wide with
surprise, was presenting him with a document for signing.
Semipalatov knitted his brow: prose had displaced poetry at the
most interesting moment.

"I could deal with this later," he said. "Surely you can see I'm
having a conversation. What terribly ill-bred, insensitive people!
Well, Mr Galamidov... You were saying we no longer have Gogol
types... But here you are! Is he not the type? Scruffy, out at elbow,
squint-eyed... never combs his hair... And look at how he writes!
It's the devil knows what! He writes illiterately, senselessly... like
a cobbler! Have a look!"

"M-ye-ss..." muttered Galamidov after looking at the document. "Really, Mr Merdyayev, you probably don't read enough."

"You can't go on like this, my dear fellow," continued the boss. "I am ashamed for you. You really should read books, shouldn't you?"

"It's important to read," said Galamidov, sighing theatrically. "Very important. You read and will see at once how your outlook immediately changes – and you can get books anywhere you like. I have, for example... I will, with pleasure... I shall bring some tomorrow, if you wish."

"Thank you, my friend," said Semipalatov.

Merdyayev bowed awkwardly, muttered something and went out.

The next day Galamidov arrived in our office with a bundle of books. And from that moment the story begins. Posterity will never forgive Semipalatov for his thoughtless action! It might have been possible, perhaps, to forgive a youth – but an experienced, full state councillor, never! On the arrival of the impresario, Merdyayev was summoned to the office.

"So here you are: read, my dear fellow!" said Semipalatov, handing him a book. "Read attentively."

Merdyayev took the book with trembling hands and left the office. He was pale. His squinting eyes were moving uneasily and seemed to be looking for help in the surrounding objects. We took the book from him and examined it carefully.

The book was *The Count of Monte Cristo.**

"You can't oppose his will!" said our old bookkeeper Prokhor Semyonych Budylda with a sigh. "Try hard somehow, make an effort... Read a little at a time, and then, God willing, he'll forget, and you'll be able to stop. Don't be afraid... But the main thing is: don't take it too seriously... Don't go into it in too much detail."

Merdyayev wrapped the book in paper and sat down to write. But he did not feel like writing now. His hands were shaking, and he was casting sidelong looks all around – now at the ceiling, now at the inkwell. The next day he came to work with a tear-stained face.

"I have already begun four times," he said, "but can understand nothing... It's about some foreigners..."

Five days later Semipalatov, walking among the desks, stopped in front of Merdyayev and asked:

"Well then, did you read the book?"

"I read it, Your Excellency."

"So what did you read about, my good man? Come on, tell me."

Merdyayev raised his head. His lips began to tremble.

"I have forgotten, Your Excellency," he said a minute later.

"It means you did not read or, ah-h-h… read inattentively. Me-chan-i-cal-ly! That's no good. Read it through once again. That's what I always recommend, gentlemen. Be so good as to read! Everyone read! Take the books by my window there and read. Paramonov, go and take a book. Podkhodtsev, my dear man, you go too. Smirnov – you too. All of you, gentlemen. Please!"

They all went and took themselves a book. Only Budylda dared to voice a protest. He threw up his hands, shook his head and said:

"Excuse me, Your Excellency… I'd rather resign… I know what these writers and their works bring. Because of them my eldest grandson calls his mother a fool to her face, and all during Lent drinks milk. Excuse me, sir!"

"You don't understand anything," said Semipalatov, who usually forgave the old man all his rudeness.

But Semipalatov was mistaken: the old man understood everything. Just a week later we saw the fruits of this reading. Podkhodtsev, who was reading the second volume of *The Wandering Jew*,* called Budylda a "Jesuit"; Smirnov began to come to work drunk. But no one was so affected by the reading as Merdyayev. He lost weight, grew thin and started to drink.

"Prokhor Semyonych!" he implored Budylda. "Force me to pray eternally to God!* Ask His Excellency to forgive me… I cannot read. I read day and night – don't sleep, don't eat. My wife is exhausted, reading aloud, but, God strike me dead, I understand nothing. For Heaven's sake!"

Budylda tried several times to report to Semipalatov, but he only waved his hands and, pacing back and forth in the office with Galamidov, reproached them all for ignorance. Two months passed in this way, and the story ended in the most terrible way.

One day Merdyayev, having come to work, instead of sitting down at his desk, knelt before his colleagues, began to cry and said:

"Forgive me, Christian people, for having made counterfeit banknotes!"

Then he went into the office and, kneeling before Semipalatov, said:

"Forgive me, Your Excellency: yesterday I threw a small child into a well!"

He knocked his head on the floor and began to sob...

"What does this mean?" asked Semipalatov in amazement.

"It means, Your Excellency," said Budylda, coming forward with tears in his eyes, "that he's lost his mind. You see what your little Galamidov has done with his books! God sees everything, Your Excellency. But if my words are unpleasing to you, then dismiss me. Better to die of hunger than to see this in old age."

Semipalatov went pale and began to pace back and forth.

"I'm not receiving Galamidov," he said in a muffled voice. "And you, gentlemen, calm down. I now see my mistake. Thank you, old man!"

After that, nothing more happened to us. Merdyayev recovered, but not completely. Even now, at the sight of a book, he trembles and looks away.

She Left Him

THEY HAD DINED. The stomachs were feeling blissfully replete, the mouths were beginning to yawn, the eyes narrowing from sweet doziness. The husband lit a cigar, stretched and lay down on the couch. The wife sat on the side of the bed and sighed with content... Both were happy.

"Tell me something," yawned the husband.

"What should I tell you? M-m-m... Oh yes! Did you hear? Sophie Okurkova married this... what's his name... this Von Tramb! What a scandal!"

"So what's the scandal?"

"Well, Tramb really is a scoundrel! He's such a swine... Such an unscrupulous man! Without any principles! A depraved individual! He was the count's bailiff – got rich, now works for the railway and embezzles... He robbed his sister... In a word, he is a scoundrel and a thief. And to marry such a man? To live with him? I'm astonished! Such a moral girl and... well, there you are! Not for anything in the world would I marry such a fellow. Even if he were a millionaire! Even if he were I don't know how handsome. I would spit on him! I cannot imagine having such a bastard for a husband!

His wife leapt up and, going red and becoming indignant, began to pace back and forth in the room. Her eyes were burning with anger. Her sincerity was evident...

"That Tramb is such a swine! Those women who marry such men are a thousand times stupid and vulgar!"

"Y-e-s-s... You, of course, would not marry... Y-e-s-s... But if you were now to learn that I also... am a scoundrel? What would you do?"

"I? I would leave you! I would not stay a single second with you! I can only love an honest man! If I learnt that you had done even a hundredth part of what Tramb did, I... in an instant! *Adieu*, then!"

"Y-e-s-s... Hm... What a woman you are... And I didn't even know. Hee-hee-hee... The woman lies without blushing!"

"I never lie! Just try doing something dishonest, then you will see!"

"Why should I try? You yourself know... I go one better than your Von Tramb... Tramb... is comparatively small fry. Why are you staring at me? It's strange... What is my salary?" he asked after a pause.

"Three thousand a year."

"And how much was the necklace that I bought for you last week? Two thousand... Wasn't it? And yesterday's dress cost five hundred... Two thousand for the dacha... Hee-hee-hee. Yesterday your papa cadged a thousand from me..."

"But Pierre, of course there is income on the side..."

"Horses... Private doctor... Milliner's bills. Day before yesterday you lost a hundred roubles playing *stukolka*..."

The husband raised himself and, supporting his head on his fists, read the whole act of indictment. Going to the writing table, he showed his wife all the evidence...

"Now you see, my dear, that your Von Tramb is nothing, just a little pickpocket compared to me... *Adieu!* Go away and from now on don't judge!"

That's the end. Perhaps the reader will still ask:

"Did she leave her husband?"

Yes, she left him... for the other room.

The Absolute Truth

SIX COLLEGIATE REGISTRARS and one with no rank were sitting in a suburban grove and drinking heavily.

In their drunken state they were noisy, but gloomy and sad. There were no smiles or joyful gestures, no laughter or happy chatter. There was a sense of mourning...

Less than a week before, Collegiate Registrar Kanifolev, who had come to the office drunk, slipped on someone's spittle and fell against a glass cupboard, breaking it and hurting himself badly. The day after this fall, he lost two documents from case No. 2423. Moreover... he arrived in the office with powder and shot in his pocket. In general, he leads an intemperate and tempestuous life. All was taken into account. He was dismissed from his job and was now eating a farewell dinner.

"We shall always remember you, Alyosha!" his former colleagues said before each glass, turning to Kanifolev. "Amen to you!"

After the voicing of each such sentiment, Kanifolev, a little man with a long, tear-stained face, sobbed, banged his fist on the table and said:

"I've come to the end at last!"

The dismissed man drained his glass, sobbed loudly and rose to kiss his friends.

"They drove me away!" he said, shaking his head in misery. "They dismissed me because I'm a drunkard! But they don't understand that I drink from grief, from melancholy!"

"From what grief?"

"The grief is that I couldn't bear their lies. Their despicable lies ate at my heart! I could not ignore their dirty dealings. They refuse to understand that... Very well, then! I'll show them I know what to do about it. I'll show them! I'll go and spit right in their eye. I'll tell them the absolute truth, the whole truth!"

"No you won't... You're only boasting... We can all speak our mind when drunk, but then we back down... And you are the same..."

"You think I won't tell them? You think so? Ah-h-h... So you think so... All right... Very well, you'll see... Be I three times damned... struck dead... Call me a scoundrel to my face, then spit at me, if I don't tell them!"

Kanifolev struck his fist on the table and turned red.

"I've come to the end at last! I shall go right now and tell them what I think. This minute! He's at home with his wife not far from here! You'll see what will happen. To hell with it. I'll open their eyes! I'll bring everything out into the open! They'll see the real Alyoshka Kanifolev!"

Kanifolev rushed from the room and, swaying unsteadily, ran off... Before his friends could stretch out their hands to restrain him he was already far away. And by the time they thought of running after and catching him, he was already standing before the desk at which his boss was sitting, and saying:

"Your Excel... lency, I've come into your house unannounced, but I've done it as a honest man, and therefore, excuse me... I, Your Excel... lency, am drunk, it's true," he said, "but I do remember th-th-things! Drunkenness reveals what soberness conceals,* and I am going to tell you the complete truth! Yes, sir, Your Excel... lency! I have suffered enough! Why, for example, have our office floors not been painted for so long? Why do you allow the book-keeper to sleep till eleven o'clock? Why do you allow Mityayev to take home the newspapers, but don't allow the others? I've come to the end at last, and I'm going to tell you the absolute truth..."

And this absolute truth Kanifolev spoke with a tremor in his voice, with tears in his eyes, beating his chest with his fist.

His boss looked at him, eyes wide open, without understanding what it was all about.

The Rebel

A New Year's Tale

T HE FIRST DAY OF THE NEW YEAR revealed a beautiful and moving picture of mankind. All rejoiced, exulted and congratulated each other. The air resounded with the most sincere and heartfelt best wishes. All were happy and at peace.

Only a provincial secretary, Ponimayev, was dissatisfied. At noon of New Year's Day he was standing on one of the streets of the capital and ranting. Embracing a lamp-post with his right hand and waving away some imaginary opponent with his left, he was muttering vague, unforgivable things... His wife was standing next to him and pulling him by the sleeve. Misery was written on her tearful face.

"You're a disgrace!" she was saying. "You're my punishment. You're shameless, you infidel! Go, I tell you! Go while there is still time, and sign! Go, drunken scum!"

"In no way! I'm an educated man and won't submit to ignorance! Go yourself and sign, if you wish, but leave me alone!... I won't be a slave."

"Go! If you don't sign, you'll be sorry! You will be dismissed, you scoundrel, and then I shall die of hunger. Go, you dog!"

"Very well... And then I shall be the one to die... For speaking the truth? Straightaway!"

Ponimayev raised a hand to push aside his wife, and described a semicircle in the air... A police inspector in a new greatcoat who was walking past stopped for a second, and, turning to Ponimayev, said:

"Shame on you! Behave yourself, like a decent person."

Ponimayev felt ashamed. He blinked with embarrassment and withdrew his hand from the lamp-post. His wife seized the

180

moment and began to drag him by the sleeve along the street, carefully avoiding anything he could grasp. Ten minutes later, not more, she had dragged her husband to the house of his section head.

"Go now, Alyosha!" she said tenderly, leading him on to the porch. "Go Alyoshechka! Just sign, and come back. And for that I shall buy you brandy for your tea. I shall not scold you if you get drunk... Don't destroy me, a poor soul!"

"Ahh... Hm... Is this, therefore, his house? Excellent! Very well, madam! I shall sign, let the devil take it. I'll sign in a way he'll remember for a long time! I shall tell him what I think! Then let him dismiss me! And if he dismisses me, you'll be to blame! You!"

Ponimayev tottered, pushed the door with his shoulder and noisily went into the hall. Standing there by the door, displaying a clean-shaven New Year's face, was the porter Yegor. Near a little table with a sheet of paper on it stood Vezuvyev and Chernosvinsky, two colleagues of Ponimayev. The tall, gaunt Vezuvyev was signing the sheet, while Chernosvinsky, a small man with a pockmarked face, awaited his turn. On both their faces was written: "Best wishes for the New Year!" It was clear that they were signing not just according to form, but with true feeling. Seeing them, Ponimayev smirked disdainfully and indignantly pulled his fur coat around himself.

"Of course," he began. "Of course! How can we not congratulate His Excellency? It's impossible not to congratulate him! Ha, ha! We have to express our servile feelings!"

Vezuvyev and Chernosvinsky looked at him with astonishment. Never in their life had they heard such a sentiment.

"Is this not really ignorance, slavishness?" continued Ponimayev. "Leave it alone, don't sign! Make a protest!"

He struck the sheet with his fist, smudging Vezuvyev's signature.

"You are inciting rebellion, Your Honour!" said Yegor, running up to the table and waving the sheet over their heads. "For this, Your Honour, you and your kind would be dealt with... you know how?"

Just then the door opened, and there came into the hall a tall, elderly man wearing a bearskin coat and a three-cornered hat embroidered in gold. This was Ponimayev's chief, Veleleptov. On his entry, Yegor, Vezuvyev and Chernosvinsky drew themselves up and stood to attention. Ponimayev also drew himself up, but gave a smirk and twirled his whiskers.

"Ah!" said Veleleptov, seeing the employees. "You... are here? M-yes... friends... Of course..." Evidently His Excellency was slightly tipsy. "Of course... and you too... Thank you for not forgetting... Thank you... M-yes... Delighted to see you... I wish you... And you, Ponimayev, are already drunk? It doesn't matter, don't be embarrassed... Drink, but know your business.* Drink and enjoy yourselves..."

"All grains are for the use of man,* Your Excellency," Vezuvyev ventured to interject.

"Well, yes, of course... What did you say? What about grains? Well, go home... God speed... Or no... Have you already been to Nikita Prokhorych? You haven't been yet? Excellent. I shall give you some books... take them to him... He gave me the last two years' issues of *Strannik** to read... So they have to be returned to him... Come with me, I'll give them to you... Take off your coats."

The callers took off their coats and followed Veleleptov. They went through the reception hall into a big, luxuriously decorated room where the host's wife was sitting at a round table. Beside her were sitting two young women, one wearing white gloves, the other dressed in black. Veleleptov left the guests in the room and went to his study. The guests were embarrassed.

They stood in silence for ten minutes without moving or knowing what to do with their hands. The ladies were speaking French – from time to time they looked up at the men... It was torture! At last Veleleptov returned from the study, carrying in both hands bound copies of the magazine.

"Here," he said. "Give these to him with thanks... They are copies of *Strannik*. I sometimes read them in the evenings...

As for you... thank you for not forgetting... for coming to pay your respects..." Veleleptov turned to the ladies. "Have you been having a good look at my staff? Hee-hee... Have a look, have a look... This here is Vezuvyev, this is Chernosvinsky... and this is my Ponimayev. One day I went into the duty room and found him, this Ponimayev, imitating a train. And how was he doing it? Pssh! Pssh! Pssh! He was whistling like that, and stamping his feet... It was just like a train... M-yes... So then, show us! Come on, entertain us."

The ladies directed their gaze at Ponimayev and broke into smiles. He coughed.

"I can't... I have forgotten, Your Excellency," he muttered. "I can't and don't wish to."

"You don't wish to?" said Veleleptov in surprise. "Really? It's a pity... it's a pity you can't humour an old man... Goodbye... It's a shame... Go away..."

Vezuvyev and Chernosvinsky poked Ponimayev in the side. And even he was frightened by his refusal. His sight became blurred... The black gloves mingled with the white – the faces began to drift before his eyes, the furniture to jump, and Veleleptov himself turned into a big wagging finger. After standing for a while and muttering something, Ponimayev pressed the copies of *Strannik* to his chest and went out to the street. There he saw his wife, pale and shivering from the cold and the fright. Vezuvyev and Chernosvinsky were standing next to her and, gesticulating vigorously with their hands, were relating something fearful straight into her ears. "What will happen now?" was the question that could be read in their faces and movements. Ponimayev looked despairingly at his wife and, carrying the magazines, trudged away behind his friends.

Returning home, he did not eat dinner or even have tea... During the night he was awakened by a nightmare.

He rose and stared into the darkness. Black and white gloves, Veleleptov's side whiskers – all these began to dance before his eyes, began to whirl, as he recalled what had happened.

"I'm a swine, a swine!" he muttered. "You can protest if you wish, you ass, but don't dare to show disrespect to your superiors! What would it have cost you to imitate a train?"

He could not fall asleep again. All night, until morning itself, he was tormented by pangs of regret, misery and the sobbing of his wife. Looking the next morning in the mirror, he saw not himself, but some other face – pale, exhausted, sad…

"I shall not go to work," he decided. "It's all the same… It'll be all the same in the end."

All that second day of the New Year he abandoned himself to pacing back and forth in the room.

As he walked, he kept sighing and thinking:

"Where can I get a revolver? Rather than live like this, it would be better… really… Bullet in the head, and that's the end…"

On the third day he went in sadness to work.

"What's going to happen?" thought all his colleagues, looking at him from behind their inkwells.

And Ponimayev asked himself the same question.

"So, then," he whispered to Vezuvyev. "Let him dismiss me. He'll feel really bad if I do away with myself."

Veleleptov arrived at eleven o'clock. Going past Ponimayev and looking at his pale, thin, frightened face, he stopped, shook his head and said:

"You drank a lot the other day, my friend! Even now your face looks unwell. You should be more temperate, my friend… It's not good… You'll soon lose your health."

And, slapping Ponimayev on the shoulder, Veleleptov walked on.

"Just that?" thought everyone in the office.

Ponimayev began to laugh with delight. He was so pleased that he even whistled like a bird. But soon his face changed… He frowned and grinned contemptuously.

"You were lucky I was drunk!" he muttered aloud behind Veleleptov's back. "You were lucky, otherwise I would have… Do you remember, Vezuvyev, how I mocked him?"

Arriving home from work, Ponimayev dined with great appetite.

Women's Privileges

THEY WERE BURYING Lieutenant General Zapupyrin. To the house of the deceased, where shouted instructions and the droning of funeral music could be heard, crowds were running from all directions in the hope of seeing the coffin being carried out. In one of these groups that were hurrying to the cortège were state officials Probkin and Svistkov. Both were with their wives.

"You can't go through!" They were stopped by a security guard with a kind, sympathetic face when they came up to the chain barrier. "Can't... go... through! Plee-ease step back a little! Gentlemen, we really don't set the rules. I ask you to step back. The ladies, however, can go through... if you please, *mesdames*, but, gentlemen, for God's sake..."

The wives of Probkin and Svistkov blushed from the unexpected kindness of the guard and passed through the barrier, but their husbands were stopped on the other side of the throng of people and busied themselves watching the backs of the guards on foot and horseback.

"They got through!" said Probkin, looking with envy and a touch of disgust at the women who were moving away. "The luck, truly, of these chignons!* The male sex will never have such privileges as those of the female. So what is special about them? Women, one can say, are quite ordinary, with their shortcomings, but they are let through – but you and I, even if we'd been state councillors, would never have been allowed to pass."

"Your reasoning is strange, sir," said a policeman, looking reproachfully at Probkin. "If you were let through, you would immediately start to push and make a nuisance of yourselves – but ladies, because of their delicate nature, would never do anything of the kind."

"Less of that, please!" Probkin said angrily. "A woman in a crowd is always the first to push. A man stands in one spot and looks, but a woman spreads her elbows and pushes, so that her clothes don't get crumpled. There is nothing more to say! The female sex is always fortunate in everything. Women don't have to be soldiers – they don't have to pay to go to dances, and they're exempt from corporal punishment. And why, I ask you, do they deserve it? A young girl drops her handkerchief – you have to pick it up; she enters – you get up and give her your chair; she leaves – you see her off... And consider ranks! In order to become, let's say, a state councillor, you or I have to work hard all our life, but a girl in just half an hour gets married to a state councillor – and she's already a somebody. If I want to be made a prince or count, I have to conquer the whole world, to capture Shipka*, to be a minister, but some – God help me – Varyenka or Katyenka, barely out of nappies, flounces around a count, flutters her eyelashes, and there she is... Her Highness... You, Svistkov, are now a provincial secretary... This rank, I may say, you achieved yourself with blood and sweat. But your Marya Fominishna? Why is she a provincial secretary? From a priest's daughter straight to being an official! Some official! Give her our work to do, and she'll just put the contents of the in-tray into the out-tray."

"But she gives birth in pain," remarked Svistkov.

"Great achievement! If she had to stand in front of our boss when he was in a bad mood, having children would seem a pleasure, by comparison. In all things and everything, they are privileged! Any girl or lady in our circle may blurt out something to a general that you would not dare to say even in the presence of a high official. Yes... Your Marya Fomishna may boldly stroll arm in arm with a state councillor, but you try and take a state councillor by the arm! Just go and try it! Just below us in our house, my friend, lives a certain professor and his wife... A general, you understand, with the St Anna of the first class, but you constantly hear how his wife nags him: 'You fool! Fool! Fool!' She's really a simple woman, from the petty bourgeoisie. But she's his lawful wife, so that's the way it is... From time immemorial it's been accepted that lawfully married couples can quarrel – but look at the unmarried ones! What *they* allow themselves to do! I'll never forget one example. I nearly died, and only survived thanks to the prayers of my parents. Last year, you remember, our general, when he left for a holiday at his place in the country, took me with him to deal with his correspondence... It was an easy job, an hour's work a day. I would finish work and go off for a walk in the forest, or listen to the songs of the servants. Our general is an unmarried man. His house is richly furnished; he has servants aplenty, but no wife, no one to run the place. The people are all undisciplined, disobedient... and an old woman bosses everyone around – the housekeeper Vera Nikitishna. She pours the tea, and orders the supper, and shouts at the servants... The woman, my dear man, is nasty and malicious, like Satan. She is fat, red-faced and shrill... When she starts to shout at someone, when she raises a scream, it's enough to try the patience of a saint. It's not her shouting so much as her scream that's wearing. Oh, God! She made life unbearable for everyone. She tore into not only the servants, but me as well, the bitch... Well, I thought, just you wait – I shall find a moment and tell the general all about you. He's busy, I thought, with his work, and doesn't see how you are robbing him and mistreating the servants. Just you wait, I shall open his eyes. And I opened his eyes, my friend, I so opened them that if my own eyes were to close for ever, I would even now be able to remember the horror that followed. I was walking along the corridor once and suddenly heard a scream. At first I thought a pig was being slaughtered, but then I listened, and heard that it was Vera Nikitishna, swearing at someone: 'Swine! What a scoundrel you are! Devil!' 'Who is that?' I thought. And suddenly, my dear man, I saw the door open and our general come flying out, all red in the face, eyes goggling, and hair as if the Devil had blown on it. And she was behind him, shouting: 'Scoundrel! Devil!'"

"You lie!"

"My word of honour. You know, I went hot all over. Our general retreated back into his room. I stood in the corridor like a fool, completely at a loss. A simple, uneducated woman, a cook,

a peasant – and suddenly she allowed herself to utter such words
and to behave like that. I suspect the general wanted to dismiss her,
and she took the opportunity, while there was no witness, to tell
him what she thought of him. It's all the same to me, I thought,
I'll be leaving. I was boiling with rage... I went to her room and
said: 'How dare you, you worthless creature, say such things to a
highly placed personage? Do you think that because he is a weak
old man there is no one to stand up for him?' I went and smacked
her twice on her fat cheek. My dear fellow, what a scream she
raised, how she started to bawl, be she three times cursed, God
save me! I plugged my ears and went to the forest. Then about
two hours later a boy comes running towards me. 'Please come
to see the *barin*.' I go. I enter his room. He sits, having knitted
his face into a frown like a turkey-cock, and doesn't look at me.

"'So what,' he says, 'is this that you are doing in my house?'
'What do you mean?' I say. 'If,' I say, 'this is about Nikitishna, Your
Excellency, then I had to stand up for you.' 'It's not your business,'
he says, 'to interfere in other families' affairs.' You understand?
Families! And how, my friend, he began to tell me off, how he began
to grill me – I almost died! He spoke and spoke, grumbled and
grumbled – and suddenly, my friend, for no reason at all, he began
to laugh. 'But how,' he says, 'were you able to do this?! How could
you find the courage? It was wonderful! But I hope, my friend, that
all this remains between us... Your impulsiveness is understand-
able to me, but let's agree that it's impossible for you to stay in my
house any longer...' There you are, my friend! He thought it was
wonderful how I could discipline such a self-important peahen. He
was blinded by the woman! A privy councillor, who has the Order
of the White Eagle, no one higher than himself in the pecking order,
yet he is under the thumb of a woman... The female sex has b–i–i–g
privileges, my friend! But... take off your hat! They're carrying out
the general... Good Lord, how many decorations he has! But why,
really, were the ladies allowed to go forward? Do they really know
anything about decorations?"

The music began to play.

New Year's Great Martyrs

O N THE STREETS is a picture of hell in a golden frame. If there were not holiday expressions on the faces of the street-sweepers and policemen, it would be possible to think that the enemy is approaching the capital. Back and forth, with fuss and noise, dash ceremonial sleighs and carriages... Along the pavement run callers, their eyes bulging and their tongues hanging out from breathlessness... They run with such excitement that, had the wife of Potiphar* grabbed some collegiate registrar by the coat-tails, she would have in her hands not only the coat-tails but the whole side of the official's body complete with liver and spleen...

Suddenly a piercing police whistle is heard. What's happening? The street-sweepers leave their work and run towards the whistle...

"Disperse! Keep going! There is nothing here for you to see! Have you never seen a dead body? Oh, people!..."

By one of the doorways on the pavement lies a well-dressed man in a beaver-fur coat and new galoshes... Next to his deathly-pale, clean-shaven face lies a pair of broken glasses. His fur coat is thrown open at the chest, and the crowd that had gathered sees a part of his tailcoat and the Stanislav of the third class. His chest rises and falls slowly and heavily as he breathes; his eyes are closed...

"Sir!" A policeman pushes the official. "Sir, it's forbidden to lie here! Your Honour!"

But there is no response from the gentleman... After spending five minutes with him without being able to bring him round, the police place him in a cab and take him to the casualty ward...

"Good trousers!" says the policeman, helping the medical assistant to undress the patient. "They must have cost about six roubles. And the waistcoat is smart... Judging by the trousers, this one is from the upper class."

In the casualty ward, after lying down for about an hour and a half and drinking a whole phial of valerian, the official comes to... They learn that he is Titular Councillor Gerasim Kuzmich Sinkletyeyev.

"What's wrong with you?" the police doctor asks him.

"Happy New Year," he mutters, looking dully at the ceiling and breathing heavily.

"And to you too... But... what's the matter with you? Why did you fall? Try and remember. Did you drink something?"

"N... no..."

"So why did you feel faint?"

"I went crazy, sir... I... I was making calls..."

"Did you make many calls?"

"N... no, not many, sir... Having gone home after matins, I had tea and went to Nikolai Mikhailych... There, of course, I signed... From there I went to Ofitserskaya Street... to Kachalkin's... I signed there too... I also remember, there in the hall I caught a chill... From Kachalkin's I went to the Viborg district, to Ivan Ivanych's... I signed..."

"One more official has been brought in!" reports the policeman.

"From Ivan Ivanych's," continues Sinkletyeyev, "it's not far to the merchant Khrymov... I dropped in to congratulate... him and his family... They offered me a drink for the occasion... Why not have a drink? You will offend people by not drinking... Well, I drank three glasses... had some salami *zakuski*... From the St Petersburg side I went to Likhodeyev's... A good man..."

"And all on foot?"

"On foot, sir... I signed at Likhodeyev's... From his place I went to Pelageya Yemelyanovna... They invited me for breakfast and gave me coffee. I broke into a sweat from the coffee, and it must have gone to my head... From Pelageya Yemelyanovna's I went to Vasily Obleukhov's. It is his name-day... He would have been offended if I had not eaten a slice of his name-day *pirog*."*

"A retired military officer and two civil servants have been brought in," reports the policeman...

"I ate a slice of *pirog*, drank rowan-berry vodka and went to Sadovaya, to Izyumov's... At Izyumov's I drank cold beer... developed a sore throat... From Izyumov's I went to Koshkin's, then to Karl Karlych's... From there to Uncle Pyotr Semyonych... His niece Nastya gave me hot chocolate... Then I called in at Lyapkin's... No, I lie, not at Lyapkin's, but at Darya Nikodimovna's... It was from her that I went to Lyapkin's... Well, sir, I felt well everywhere... Then I was at Ivanov's, Kurdyukov's and Schiller's, and at Colonel Poroshkov's, and felt well there... I was at the merchant Dunkin's... He pressed me to drink some brandy and eat sausage and cabbage... I drank three glasses... ate a couple of sausages – and still felt nothing wrong... Only when I was leaving Ryzhov's did I feel in my head... a shimmering... I felt weak... I don't know why..."

"You are tired... Rest a little, and we'll send you home..."

"I can't go home," groans Sinkletyeyev. "I still have to go to my brother-in-law Kuzma Vavilych... to the director of supplies, to Natalya Yegorovna... There are still many I haven't visited."

"But you don't have to go."

"Impossible... How can I not offer my congratulations on New Year's Day? I must, sir... If I don't go to Natalya Yegorovna, life won't be worth living... You have to release me, doctor, sir, don't force me..."

Sinkletyeyev rises and reaches for his clothes.

"You may go home if you wish," says the doctor, "but don't even think about making visits."

"It's all right, sir, with God's help," sighs Sinkletyeyev, "I shall go very carefully..."

The official dresses slowly, muffles up in his fur coat and, swaying, goes out to the street.

"Five more officials have been brought in!" reports the policeman. "Where do you want them put?"

Notes

p. 3, *tessarakonta... oktokaideka*: "Forty... eighteen" (Greek).

p. 5, *He referred to learning, to light and darkness*: A reference to the Russian proverb "Knowledge is light, ignorance is darkness".

p. 9, *My cup is mingled with tears*: Psalms 102:9.

p. 10, *Mount Athos*: A monastery believed to cure with miracles.

p. 13, *To whom shall I tell my sorrow?*: A line from a folk song.

p. 14, *barin*: A landowner or gentleman, a man deserving of respect.

p. 16, *Serpent Gorynych*: An evil creature in Russian fairy tales.

p. 21, *balik*: Cured fillet of sturgeon (pl. *baliki*).

p. 23, *thirty-five degrees of frost*: Around −20°C.

p. 24, *blinis*: Pancakes, often with a filling of meat, made from buckwheat flour.

p. 26, *I thought the heavens had opened!*: An allusion to Mark 1:10: "And straightway coming up out of the water, he saw the heavens opened, and the Spirit like a dove descending upon him."

p. 26, *"Die, perfidious one! I thirst for blood!"*: A parody of the death of Desdemona in Shakespeare's *Othello* (Act V, Sc. 2).

p. 31, *pirozhki*: A *pirozhok* (pl. *pirozhki*, dimin. of *pirog*) is a pie, usually of meat or cabbage.

p. 32, *shchi*: Cabbage soup.

p. 34, *With a jawbone like that, Samson slew the Philistines*: Judges 15:15.

p. 36, *vinum gallicum rubrum*: "French red wine" (Latin).

p. 36, *Quantum satis*: "As much as needed" (Latin).

p. 36, *per se*: "As it comes" (Latin). Literally, "by itself".

p. 37, *Griboyedov... Saratov*: A quotation from *Woe from Wit* (Act IV, Sc. 14), a verse comedy by Alexander Griboyedov (1795–1829).

p. 37, *"It was blissful in one's youth to be young!"*: It is actually Alexander Pushkin, not Shakespeare, who wrote these words in his *Eugene Onegin* (VIII, 10, l. 1).

p. 42, *Okroshka*: A cold soup of kvass and vegetables.

p. 50, *eleven versts*: A verst is about 1.1 km (0.66 miles).

p. 52, *The Charcot shower*: Named after Jean-Martin Charcot (1825–93), a French clinician.

p. 60, *Gogol or Krylov*: The Russian writers Nikolai Gogol (1809–52) and Ivan Krylov (1769–1844).

p. 61, *a one*: The lowest grade awarded in a subject.

p. 63, *the Trinity Lavra of St Sergius*: The most important Russian monastery of the Russian Orthodox Church.

p. 63, *Aras River*: A river in the Caucasus.

p. 65, *Bring Tyapkin-Lyapkin here!*: The reference is to the summons issued by the government inspector, travelling incognito, in Gogol's play of the same name.

p. 78, *You can help me lay the table*: The end of the Lenten fast is at midnight before Easter Sunday.

p. 79, *zakuski*: Little snacks or hors-d'oeuvres (sing. *zakuska*).

p. 79, *paskha*: A sweet dish made chiefly from cottage cheese, usually served at Easter.

p. 80, *pour manger*: "To eat" (French).

p. 83, *hapyen zee gevezyen*: An attempt at transliterating German words implying "saw the chance to make a little something".

p. 85, *arshins*: The *arshin* is a unit of length equivalent to about 71 cm.

p. 85, *vershoks*: The *vershok* is a unit of length equivalent to about 4.45 cm.

p. 86, *stukolka*: A card game of chance with simple rules.

p. 89, *Novoye Vremya*: A conservative St Petersburg newspaper (literally, "New Time") published between 1868 and 1917.

NOTES

p. 89, *Golos*: A St Petersburg newspaper (literally, "The Voice") of moderately liberal tendency published between 1863 and 1885.

p. 89, *Sic transit gloria mundi!*: "Thus passes the glory of the world!" (Latin).

p. 90, *Digging through... Krylov*: From Krylov's fable 'The Cockerel and the Pearl' (*Fables*, Book 2, XVIII, ll. 1–2).

p. 90, *the flames... she revived*: The source of this quote (if indeed it is a literary quotation) has not been identified.

p. 92, *my name... my own anthill*: A reference to Krylov's fable 'The Ant' (Book 6, XIV).

p. 92, *Trediakovsky*: The Russian poet and translator Vasily Trediakovsky (1703–69).

p. 94, *Kasha*: A form of gruel, made from buckwheat.

p. 103, *ma chère*: "My dear" (French).

p. 106, *cunning simpletons... Woe from Wit*: From Act IV, Sc. 14 of Griboyedov's *Woe from Wit*.

p. 109, *Merci*: "Thank you" (French).

p. 112, *five*: The highest mark.

p. 114, *I loved you, love is still perhaps*: A popular romance to words by Pushkin.

p. 114, *je vous prie*: "Please" (French).

p. 115, *The knights have love and honour*: From Sc. 12 of the vaudevillian opera *A New Prank, or A Theatrical Battle* (1822) by the Russian dramatist Nikolai Khmelnitsky (1789–1845), with music by Alexander Alyabyev (1787–1851), Ludwig Wilhelm Maurer (1789–1878) and Alexei Verstovsky (1799–1862).

p. 117, *Pereat*: "Let him die" (Latin).

p. 117, *our Renan and Spinoza*: A reference to the French scholar Ernest Renan (1823–92) and to the Dutch philosopher Baruch Spinoza (1632–77).

p. 119, *L.I. Palmin*: The Russian poet and translator Liodor Palmin (1841–91).

p. 119, *As you measure... measured unto you*: Matthew 7:2.

p. 125, *Business is not… to the forest*: A Russian proverb.

p. 125, *Palkin's*: An expensive restaurant on Nevsky Prospekt in St Petersburg.

p. 127, *mon oncle*: "Uncle" (French).

p. 131, *'Luchinushka'*: A popular folk song of melancholy and yearning (literally, "Little Splinter").

p. 132, *Gambetta*: The French republican politician Léon Gambetta (1838–82), who proclaimed the French Third Republic in 1870. He died prematurely of stomach cancer in December 1882.

p. 132, *Bismarck's purposes*: A reference to the German statesman Otto von Bismarck (1815–98).

p. 137, *Lassalle*: An allusion to the German socialist and political activist Ferdinand Lassalle (1825–64).

p. 138, *fire horses can't be fed with oats*: Oats, being a high-energy food, would make the horses too lively and unmanageable in a dangerous situation.

p. 138, *Vyestnik Yevropi*: A liberal magazine published between 1866 and 1918 (literally, "Messenger of Europe").

p. 138, *na zapyatka*: At the back of the carriage, where the servants travelled standing.

p. 139, *kalatches*: Bread rolls baked in the form of a padlock.

p. 147, *fructus*: "Fruit" (Latin).

p. 147, *Kühner's grammar*: The German philologist and classical scholar Raphael Kühner (1802–78) was the author of a popular Latin grammar.

p. 148, *meus filius*: "My son" (Latin).

p. 148, *dea*: "Goddess" (Latin).

p. 148, *bonus*: "Good" (Latin).

p. 148, *antropos*: *Anthropos* is actually Greek for "human being".

p. 156, *shaking his rattle*: Watchmen traditionally carried a rattle on their rounds.

p. 158, *Here the children don't walk out carrying a star*: A Russian custom at Christmas.

p. 158, *pood*: A unit of weight equivalent to about 16.38 kg.

p. 166, *Get thee behind me, Satan*: Mark 8:33, Matthew 16:23, Luke 4:8.

p. 173, *The Count of Monte Cristo*: The famous adventure novel by Alexandre Dumas (1802–70).

p. 174, *The Wandering Jew*: An 1844 novel by Eugène Sue (1804–57).

p. 174, *Force me to pray eternally to God*: An implied reference to the Russian proverb: "Force a fool to pray, and he'll crack his skull" (when prostrating himself).

p. 179, *Drunkenness reveals what soberness conceals*: A well-known Russian proverb.

p. 182, *Drink, but know your business*: A well-known saying in Russia.

p. 182, *All grains are for the use of man*: Another Russian saying.

p. 182, *Strannik*: A Russian magazine published between 1860 and 1917 (literally, "The Wanderer").

p. 185, *chignons*: A fashionable women's hairstyle consisting of a coil of hair worn on the nape of the neck or back of the head – here a synecdoche for the women themselves.

p. 186, *Shipka*: A town in central Bulgaria overrun by the Russians in the Russo-Turkish War of 1877–78.

p. 189, *the wife of Potiphar*: A reference to the biblical story of Joseph and Potiphar's wife narrated in Genesis 39.

p. 190, *pirog*: See note to p. 31.

Extra Material

on

Anton Chekhov's

*Small Fry
and Other Stories*

Anton Chekhov's Life

Anton Pavlovich Chekhov was born in Taganrog, on the Sea Birth and Background
of Azov in southern Russia, on 29th January 1860. He was the
third child of Pavel Yegorovich Chekhov and his wife Yevgenia
Yakovlevna. He had four brothers – Alexander (born in 1855),
Nikolai (1858), Ivan (1861) and Mikhail (1865) – and one
sister, Marya, who was born in 1863. Anton's father, the owner
of a small shop, was a devout Christian who administered
brutal floggings to his children almost on a daily basis. Anton
remembered these with bitterness throughout his life, and
possibly as a result was always sceptical of organized religion.
The shop – a grocery and general-supplies store which sold
such goods as lamp oil, tea, coffee, seeds, flour and sugar –
was kept by the children during their father's absence. The
father also required his children to go with him to church at
least once a day. He set up a liturgical choir which practised
in his shop, and demanded that his children – whether they
had school work to do or not, or whether they had been in the
shop all day – should join the rehearsals to provide the higher
voice parts.

Chekhov described his home town as filthy and tedious, and Education and
the people as drunk, idle, lazy and illiterate. At first, Pavel tried Childhood
to provide his children with an education by enrolling the two
he considered the brightest, Nikolai and Anton, in one of the
schools for the descendants of the Greek merchants who had
once settled in Taganrog. These provided a more "classical"
education than their Russian equivalents, and their standard
of teaching was held in high regard. However, the experience
was not a successful one, since most of the other pupils spoke
Greek among themselves, of which the Chekhovs did not
know a single word. Eventually, in 1868, Anton was enrolled

in one of the town's Russian high schools. The courses at the Russian school included Church Slavonic, Latin and Greek, and if the entire curriculum was successfully completed, entry to a university was guaranteed. Unfortunately, as the shop was making less and less money, the school fees were often unpaid and lessons were missed. The teaching was generally mediocre, but the religious education teacher, Father Pokrovsky, encouraged his pupils to read the Russian classics and such foreign authors as Shakespeare, Swift and Goethe. Pavel also paid for private French and music lessons for his children.

Every summer the family would travel through the steppe by cart some fifty miles to an estate where their paternal grandfather was chief steward. The impressions gathered on these journeys, and the people encountered, had a profound impact on the young Anton, and later provided material for one of his greatest stories, 'The Steppe'.

At the age of thirteen, Anton went to the theatre for the first time, to see Offenbach's operetta *La Belle Hélène* at the Taganrog theatre. He was enchanted by the spectacle, and went as often as time and money allowed, seeing not only the Russian classics, but also foreign pieces such as *Hamlet* in Russian translation. In his early teens, he even created his own theatrical company with his school friends to act out the Russian classics.

Adversity   In 1875 Anton was severely ill with peritonitis. The high-school doctor tended him with great care, and he resolved to join the medical profession one day. That same year, his brothers Alexander and Nikolai, fed up with the beatings they received at home, decided to move to Moscow to work and study, ignoring their father's admonitions and threats. Anton now bore the entire brunt of Pavel's brutality. To complicate things further, the family shop ran into severe financial difficulties, and was eventually declared bankrupt. The children were withdrawn from school, and Pavel fled to Moscow, leaving his wife and family to face the creditors. In the end, everybody abandoned the old residence, with the exception of Anton, who remained behind with the new owner.

Although he was now free of his father's bullying and the hardship of having to go to church and work in the shop, Anton had to find other employment in order to pay his rent and bills, and to resume his school studies. Accordingly, at the age of fifteen, he took up tutoring, continuing voraciously to read books of Russian and foreign literature, philosophy and science, in the town library.

In 1877, during a summer holiday, he undertook the seven-hundred-mile journey to Moscow to see his family, and found them all living in one room and sleeping on a single mattress on the floor. His father was not at all abashed by his failures: he continued to be dogmatically religious and to beat the younger children regularly. On his return to Taganrog, Anton attempted to earn a little additional income by sending sketches and anecdotes to several of Moscow's humorous magazines, but they were all turned down.

The young Chekhov unabatedly pursued his studies, and in June 1879 he passed the Taganrog High School exams with distinction, and in the autumn he moved to Moscow to study medicine. The family still lived in one room, and Alexander and Nikolai were well on the way to becoming alcoholics. Anton, instead of finding his own lodgings, decided to support not only himself, but his entire family, and try to re-educate them. After a hard day spent in lectures, tutorials and in the laboratories, he would write more sketches for humorous and satirical magazines, and an increasing number of these were now accepted: by the early 1880s, over a hundred had been printed. Anton used a series of pseudonyms (the most usual being "Antosha Chekhonte") for these productions, which he later called "rubbish". He also visited the Moscow theatres and concert halls on numerous occasions, and in 1880 sent the renowned Maly Theatre a play he had recently written. Only a rough draft of the piece – which was rejected by the Maly and published for the first time in 1920, under the title *Platonov* – has survived. Unless Chekhov had polished and pruned his lost final version considerably, the play would have lasted around seven hours. Despite its poor construction and verbosity, *Platonov* already shows some of the themes and characters present in Chekhov's mature works, such as rural boredom and weak-willed, supine intellectuals dreaming of a better future while not doing anything to bring it about.

As well as humorous sketches and stories, Chekhov wrote brief résumés of legal court proceedings and gossip from the artistic world for various Moscow journals. With the money made from these pieces he moved his family into a larger flat, and regularly invited friends to visit and talk and drink till late at night.

Studies in Moscow and Early Publications

203

In 1882, encouraged by his success with the Moscow papers, he started contributing to the journals of the capital St Petersburg, since payment there was better than in Moscow. He was eventually commissioned to contribute a regular column to the best-selling journal *Oskolki* ("Splinters"), providing a highly coloured picture of Moscow life with its court cases and bohemian atmosphere. He was now making over 150 roubles a month from his writing – about three times as much as his student stipend – although he managed to save very little because of the needs of his family. In 1884 Chekhov published, at his own expense, a booklet of six of his short stories, entitled *Tales of Melpomene*, which sold quite poorly.

Start of Medical Career   There was compensation for this relative literary failure: in June of that year Anton passed all his final exams in medicine and became a medical practitioner. That summer, he began to receive patients at a village outside Moscow, and even stepped in for the director of a local hospital when the latter went on his summer vacation. He was soon receiving thirty to forty patients a day, and was struck by the peasants' ill health, filth and drunkenness. He planned a major treatise entitled *A History of Medicine in Russia* but, after reading and annotating over a hundred works on the subject, he gave the subject up and returned to Moscow to set up his own medical practice.

First Signs of   Suddenly, in December 1884, when he was approaching the
Tuberculosis achievement of all his ambitions, Chekhov developed a dry cough and began to spit blood. He tried to pretend that these were not early symptoms of tuberculosis but, as a doctor, he must have had an inkling of the truth. He made no attempt to cut down his commitments in the light of his illness, but kept up the same punishing schedule of activity. By this time, Chekhov had published over three hundred items, including some of his first recognized mature works, such as 'The Daughter of Albion' and 'The Death of an Official'. Most of the stories were already, in a very understated way, depicting life's "losers" – such as the idle gentry, shopkeepers striving unsuccessfully to make a living and ignorant peasants. Now that his income had increased, Chekhov rented a summer house a few miles outside Moscow. However, although he intended to use his holiday exclusively for writing, he was inundated all day with locals who had heard he was a doctor and required medical attention.

Chekhov made a crucial step in his literary career, when in *Trip to St Petersburg and* December 1885 he visited the imperial capital St Petersburg *Meeting with Suvorin* for the first time, as a guest of the editor of the renowned *St Petersburg Journal*. His stories were beginning to gain him a reputation, and he was introduced at numerous soirées to famous members of the St Petersburg literary world. He was agreeably surprised to find they knew his work and valued it highly. Here for the first time he met Alexei Suvorin, the press mogul and editor of the most influential daily of the period, *Novoye Vremya (New Times)*. Suvorin asked Chekhov to contribute stories regularly to his paper at a far higher rate of pay than he had been receiving from other journals. Now Chekhov, while busy treating numerous patients in Moscow and helping to stem the constant typhus epidemics that broke out in the city, also began to churn out for Suvorin such embryonic masterpieces as 'The Requiem' and 'Grief' – although all were still published pseudonymously. Distinguished writers advised him to start publishing under his own name and, although his current collection *Motley Stories* had already gone to press under the Chekhonte pseudonym, Anton resolved from now on to shed his anonymity. The collection received tepid reviews, but Chekhov now had sufficient income to rent a whole house on Sadova-Kudrinskaya Street (now maintained as a museum of this early period of Chekhov's life), in an elegant district of Moscow.

Chekhov's reputation as a writer was further enhanced *Literary Recognition* when Suvorin published a collection of sixteen of Chekhov's short stories in 1887 – under the title *In the Twilight* – to great critical acclaim. However, Chekhov's health was deteriorating and his blood-spitting was growing worse by the day. Anton appears more and more by now to have come to regard life as a parade of "the vanity of human wishes". He channelled some of this ennui and his previous life experiences into a slightly melodramatic and overlong play, *Ivanov*, in which the eponymous hero – a typical "superfluous man" who indulges in pointless speculation while his estate goes to ruin and his capital dwindles – ends up shooting himself. *Ivanov* was premiered in November 1887 by the respected Korsh Private Theatre under Chekhov's real name – a sign of Anton's growing confidence as a writer – although it received very mixed reviews.

However, in the spring of 1888, Chekhov's story 'The Steppe' – an impressionistic, poetical recounting of the experiences of a young boy travelling through the steppe on a cart – was published in *The Northern Herald*, again under his real name, enabling him to reach another milestone in his literary career, and prompting reviewers for the first time to talk of his genius. Although Chekhov began to travel to the Crimea for vacations, in the hope that the warm climate might aid his health, the symptoms of tuberculosis simply reappeared whenever he returned to Moscow. In October of the same year, Chekhov was awarded the prestigious Pushkin Prize for Literature for *In the Twilight*. He was now recognized as a major Russian writer, and began to state his belief to reporters that a writer's job is not to peddle any political or philosophical point of view, but to depict human life with its associated problems as objectively as possible.

Death of his Brother   A few months later, in January 1889, a revised version of *Ivanov* was staged at the Alexandrinsky Theatre in St Petersburg, arguably the most important drama theatre in Russia at the time. The new production was a huge success and received excellent reviews. However, around that time it also emerged that Anton's alcoholic brother, Nikolai, was suffering from advanced tuberculosis. When Nikolai died in June of that year, at the age of thirty, Anton must have seen this as a harbinger of his own early demise.

Chekhov was now working on a new play, *The Wood Demon*, in which, for the first time, psychological nuance replaced stage action, and the effect on the audience was achieved by atmosphere rather than by drama or the portrayal of events. However, precisely for these reasons, it was rejected by the Alexandrinsky Theatre in October of that year. Undeterred, Chekhov decided to revise it, and a new version of *The Wood Demon* was put on in Moscow in December 1889. Lambasted by the critics, it was swiftly withdrawn from the scene, to make its appearance again many years later, thoroughly rewritten, as *Uncle Vanya*.

Journey to   It was around this time that Anton Chekhov began con-
Sakhalin Island templating his journey to the prison island of Sakhalin. At the end of 1889, unexpectedly, and for no apparent reason, the twenty-nine-year-old author announced his intention to leave European Russia, and to travel across Siberia to Sakhalin, the large island separating Siberia and the Pacific Ocean, following which he would write a full-scale examination of the penal colony maintained there by the Tsarist authorities. Explanations put forward by commentators both then and since include a

search by the author for fresh material for his works, a desire to escape from the constant carping of his liberally minded colleagues on his lack of a political line; desire to escape from an unhappy love affair; and disappointment at the recent failure of *The Wood Demon*. A further explanation may well be that, as early as 1884, he had been spitting blood, and recently, just before his journey, several friends and relations had died of tuberculosis. Chekhov, as a doctor, must have been aware that he too was in the early stages of the disease, and that his lifespan would be considerably curtailed. Possibly he wished to distance himself for several months from everything he had known, and give himself time to think over his illness and mortality by immersing himself in a totally alien world. Chekhov hurled himself into a study of the geography, history, nature and ethnography of the island, as background material to his study of the penal settlement. The Trans-Siberian Railway had not yet been constructed, and the journey across Siberia, begun in April 1890, required two and a half months of travel in sledges and carriages on abominable roads in freezing temperatures and appalling weather. This certainly hastened the progress of his tuberculosis and almost certainly deprived him of a few extra years of life. He spent three months in frantic work on the island, conducting his census of the prison population, rummaging in archives, collecting material and organizing book collections for the children of exiles, before leaving in October 1890 and returning to Moscow, via Hong Kong, Ceylon and Odessa, in December of that year.

The completion of his report on his trip to Sakhalin was *Travels in Europe* to be hindered for almost five years by his phenomenally busy life, as he attempted, as before, to continue his medical practice and write at the same time. In early 1891 Chekhov, in the company of Suvorin, travelled for the first time to western Europe, visiting Vienna, Venice, Bologna, Florence, Rome, Naples and finally Monaco and Paris.

Trying to cut down on the expenses he was paying out for *Move to Melikhovo* his family in Moscow, he bought a small estate at Melikhovo, a few miles outside Moscow, and the entire family moved there. His father did some gardening, his mother cooked, while Anton planted hundreds of fruit trees, shrubs and flowers. Chekhov's concerns for nature have a surprisingly modern ecological ring: he once said that if he had not been a writer he would have become a gardener.

Although his brothers had their own lives in Moscow and only spent holidays at Melikhovo, Anton's sister Marya – who never married – lived there permanently, acting as his confidante and as his housekeeper when he had his friends and famous literary figures to stay, as he often did in large parties. Chekhov also continued to write, but was distracted, as before, by the scores of locals who came every day to receive medical treatment from him. There was no such thing as free medical assistance in those days and, if anybody seemed unable to pay, Chekhov often treated them for nothing. In 1892, there was a severe local outbreak of cholera, and Chekhov was placed in charge of relief operations. He supervised the building of emergency isolation wards in all the surrounding villages and travelled around the entire area directing the medical operations.

Ill Health Chekhov's health was deteriorating more and more rapidly, and his relentless activity certainly did not help. He began to experience almost constant pain and, although still hosting gatherings, he gave the appearance of withdrawing increasingly into himself and growing easily tired. By the mid-1890s, his sleep was disturbed almost nightly by bouts of violent coughing. Besides continuing his medical activities, looking after his estate and writing, Chekhov undertook to supervise – often with large subsidies from his own pocket – the building of schools in the local villages, where there had been none before.

Controversy around By late 1895, Chekhov was thinking of writing for the theatre
The Seagull again. The result was *The Seagull*, which was premiered at the Alexandrinsky Theatre in October 1896. Unfortunately the acting was so bad that the premiere was met by jeering and laughter, and received vicious reviews. Chekhov himself commented that the director did not understand the play, the actors didn't know their lines and nobody could grasp the understated style. He fled from the theatre and roamed the streets of St Petersburg until two in the morning, resolving never to write for the theatre again. Despite this initial fiasco, subsequent performances went from strength to strength, with the actors called out on stage after every performance.

Olga Knipper By this time, it seems that Chekhov had accepted the fact that he had a mortal illness. In 1897, he returned to Italy to see whether the warmer climate would not afford his condition some respite, but as soon as he came back to Russia the coughing and blood-spitting resumed as violently as before. It was around this time that the two founders of the

Moscow Arts Theatre, Vladimir Nemirovich-Danchenko and Konstantin Stanislavsky, asked Chekhov whether they could stage *The Seagull*. Their aims were to replace the stylized and unnatural devices of the classical theatre with more natural events and dialogue, and Chekhov's play seemed ideal for this purpose. He gave his permission, and in September 1898 went to Moscow to attend the preliminary rehearsals. It was there that he first met the twenty-eight-year-old actress Olga Knipper, who was going to take the leading role of Arkadina. However, the Russian winter was making him cough blood violently, and so he decided to follow the local doctor's advice and travel south to the Crimea, in order to spend the winter in a warmer climate. Accordingly, he rented a villa with a large garden in Yalta.

When his father died in October of the same year, Chekhov *Move to the Crimea* decided to put Melikhovo up for sale and move his mother and Marya to the Crimea. They temporarily stayed in a large villa near the Tatar village of Kuchukoy, but Chekhov had in the mean time bought a plot of land at Autka, some twenty minutes by carriage from Yalta, and he drew up a project to have a house built there. Construction began in December.

Also in December 1898, the first performance of *The Seagull* at the Moscow Arts Theatre took place. It was a resounding success, and there were now all-night queues for tickets. Despite his extremely poor health, Chekhov was still busy raising money for relief of the severe famine then scourging the Russian heartlands, overseeing the building of his new house and aiding the local branch of the Red Cross. In addition to this, local people and aspiring writers would turn up in droves at his villa in Yalta to receive medical treatment or advice on their manuscripts.

In early January 1899, Chekhov signed an agreement with *Collected Works Project* the publisher Adolf Marx to supervise the publication of a multi-volume edition of his collected works in return for a flat fee of 75,000 roubles and no royalties. This proved to be an error of judgement from a financial point of view, because by the time Chekhov had put some money towards building his new house, ensured all the members of his family were provided for and made various other donations, the advance had almost disappeared.

Chekhov finally moved to Autka – where he was to spend *Romance* the last few years of his life – in June 1899, and immediately *with Olga* began to plant vegetables, flowers and fruit trees. During a short period spent in Moscow to facilitate his work for Adolf Marx, he re-established contact with the Moscow Arts Theatre and Olga Knipper. Chekhov invited the actress to Yalta on several occasions and, although her visits were brief and at first she stayed in a hotel, it was obvious that she and Chekhov were becoming very close. Apart from occasional short visits to Moscow, which cost him a great expenditure of energy and were extremely harmful to his medical condition, Chekhov now had to spend all of his time in the south. He forced himself to continue writing short stories and plays, but felt increasingly lonely and isolated and, aware that he had only a short time left to live, became even more withdrawn. It was around this time that he worked again at his early play *The Wood Demon*, reducing the dramatis personae to only nine characters, radically altering the most significant scenes and renaming it *Uncle Vanya*. This was premiered in October 1899, and it was another gigantic success. In July of the following year, Olga Knipper took time off from her busy schedule of rehearsals and performances in Moscow to visit Chekhov in Yalta. There was no longer any attempt at pretence: she stayed in his house and, although he was by now extremely ill, they became romantically involved, exchanging love letters almost every day.

By now Chekhov had drafted another new play, *Three Sisters*, and he travelled to Moscow to supervise the first few rehearsals. Olga came to his hotel every day bringing food and flowers. However, Anton felt that the play needed revision, so he returned to Yalta to work on a comprehensive rewrite. *Three Sisters* opened on 31st January 1901 and – though at first well received, especially by the critics – it gradually grew in the public's estimation, becoming another great success.

Wedding and But Chekhov was feeling lonely in Yalta without Olga, and *Honeymoon* in May of that year proposed to her by letter. Olga accepted, and Chekhov immediately set off for Moscow, despite his doctor's advice to the contrary. He arranged a dinner for his friends and relatives and, while they were waiting there, he and Olga got married secretly in a small church on the outskirts of Moscow. As the participants at the dinner received a telegram with the news, the couple had already left for their honeymoon. Olga and Anton sailed down the Volga, up the Kama River and along the Belaya River to the village of Aksyonovo, where they checked into a sanatorium. At this establishment Chekhov drank four large bottles of fermented mare's milk every day, put on weight, and his condition seemed to improve somewhat. However, on their return to Yalta, Chekhov's health deteriorated again. He made his will, leaving his house in Yalta to Marya, all income from his dramatic works to Olga and large sums to his mother and his surviving brothers, to the municipality of Taganrog and to the peasant body of Melikhovo.

After a while, Olga returned to her busy schedule of rehears- *Difficult Relationship* als and performances in Moscow, and the couple continued their relationship at a distance, as they had done before their marriage, with long and frequent love letters. Chekhov managed to visit her in Moscow occasionally, but by now he was so ill that he had to return to Yalta immediately, often remaining confined to bed for long periods. Olga was tortured as to whether she should give up her acting career and nurse Anton for the time left to him. Almost unable to write, Anton now embarked laboriously on his last dramatic masterpiece, *The Cherry Orchard*. Around that time, in the spring of 1902, Olga visited Anton in Yalta after suffering a spontaneous miscarriage during a Moscow Art Theatre tour, leaving her husband with the unpleasant suspicion that she might have been unfaithful to him. In the following months, Anton nursed his wife devotedly, travelling to Moscow whenever he could to be near her. Olga's flat was on the third floor, and there was no lift. It took Anton half an hour to get up the stairs, so he practically never went out.

When *The Cherry Orchard* was finally completed in *Final Play* October 1903, Chekhov once again travelled to Moscow to attend rehearsals, despite the advice of his doctors that it would be tantamount to suicide. The play was premiered on 17th January 1904, Chekhov's forty-fourth birthday, and at the end of the performance the author was dragged onstage. There was no chair for him, and he was forced to stand listening to the interminable speeches, trying not to cough and pretending to look interested. Although the performance was a success, press reviews, as usual, were mixed, and Chekhov thought that Nemirovich-Danchenko and Stanislavsky had misunderstood the play.

Chekhov returned to Yalta knowing he would not live long *Death* enough to write another work. His health deteriorated even further, and the doctors put him on morphine, advising him to go to a sanatorium in Germany. Accordingly, in June 1904, he and Olga set off for Badenweiler, a spa in the Black Forest. The German specialists examined him and reported that they could do nothing. Soon oxygen had to be administered to him, and he became feverish and delirious. At 12.30 a.m. on 15th July 1904, he regained his mental clarity sufficiently to tell Olga to summon a doctor urgently. On the doctor's arrival, Chekhov told him, "*Ich sterbe*" ("I'm dying"). The doctor gave him a strong stimulant, and was on the point of sending for other medicines when Chekhov, knowing it was all pointless, simply asked for a bottle of champagne to be sent to the room. He poured everybody a glass, drank his off, commenting that he hadn't had champagne for ages, lay down, and died in the early hours of the morning.

Funeral   The coffin was transported back to Moscow in a filthy green carriage marked "FOR OYSTERS", and although it was met at the station by bands and a large ceremonial gathering, it turned out that this was for an eminent Russian General who had just been killed in action in Manchuria. Only a handful of people had assembled to greet Chekhov's coffin. However, as word got round Moscow that his body was being transported to the graveyard at the Novodevichy Monastery, people poured out of their homes and workplaces, forming a vast crowd both inside and outside the cemetery and causing a large amount of damage to buildings, pathways and other graves in the process. The entire tragicomic episode of Chekhov's death, transportation back to Moscow and burial could almost have featured in one of his own short stories. Chekhov was buried next to his father Pavel. His mother outlived him by fifteen years, and his sister Marya died in 1957 at the age of ninety-four. Olga Knipper survived two more years, dying in 1959 at the age of eighty-nine.

Anton Chekhov's Works

Early Writings   When Chekhov studied medicine in Moscow from 1879 to 1884, he financed his studies by writing reports of law-court proceedings for the newspapers and contributing, under a whole series of pseudonyms, hundreds of jokes, comic sketches and short stories to the numerous Russian humorous magazines and more serious journals of the time. From 1885, when he began to practise as a doctor, he concentrated far more on serious literary works, and between then and the end of his life he produced over 200 short stories, plus a score or so of dramatic pieces, ranging from monologues through one-act to full-length plays. In 1884 he also wrote his only novel, *The Hunting Party*, which was a rather wooden attempt at a detective novel.

A number of his stories between the mid-Eighties and his journey to Sakhalin were vitiated by his attempt to propagate the Tolstoyan moral principles he had espoused at the time. But even before his journey to the prison island he was realizing that laying down the law to his readers, and trying to dictate how they should read his stories, was not his job: it should be the goal of an artist to describe persons and events non-judgementally, and let the reader draw his or her own conclusions. This is attested by his letter to Suvorin in April 1890: "You reproach me for 'objectivity', calling it indifference to good and evil, and absence of ideals and ideas and so forth. You wish me, when depicting horse thieves, to state: stealing horses is bad. But surely people have known that for ages already, without me telling them so? Let them be judged by jurymen – my business is to show them as they really are. When I write, I rely totally on the reader, supposing that he himself will supply the subjective factors absent in the story." After Chekhov's return from Sakhalin, this objectivity dominated everything he wrote.

Invention of a New, "Objective" Style of Writing

A further feature of Chekhov's storytelling, which developed throughout his career, is that he does not so much describe events taking place, but rather depicts the way that characters react to those – frequently quite insignificant – events, and the way people's lives are often transformed for better or worse by them. His dramatic works from that time also showed a development from fully displayed events and action – sometimes, in the early plays, quite melodramatic – to, in the major plays written in the last decade or so of his life, depicting the effects on people's lives of offstage events, and the way the characters react to those events.

His style in all his later writing – especially from 1890 onwards – is lucid and economical, and there is a total absence of purple passages. The works of his final years display an increasing awareness of the need for conservation of the natural world in the face of the creeping industrialization of Russia. The breakdown of the old social order in the face of the new rising entrepreneurial class is also depicted non-judgementally; in Chekhov's last play, *The Cherry Orchard*, an old estate belonging to a long-established family of gentry is sold to a businessman, and the final scenes of the play give way to the offstage sounds of wood-chopping, as the old cherry orchard – one of the major beauties of the estate – is cut down by its new owner to be sold for timber.

Major Short Stories It is generally accepted that Chekhov's mature story-writing may be said to date from the mid-1880s, when he began to contribute to the "thick journals". Descriptions of a small representative selection of some of the major short stories – giving an idea of Chekhov's predominant themes – can be found below.

On the Road In 'On the Road' (1886), set in a seedy wayside inn on Christmas Eve, a man, apparently from the privileged classes, and his eight-year-old daughter are attempting to sleep in the "travellers' lounge", having been forced to take refuge from a violent storm. The little girl wakes up, and tells him how unhappy she is and that he is a wicked man. A noblewoman, also sheltering from the storm, enters and comforts the girl. The man and the woman both tell each other of the unhappiness of their lives: he is a widowed nobleman who has squandered all his money and is now on his way to a tedious job in the middle of nowhere; she is from a wealthy family, but her father and her brothers are wastrels, and she is the only one who takes care of the estate. They both part in the morning, on Christmas Day, profoundly unhappy, and without succeeding in establishing that deep inner contact with another human being which both of them obviously crave.

Enemies Chekhov's 1887 tale 'Enemies' touches on similar themes of misery and incomprehension: a country doctor's six-year-old son has just died of diphtheria, leaving him and his wife devastated; at precisely this moment, a local landowner comes to his house to call him out to attend to his wife, who is apparently dangerously ill. Though sympathetic to the doctor's state, he is understandably full of anxiety for his wife, and insists that the doctor come. After an uncomfortable carriage journey, they arrive at the landowner's mansion to discover that the wife was never ill at all, but was simply getting rid of her husband so that she could run off with her lover. The landowner is now in a state of anger and despair, and the doctor unreasonably blames him for having dragged him out under false pretences. When the man offers him his fee, the doctor throws it in his face and storms out. The landowner also furiously drives off somewhere to assuage his anger. Neither man can even begin to penetrate the other's mental state because of their own problems. The doctor remains full of contempt and cynicism for the human race for the rest of his life.

In 1888, Chekhov's first indubitably great narrative, the *The Steppe* novella-length 'The Steppe', was published to rapturous reviews. There is almost no plot: in blazing midsummer, a nine-year-old boy sets out on a long wagon ride, lasting several days, from his home in a small provincial town through the steppe, to stay with relatives and attend high school in a large city. The entire story consists of his impressions of the journey – of his travelling companions, the people they meet en route, the inns at which they stay, the scenery and wildlife. He finally reaches his destination, bids farewell to his travelling companions, and the story ends with him full of tears of regret at his lost home life, and foreboding at what the future in this strange new world holds for him.

Another major short story by Chekhov, 'The Name-Day *The Name-Day Party* Party' (also translated as 'The Party'), was published in the same year as 'The Steppe'. The title refers to the fact that Russians celebrate not only their birthdays, but the day of the saint after whom they are named. It is the name day of a selfish lawyer and magistrate; his young wife, who is seven-months pregnant, has spent all day organizing a banquet in his honour and entertaining guests. Utterly exhausted, she occasionally asks him to help her, but he does very little. Finally, when all the guests have gone home, she, in extreme agony, gives birth prematurely to a stillborn baby. She slips in and out of consciousness, believes she too is dying, and, despite his behaviour, she feels sorry for her husband, who will be lost without her. However, when she regains consciousness he seems to blame her for the loss of the child, and not his own selfishness, leading to her utter exhaustion at such a time.

'A Dreary Story' (also known as 'A Tedious Story') is one *A Dreary Story* of Chekhov's longer stories, originally published in 1889. In a tour de force, the twenty-nine-year-old Chekhov penetrates into the mind of a famous sixty-two-year-old professor – his interior monologue constituting the entire tale. The professor is a world expert in his subject, fêted throughout Russia, yet has a terminal disease which means he will be dead in a few months. He has told nobody, not even his family. This professor muses over his life, and how his body is falling apart, and he wonders what the point of it all was. He would gladly give all his fame for just a few more years of warm, vibrant life. Chekhov wrote this story the year before he travelled to Sakhalin, when he was beginning to display the first symptoms of the tuberculosis which was to kill him at the age of forty-four.

The Duel   In Chekhov's 1891 story 'The Duel', a bored young civil servant has lost interest in everything in life, including his lover. When the latter's husband dies, she expects him to marry her, but he decides to borrow money and leave the town permanently instead. However, the acquaintance from whom he tries to borrow the money refuses to advance him the sum for such purposes. After a heated exchange, the civil servant challenges the acquaintance to a duel – a challenge which is taken up by a friend of the person who has refused to lend the money, disgusted at the civil servant's selfish behaviour. Both miss their shot, and the civil servant, realizing how near he has been to death, regains interest in life, marries his mistress, and all are reconciled.

Ward Six   In 'Ward Six' (1892), a well-meaning but apathetic and weak provincial hospital director has a ward for the mentally disturbed as one of his responsibilities. He knows that the thuggish peasant warden regularly beats the lunatics up, but makes all kinds of excuses not to get involved. He ends up being incarcerated in his own mental ward by the ruse of an ambitious rival, and is promptly beaten by the same warden who used to call him "Your Honour", and dies soon afterwards. This is perhaps Chekhov's most transparent attack on the supine intelligentsia of his own time, whom he saw as lacking determination in the fight against social evils.

Three Years   In 1895, Chekhov published his famous story 'Three Years', in which Laptev, a young Muscovite, is nursing his seriously ill sister in a small provincial town, and feels restricted and bored. He falls in love with the daughter of her doctor and, perhaps from loneliness and the need for companionship, proposes marriage. Although she is not in love with him, she accepts, after a good deal of hesitation, because she is afraid this might be her only offer in this dull town. For the first three years this marriage – forged through a sense of isolation on one side and fear of spinsterhood on the other – is passionless and somewhat unhappy. However, after this period, they manage to achieve an equable and fulfilling relationship based on companionship.

In the 'The House with a Mezzanine' (1896), a talented but lazy young artist visits a rich landowning friend in the country. They go to visit the wealthy family at the title's "house with a mezzanine", which consists of a mother and two unmarried daughters. The artist falls in love with the younger daughter, but her tyrannical older sister sends both her and her mother abroad. The story ends some years later with the artist still wistfully wondering what has become of the younger sister. *The House with a Mezzanine*

In 'Peasants' (1897), Nikolai, who has lived and worked in Moscow since adolescence, and now works as a waiter at a prestigious Moscow hotel, is taken very ill and can no longer work, so he decides to return to the country village of his childhood, taking with him his wife and young daughter, who was born in Moscow. He has warm recollections of the village, but finds that memory has deceived him. The place is filthy and squalid, and the local inhabitants all seem to be permanently blind drunk. Since anybody with any intelligence – like Nikolai himself – is sent to the city as young as possible to work and send money back to the family, the level of ignorance and stupidity is appalling. Nikolai dies, and the story ends with his wife and daughter walking back to Moscow, begging as they go. *Peasants*

In 1898, Chekhov published 'The Man in a Case', in which the narrator, a schoolmaster, recounts the life of a recently deceased colleague of his, Byelikov, who taught classical Greek. A figure of ridicule for his pupils and colleagues, Byelikov is described as being terrified of the modern world, walking around, even in the warmest weather, in high boots, a heavy overcoat, dark spectacles and a hat with a large brim concealing his face. The blinds are always drawn on all the windows in his house, and these are permanently shut. He threatens to report to the headmaster a young colleague who engages in the appallingly immoral and progressive activity of going for bicycle rides in the countryside. The young man pushes him, Byelikov falls down and, although not hurt, takes to his bed and dies, apparently of humiliation and oversensitivity. *The Man in a Case*

The Lady with   'The Lady with the Little Dog' (1899) tells the story of a bored
the Little Dog   and cynical bank official who, trapped in a tedious marriage in
Moscow, takes a holiday by himself in Yalta. There he meets
Anna, who is also unhappily married. They have an affair, then
go back to their respective homes. In love for possibly the first
time in his life, he travels to the provincial town where she lives,
and tracks her down. They meet in a theatre, and in a snatched
conversation she promises to visit him in Moscow. The story
ends with them both realizing that their problems are only just
beginning.

Sakhalin Island   As well as being a prolific writer of short fiction, Chekhov
also wrote countless articles as a journalist, and the volume-
length *Sakhalin Island* ranks as one of the most notable
examples of his investigative non-fiction. As mentioned above,
Chekhov's decision to travel to Sakhalin Island in easternmost
Siberia for three months in 1890 was motivated by several
factors, one of them being to write a comprehensive study of
the penal colonies on the island.

Chekhov toured round the entire island, visiting all the
prisons and most of the settlements, and generally spending up
to nineteen hours a day gathering material and writing up his
findings. Chekhov returned from Sakhalin at the end of 1890,
but it took him three years to write up and start publishing
the material he had collected. The first chapter was published
in the journal *Russian Thought* (*Russkaya Mysl*) in late 1893,
and subsequent material appeared regularly in this magazine
until July 1894, with no objection from the censor, until finally
the chapters from number twenty onwards were banned from
publication. Chekhov took the decision to "publish and be
damned" – accordingly the whole thing appeared in book
form, including the banned chapters, in May 1895.

The book caused enormous interest and discussion in
the press, and over the next decade a number of substantial
ameliorations were brought about in the criminals' lives.

Major Plays   Chekhov first made his name in the theatre with a series
of one-act farces, most notably *The Bear* and *Swan Song*
(both 1888). However, his first attempts at full-length plays,
Platonov (1880), *Ivanov* (1887) and *The Wood Demon* (1889),
were not entirely successful. The four plays which are now
considered to be Chekhov's masterpieces, and outstanding
works of world theatre, are *The Seagull* (1896), *Uncle Vanya*
(1899), *Three Sisters* (1901) and *The Cherry Orchard* (1904).

The central character in *The Seagull* is an unsuccessful
playwright, Treplyov, who is in love with the actress Nina.
However, she falls in love with the far more successful writer
Trigorin. Out of spite and as an anti-idealist gesture, Treplyov
shoots a seagull and places it in front of her. Nina becomes
Trigorin's mistress. Unfortunately their baby dies, Nina's career
collapses and Trigorin leaves her. However, on Treplyov renewing
his overtures to Nina, she tells him that she still loves Trigorin.
The play ends with news being brought in that Treplyov has
committed suicide offstage.

The second of Chekhov's four dramatic masterpieces, *Uncle*
Vanya, a comprehensive reworking of the previously unsuccessful *Wood Demon*, centres on Vanya, who has for many
years tirelessly managed a professor's estate. However, the
professor finally retires back to his estate with his bored and idle
young wife, with whom Vanya falls in love. Vanya now realizes
that the professor is a thoroughly selfish and mediocre man
and becomes jealous and embittered at his own fate, believing
he has sacrificed his own brilliant future. When the professor
tells him that he is going to sell the estate, Vanya, incensed, fires
a pistol at him at point-blank range and misses – which only
serves to compound his sense of failure and frustration. The
professor and his wife agree not to sell up for the time being
and leave to live elsewhere. Vanya sinks back into his boring
loveless life, probably for ever.

In *Three Sisters*, Olga, Masha and Irina live a boring life in
their brother's house in a provincial town, remote from Moscow
and St Petersburg. All three remember their happy childhood
in Moscow and dream of one day returning. A military unit
arrives nearby, and Irina and Masha start up relationships with
officers, which might offer a way out of their tedious lives.
However, Irina's fiancé is killed in a duel, Masha's relationship
ends when the regiment moves on, and Olga, a schoolteacher,
is promoted to the post of headmistress at her school, thus
forcing her to give up any hope of leaving the area. They all
relapse into what they perceive to be their meaningless lives.

The Cherry Orchard, Chekhov's final masterpiece for the
theatre, is a lament for the passing of old traditional Russia
and the encroachment of the modern world. The Ranevsky
family estate, with its wonderful and famous cherry orchard,
is no longer a viable concern. Various suggestions are made to
stave off financial disaster, all of which involve cutting down

the ancient orchard. Finally the estate is auctioned off, and in the final scene, the orchard is chopped down offstage. The old landowning family move out, and in a final tragicomic scene, they forget to take an ancient manservant with them, accidentally locking him in the house and leaving him feeling abandoned.

Select Bibliography

Biographies:

Hingley, Ronald, *A New Life of Anton Chekhov* (Oxford: Oxford University Press, 1976)

Pritchett, V.S., *Chekhov: A Spirit Set Free* (London: Hodder & Stoughton, 1988)

Rayfield, Donald, *Anton Chekhov* (London: HarperCollins, 1997)

Simmons, Ernest, *Chekhov: A Biography* (London: Jonathan Cape, 1963)

Troyat, Henri, *Chekhov*, tr. Michael Henry Heim (New York: Dutton, 1986)

Additional Recommended Background Material:

Hellman, Lillian, ed., *Selected Letters of Anton Chekhov* (New York: Farrar, Straus and Giroux, 1984)

Magarshack, David, *Chekhov the Dramatist*, 2nd ed. (London: Eyre Methuen, 1980)

Malcolm, Janet, *Reading Chekhov: A Critical Journey* (London: Granta, 2001)

Pennington, Michael, *Are You There, Crocodile?: Inventing Anton Chekhov* (London: Oberon, 2003)

EVERGREENS SERIES

Beautifully produced classics, affordably priced

Alma Classics is committed to making available a wide range of literature from around the globe. Most of the titles are enriched by an extensive critical apparatus, notes and extra reading material, as well as a selection of photographs. The texts are based on the most authoritative editions and edited using a fresh, accessible editorial approach. With an emphasis on production, editorial and typographical values, Alma Classics aspires to revitalize the whole experience of reading classics.

For our complete list and latest offers visit

almabooks.com/evergreens

ALMA CLASSICS

ALMA CLASSICS aims to publish mainstream and lesser-known European classics in an innovative and striking way, while employing the highest editorial and production standards. By way of a unique approach the range offers much more, both visually and textually, than readers have come to expect from contemporary classics publishing.

LATEST TITLES PUBLISHED BY ALMA CLASSICS

www.almaclassics.com